Watchers

MICHAEL E. REGISTER

Watchers

By Michael E. Register

www.thegenesischronicles.com
www.michaelregister.com

Published in Benedict, Maryland, by Calamus Crest.

International Standard Book Number: 978-0983997740

For Yeshua Ha-Mashiach,
The First and the Last
The King of Angels

Dramatis Personae

Abel - A breath - Second born son of Adam and Eve, he was devoted to God and paid special attention to the ways and disciplines of a Godly lifestyle. He was murdered by his brother Cain in a fit of rage and the Earth would not allow Cain to hide his brother's body in burial. Cain tried to bury Abel's body three times and each time the Earth spit the body out, inciting more rage from Cain.

Anarkum - First son of the fallen angel Azazel and later King of the city called Enoch. He was a tyrant, and devourer of all manner of flesh, including man.

Archangel - In the hierarchy of angels, Archangel is similar to a general, or one in charge of millions.

Ariel - Lion of God - An angel in Raphael's choir, she administers healing and comfort in the measure she is given.

Armaros - Fallen angel and one of the Watchers, he simplified the workings of enchantments in order that they might be understood, while holding back the knowledge of their consequences.

Arteqoph - The Earth is powerful - Fallen angel and one of the Watchers. He taught the "signs of the Earth."

Awan - The meaning of this name is unclear, it is similar to the Hebrew word "אוֹן" meaning: strength, power. One of the daughters of Adam and Eve, she was the fraternal twin of their first son, Cain.

Azazel - Fallen angel and one of the Watchers - This general, known as an excellent strategist, answers directly to Lucifer. He taught men to make swords, knives, shields, and breastplates, and made known the various metals of the Earth and the working of them. He also taught men how to make bracelets, ornaments and the use of antimony, as well as how to beautify the eyelids (cosmetics) and how to prepare and administer—either by inhalation or tonic form—hallucinogenics, alcohol, and other drugs derived from plants (development of tinctures).

Azura - Sky blue - Abel's fraternal twin sister. She later married her younger brother, Seth.

Baraka - Blessings - Jarod's wife and first cousin.

Barry - An archeology professor at the University of Maryland, Barry works in the lab environment and knows the nitty-gritty of taking samples and sending them out for testing. He runs the "lab" portions of courses and is very adept at teaching students to find truth through experimentation and rational thinking. Barry and Jessica are good friends and met when Jessica joined the department a year prior to her husband's death. Barry is married to Sara, a highly intuitive person who bases her decision-making more on spiritual meaning than physical evidence. Two more different individuals would be hard to imagine.

Behemoth - The male monster that trampled the forests of the province of Duidain into a wasteland. See also, Celestrel.

Belle - Jessica's administrative assistant, twenty-something, is a natural editor-proofreader. Belle comes from a long line of writers and hopes someday to be published.

Cain - The first born son of Woman, Cain is infamous for the murder of his brother Abel, and to a lesser degree, for his aptitude in regard to agriculture. He also laid the foundations for the first city, which he names after his first son. He was said to also have developed a tremor after he murdered his brother, which made him appear unsteady and feeble.

Celestrel - The fallen angel that was split in two during the war in Paradise. The two halves healed and the male half became known as Behemoth and the female half, Leviathan.

Cherubim - Angels. Similar in appearance to Man. Set apart by their size, they are much larger than Man, ranging from seven to twelve feet tall. Their wingspans are large and range from twice their height to two-and-a-half times their height.

Dr. Angelo - See Michael - This is Michael when he appears in human form.

Ebal - This creature lived in the garden of Eden, he was a serpent who originally had arms, legs, wings, and a long tail. He lost all of his appendages except his tail as a result of the part he played in the demise of mankind.

Elohim - The Creator - This individual is the most mysterious of all. Being everywhere at once, and existing outside of time, this being is the one who creates life with a spoken word. Even Elohim's names are mysteries and many are considered too sacred to write in a novel. This name, "Elohim" is considered common and therefore safe for this purpose.

Ermiel - Close friend and confidant of Jabal.

Falk - Among the fastest of the angels, this Cherubim is one of the smaller messenger angels. He is known to be fierce and highly unpredictable.

Feivel - Bright one - An angel in Michael's choir.

Gabriel - Archangel who stands at the left hand of the throne, he represents the "message" of Elohim.

Hermani - Fallen angel and one of the Watchers who taught magic and sorcery, for the loosing of spells.

Jabal - A descendant of Cain, he was one of the first leaders of the city of Enoch once Cain's tremors became so bad that he could no longer stand in charge of the great city. He was a son of Lamech and Adah, the brother of Jubal, and half-brother of Tubal Cain and Naamah.

Jarod - Shall come down - Son of Mahalalel, and the sixth generation of Adam.

Jeremiel - Archangel of Hope - As carrier of the sound of Paradise, this angel is charged with creating thunder when called upon.

Jessica Mozes - Archeologist and professor at the University of Maryland. Having lost her husband, Stephen, to a chronic illness eighteen months earlier, she finds the steady interaction with students and faculty tiring and would like nothing less than to bury herself in studies.

Jubal - A descendant of Cain, he was a son of Lamech and Adah, the Brother of Jabal, and half-brother of Tubal Cain and Naamah. He was known as the father of musicians.

Karmiel - God is my protection - One of the many guardians of the East Wind - An angel in Michael's Choir.

Kasdeya - Fallen angel and one of the Watchers - Taught the knowledge of plants and herbs, and how to combine them to effect the body in different ways, ie. taught the making of a "draught" that would induce miscarriages.

Katriel - Crown of God - An angel in Michael's Choir.

Kokabel - Star of God - Fallen angel and one of the Watchers. Taught the signs of the stars - Astrology, and the constellations.

Leibel - Lion - An angel in Michael's Choir.

Leviathan - The female coiling sea monster that dwells in the ocean abyss. See also, Celestrel.

Lucifer - Seraphim - This red serpent/dragon was created to be the Commander of the angelic host in Paradise. He was responsible for the angels' initial training.

Mahalalel - Praise of Elohim - Son of Kenan and fifth generation of Adam.

Metatron - Ancient scribe of the throne room. While he is thought to be an angel, he is the only being that sits in the throne room other than Elohim himself. He was also not created at the time the other angels were created and no one knows exactly when he came to be. Some have called him, The Angel of The Lord.

Methuselah - His death shall bring judgement - Son of Enoch, he was the eighth generation of Adam.

Michael - Archangel, bronze skin, tawny hair and fiery blue eyes, this athletically-built angel stands nine feet tall. When he appears in man-like form, he is slightly shorter, about 6' 9", olive skin and black hair. His skin tone and hair color help him to blend in with the peoples of the Middle East, where he appears most often. He is given the task of guarding the glory of the Creator's image. Therefore this angel and all the angels under his charge protect Man (the Image of Elohim).

Naamah - A daughter of the fallen Watchers, she was an expert weaver.

Nephilim - The children of the Watchers. Generally of much taller stature than the children of Adam these mankind/angel hybrids displayed other structural anomalies including a sixth digit on each hand and foot, double rows of teeth, and taller than normal skulls (elongated).

Ophanim - Angels. These are mysterious orb-shaped beings. They worship the Creator in the throne room by orbiting the throne, forming what to many people would resemble a planetary system with the throne as the fiery central sun.

Raguel - Archangel of Justice - this angel and his kind are dark-complected and have black raven-like wings.

Raphael – Archangel of Healing - Raphael's choir tends to the mental and physical well-being of Elohim's people. Many times they are accompanied by Ophanim Orbs.

Raziel - Angel of mysteries/keeper of secrets.

Remiel - Once a guardian of Eden and one of two chief aides to the Archangel Uriel he led 365 legions into battle. Later, he switched sides and joined with the fallen angels, also known as the Watchers and taught the children of Man the signs of the Sun.

Ruach ha Kodesh - The Spirit of the Creator - Also known as the Holy Spirit.

Saba - Hebrew word meaning grandfather.

Sara - Barry's wife, Sara is a spiritual and intuitive person. She can see spiritual meaning in most of the strange occurrences of life, as well as the more normal events. It's interesting that she is drawn to Barry, the more pragmatic "if I can't prove it, it's not true" type of personality.

Satan - Enemy of Paradise - In his quest for power and his mistrust of the Creator, Lucifer-turned-Satan became the enemy of the Kingdom of Light. Satan literally means "Enemy."

Savta - Hebrew word for grandmother.

Semyaza - Seraphim Angel. Fallen angel and one of the Watchers. This general answers directly to Lucifer. He taught the art of enchantments and the cutting of roots.

Seraphim - Angels. These angels are the Dragon Serpents of Paradise, varying greatly in size and color. They also have varying numbers of horns and tail spikes. They started out with two wings, but over time many developed—two more, then more, up to thirty wings.

Seth - Appointed - Adam and Eve's third son, and brother to Cain and Abel. He was born after Cain murdered Abel and Eve believed Elohim appointed Seth to be Abel's replacement.

Tubal Cain - A son of the fallen watchers, he was an expert in the metallurgical arts, working with bronze and iron. In his day he was known to exceed all men in strength and was the inventor of many superior weapons.

Tzadkiel - An angel in Jeremiel's choir.

Uriel - Archangel. Tasked with carrying the fire of Elohim, this Cherubim, and those he leads, are completely covered in flames and to modern man they appear to have a Far Eastern appearance, as though they had originated in China, Japan or Mongolia. They are slightly smaller than most of the other angels. In the world where Michael's angels are eagles, Uriel's angels would be more like hawks.

Contents

Prologue

This Morning

"Good morning Lord,
I'm so thankful that you've given me a purpose,
something to do,
something that helps.

I hope that these books you've asked me to write make a difference.
I hope they help people to see what You want them to see.

I hope they help me to see.

Today is a big day,
the book signing.
I'm so glad Michael will be here,
he always comforts me.

Please let this day be a good one,
let me meet people you want me to encounter,
and people you want to encounter me.

Lean me into your ways, today.

In the name of Yeshua Ha-Mashiach,

Amen"

Chapter 1

Puppet

Darkness fell and Mujahid found himself alone in the desert. He looked this way and that, frustrated. He'd never had any real sense of direction, and the lack of moonlight and his unfamiliarity with stellar navigation did not help his situation. He had walked north, away from camp, and ended up between two mountains with caves along the eastern side of the western ridge, and away from the small group of what the west would call "terrorists." No one bothered to try to stop him.

Mujahid was the misfit in the group of fighters he had aligned with. The decision to join was not difficult. They paid enough that he could afford to send money home to his family, at least his wife and small children wouldn't starve. The problem was that he wasn't brave, didn't have very good aim, and didn't have the education to function as a strategist or tactician. Except for hauling gear and running errands, he was all but useless and everyone else in this small group knew it, he could see it in their eyes. He had also heard the others murmuring about how he would not last long, and would probably take some of them with him.

For many days he struggled with the idea of uselessness, it kept echoing in his head. It was as though someone continued to whisper these ideas into his ear at just the wrong times. Then, afraid of making a mistake, he would mess things up again. Not two days ago, to prove his worth, he grabbed one too many guns from the back of one of the trucks outside the cave. Surely, he could carry guns for the group. Who could mess that up?

Then, about half way to the cave, he tripped. He could have sworn someone tripped him, but of course no one was that close to him. He managed to keep all but one of the guns from falling, but the one that fell was an AK-47, and when it fell it fired off a round. Why there was a bullet in the chamber was another issue, he certainly did not load it. But of course he was blamed when one of others was shot in the leg. It was more of a scratch really, and it barely bled. But the fact that he had shot a fellow in arms wrecked whatever morale he had left.

That was the worst incident, but certainly not the only one. He finally decided he was of no use to the group and when most of them were asleep he told the look-out he had to relieve himself and left the cave. He believed they would never see him again.

He walked in the desert for what seemed like hours, buffeted about by a howling wind. With his lips dry and his eyes straining into the blackness, he fought a fear deeper than he had known before.

Then he stopped, and turned to look behind him, the darkness barred his senses from detecting even his own crooked trail.

"May the desert consume me as this darkness already has. The others will be glad I'm gone. I'm a failure to them and my family as well."

The night air was cold, very cold, and while the desert is known to get cold at night, this was different. There was a weight to the air, pressing in on him. He felt the eyes of something watching from the blackness. He began walking again, though now alternately looking over each shoulder. He was either going mad, or something ominous was out there in the dark.

He called out, "Who's there?"

No response.

The frigid air blew his breath away in wisps of white vapor. He crossed his arms in front of his chest, the hairs on the back of his neck rose to attention. He felt his spine shiver under his skin, fear radiated out and through his limbs.

The sky grew darker, the stars which should have been shining bright and clear on this moonless night were dim and pale. His heart felt like it would pound out of his chest. All at once he could not breathe. He fought for air, dizziness overtook him and he sunk to his knees to avoid falling.

He toppled over onto his back gasping, dusty air filled his lungs. He coughed and his lips became more dry with each breath. The smell of salty dirt and dust permeated his nose.

Something was doing this to him, there was no other explanation.

He stammered out the only words that came to him.

"Just kill me! Whoever you are... get it over with."

The wind took on an eerie sound, something mingled in the airy note, "What... good... would that do?"

Mujahid's breathing stopped. He froze, except for his eyes. He looked all around, or at least as much as he could without moving his head. He could not see a thing, but he was too afraid to move, much less respond.

"I... asked... you a question, Mujahid." There it was again, the wispy sound, and his name. How does it know my name? He could not tell if the voice was his imagination or if it was real.

"Yes, I know who you are. I know your name, and why you are all alone out here."

"Who are you?"

"I... am... Anarkum."

A group of four U. S. Army Rangers and three unseen companions, made their way, in the dark of night, through the hills to the north of Kandahar, Afghanistan. Satellite photos had shown a small buildup of vehicles and personnel in the confined area between two small mountains, and it was believed terrorists could be getting ready for an assault on one of the many NATO checkpoints.

The four soldiers moved at a brisk pace throughout the night toward a ridge that overlooked the encampment. Their companions walked, one on either side of the formation and one to the rear. The soldier's purpose was to set up a video camera with a satellite uplink of the site and call in air support if necessary. Two A-10's equipped with JDAM laser guided munitions would be ready for them should things get ugly, though that was not expected.

The group hiked up the side of one of the smaller mountains, no real climbing just a steady uphill hike that made their thighs and calves burn. As they neared the top ridge line the three companions fanned out and crouched into positions where they could not be seen. They formed a rough perimeter around the Rangers. Sergeant Wilders signaled to the others, palm side down. "This is it guys."

The Rangers dropped to their knees behind him as he shuffled on his belly to the top of the ridge. The Sergeant removed a night vision scope from his pack and peered past a group of small rocky crags that jutted up vertically from the top of the ridge. After about a minute he motioned for the others to follow as he moved along the top to the right, behind a second and larger group of crags.

———————

Two men stood watch at the cave's entrance. One looked to his left and saw a man walking along the road that led from the desert and in their general direction, he was still around a hundred yards out. The man slapped his companion on the chest and motioned toward the walker in the distance.

The second man peered down the road eyes squinting, then he motioned for the first man to wait. The second man walked into the cave entrance around 30 feet and nudged the leader of the group.

The leader looked up at the watchman, indignant. The watchman motioned for the leader to follow him and turned to walk back the way he came. The leader grunted as his eyes rolled in their sockets, but after a short moment pushed himself noisily from the table where he sat and arose to follow the watchman.

Once his eyes adjusted to the brightness of the sun, he mimicked both watchmen and looked down to the road and to the left.

The man was now only about 50 yards away. The leader was dumbfounded for a brief moment, and then, when he had rediscovered his voice, he blurted out, "Mujahid?"

The other two men looked at each other, then at the leader in disbelief.

"That's Mujahid," he paused and tilted his head to the side, slightly, "Something is different, he carries himself different." He looked over to one of the watchmen, "He was always crumpled up looking, no?"

The watchman shrugged his shoulders and looked back at his companion and grimaced.

The leader pushed his way past the second watchman, "You are useless!"

Mujahid climbed the rise that led to the cave entrance and as he neared the three men they moved aside. As he walked past they looked at each other, then back at Mujahid, the leader said, "What happened to you, something is different, no?"

He carried himself with poise and dignity, like a king. No effort was made to address the question. In fact, it seemed as though he did not hear it.

———————

Swanson, Gutierrez, and Hornbeck reached the top of the hill and Swanson joined Wilders. Gutierrez stopped about five meters short of the first two, removed his pack and whispered to Hornbeck, who appeared to be trying to see what the others were looking at.

"Horns!"

"What?"

"Start setting up!"

"Right."

Gutierrez looked at his watch, his right hand grasped the rim where several buttons protruded. A tiny beep indicated that a button had been pressed.

Hornbeck pulled the computer from the pack, opened it, and began the boot sequence. He reached back into the pack and pulled out two cables along with a small folded satellite antenna.

Gutierrez, busy with the camera, set up a small tripod on the top of the ridge between two of the crags. He turned just as Hornbeck reached up with a cable that would feed the camera signal into the computer.

Hornbeck turned back to his work and connected the second cable to the Satellite antenna that was now positioned atop a semi-flat rock on the backside of the hill. Using the computer interface Hornbeck was able to acquire the designated DSCS Satellite and fine-tune the antenna's direction in just under two minutes.

Gutierrez looked at his watch, under five minutes to setup a mobile video uplink, and in the dark no less. He looked over to his partner, "Not bad."

Hornbeck tipped his head back in silent acknowledgment.

While Wilders continued his scan of the many openings in the side of the opposing mountain face, Swanson resorted to counting vehicles.

"Let's see, I got seven small trucks, and two SUV's."

Wilder's kept looking, "Yeah but no people, keep scanning until you see movement."

"You got it."

Mujahid sat alone toward the rear of the cave staring into a small fire that danced before his eyes. He didn't move, stir, nor sleep. He sat throughout the night, staring into the flames, brooding.

Where had he been? No one knew. He wandered off one day. After several hours, questions began to be asked concerning his whereabouts. The camp was searched with no trace of him being found. Then, several days later, he walked back to camp. In the middle of the day, he walked back a different person. He looked like the old Mujahid, but he had changed, something was different.

His face was stern, where fear had been. His eyes, piercing, where cowardice had been. Some said he wandered off and became a man. Some said it was something else entirely.

The presence lurked within and surrounded the small man huddled at the back of the cave. The two had an agreement, the man had made a deal, not with the devil, but with something else, or rather someone else. The deal was struck in the dry lands after the man had decided to leave and never return. Walking out into the desert would have been a death sentence anyway.

Now he had something worth giving his life for, a reason not to fear anymore. His death would be heroic, his family would be compensated for his bravery and he would be remembered on Earth and welcomed into Paradise.

He had left, a fearful man, and returned, with a will not his own.

"What the... Swan, check this out. Ten o'clock, on the road."

Swanson turned his night vision monocle to see a group of Afghan soldiers, probably ten or so walking along a road that would lead them straight to the encampment.

"What do you make of that?"

"Either they don't know there's an encampment here, or they're lookin' for trouble."

"They'll get trouble, that's for sure. Is there any way to warn them?"

"Nope. We'd never make it to them in time so we're stuck here for the duration of this mission. Heck we'd be stuck here anyway. We're here to gather intel, not fight."

"I guess we're in for a show."

"No doubt. Gutierrez, what's your status?"

"Already sending video, we're online."

"Good. Make sure you're getting this."

"Don't worry about it, I'm gettin' everything..."

———————

The presence began to stir. Mujahid rose to his feet and walked toward the entrance of the cave. He could feel an anger building toward rage and allowed himself to give in to it. He walked slowly past many of his comrades, none of them had any idea what would soon occur outside in the darkness.

As he approached the cave's entrance one of the leaders, Abdur Rashid, stepped out to block his path.

Abdur addressed him with a gruff voice, "Where are you going?"

Mujahid called his bluff, expressionless, "Outside for some air."

Rashid glanced toward the cave entrance, "Don't get lost like last time."

"I won't, I'll never be lost again."

Rashid laughed and slapped Mujahid on the back as he walked by. "Something's different about you, I like the change."

———————

Hornbeck saw the movement first on his laptop screen, "I've got movement in the camp."

Gutierrez checked the camera, "What is it?"

"There's a guy walking out of one of the caves."

Swanson and Wilders turned to see the lone figure walking toward one of the small trucks that sat outside the entrance. Gutierrez zoomed his camera in to get a better view.

"Ok, he's walking to that second truck... now he's got the door open. He's looking for something..."

Hornbeck watched everything on his computer screen, "Probably guns, or food."

"Yeah maybe..."

"What's that?"

"I'm not sure, but I don't think it's a gun."

———————

Mujahid walked toward the approaching Afghan soldiers slowly, one arm behind his back. He held his head low, toward the ground. When he finally looked up, one of the soldiers pointed toward him.

"Stop right there! Put your hands in the air!"

Mujahid, continued walking. His eyes darkened under his furrowed brow. He whispered to the entity within him.

"I am ready."

Mujahid felt himself sinking away from conscious thought. He saw through his eyes, but now, somehow they didn't seem like they were his eye's anymore. He was detached, like in a dream.

He watched as his body began running toward the soldiers, slow motion. The long blade, held behind his back, slashed through the first of the patrol. Mujahid's body bound through the air, effortlessly. The blade sunk into the second soldier's chest. Popping sounds erupted around him, the soldiers must be firing at him. He felt a dull sensation in his abdomen, he was hit. It didn't matter.

His body continued as though nothing had happened. Another anesthetized pain, through his shoulder, twisted his body to the left. Then another in his chest, as he spun around, sending two more soldiers to the ground. One by one the soldiers fell around him, his sword pierced each one with a precision no machine gun could hope to achieve.

He should be feeling pain, but he was numb to everything, he must have been shot several more times, but he didn't care enough to keep track. Detached, the grimaces on the soldiers faces failed to bother him as they struggled for their last breathes. All was a fog, and he was a hero, effortlessly.

The last of the wounded soldiers struggled for air. Mujahid walked back to him and peered into his eyes. The dying soldier looked into his attacker's face, then all around it. Something sinister hovered around this small man with the sword. The soldier's face contorted and a look of horror overtook him. He expelled this last breath, eyes transfixed, mouth agape.

Mujahid stood among eleven dead bodies. Still numb, he looked down at the sword, the entire length covered with the soldier's mingled blood, the end dripped with a steady flow. With each breath, blood spurted from his own chest though he felt nothing. A sound came from behind him and he turned to see what it was.

Abdur Rashid, who was running from the cave to see what all the commotion was, slowed to a walk, the rest of the men from the caves behind him. Their faces bore the stunned look of people seeing something unbelievable.

Words poked through the numbness like a hot brand. The words felt like fire searing his mind.

"Anarkum, your father summons you."

————————

Wilders saw a swirling vapor lift over the top of the sword-wielding man. *What's that...*

————————

The bloody sword dropped to the ground and Mujahid's arms grasped for his belly, then up to his chest. His blood-soaked hands moved up to his face as he screamed. The numbness pulled away from him with such force that his insides seemed to rip away.

————————

Swanson remained riveted to the green light of his site glass. "Are you getting this? Tell me you're getting this."

Hornbeck whispered back, "I'm getting it, and headquarters is seeing it too."

"What the hell just happened down there. How was that even possible?"

The four men watched as the screaming man went limp and dropped to the ground in a heap. The others from the cave gathered around the body of their comrade.

Wilders watched the vapor move up the hill and directly toward the four Ranger's location. As it approached the top of the hill one of the companions, Ari, shot from his hiding place, and stood in front of Sergeant Wilders.

Sergeant Wilders watched the blue light move toward him, then a haze moved in front of him as the blue mist grew closer. Anarkum stopped and only the angel stood between himself and the soldier, who could apparently see him.

The standoff lasted around ten seconds, when Ari reached for his sword and muttered the words, "move along, demon."

Wilders breath became visible as he watched the vapor move on down the other side of the hill. He blew into his cupped hands as he turned to Gutierrez.

"Did the camera pick up that mist?"

"What mist?"

"You didn't see it?" His eyes drifted back to the dead man in the distance. *They hadn't seen it.* "Never mind, go ahead and pack up, the sun'll be up soon. We have everything we need."

"You got it, Sarge."

———————

The mist moved east, away from the Rangers position and toward the jagged mountains.

Chapter 2

The Second Scroll

"Falk," Metatron turned to face the approaching messenger. "You requested this assignment?"

"I did, sir, is the package ready?"

"Yes, you will deliver this directly to the writer's home in Colorado."

"Yes, of course." Falk removed his shield and turned his back to Metatron, "Will the Captain be there?"

Metatron opened the satchel on Falk's back, "No, he will not. There will, however, be a welcoming party for you, a chorus of Michael's choir is stationed there." He slid the scroll into the pouch. "You need to get to the perimeter defenses surrounding the house in

Divide." Metatron secured the top flap, then taking the messenger by the shoulder, he turned Falk to face him. "Do you understand?"

The messenger checked his armor one last time until he realized Metatron meant something more than the normal pre-flight briefing he had always heard. His eyes met the scribe's and he saw a look of concern there. Understanding washed over the messenger's face and a resolute countenance came to the forefront. "Yes, sir, get to the defenses, I understand. I will have more opposition than normal, got it."

Metatron remained silent as Falk walked to the edge of the balcony, looked over the side, and breathed in the free air of Paradise. The messenger then turned, paced off seven steps, lifted his helmet and slid it down over his head. Falk's body turned toward the scribe.

Metatron took a half step toward the messenger before he paused, "Just get to the perimeter guards, whatever the cost!"

Falk's arm raised in salute and returned to his side.

"Yes, sir." His eyes widened as a smile lifted one side of his face. With that he turned and raced for the edge of the balcony, flinging himself high into the air, arms outstretched, back arched.

The scribe walked to the edge of the balcony and watched the messenger soar toward the portal.

Jessica and Dr. Angelo arrived at the book store a full hour before it opened. They walked to the back entrance and Jessica pushed a button next to the door. A long thirty seconds later, the door opened.

A balding, round man with a cheerful face poked his head out the door, "May I help you?"

"Yes, I'm Jessica Mozes, I'm here for the..."

"Oh yes! Jessica, come on in. It'll be a little while before the store opens and we've just opened the first box containing your books."

"Oh, I'd love to see them!"

"Well, come right this way." The man held the door open for the two, then once assured it was closed, led the two to a vacant table. He walked around one side, "Here they are." He pulled two from the box and handed one to Jessica and the other to Dr. Angelo.

"I'm Wally, by the way, the Manager here this morning." Reaching out he shook Jessica's hand, "If you need anything just let me know."

Jessica placed her left hand behind her very tall companion, "This is Dr. Angelo. He'll be accompanying me during the signing."

Wally reached out and took Dr. Angelo's hand. His eyes glanced down toward their hand's embrace and he whispered, "Oh my," before catching his breath.

His look went vacant, his eyes closed slowly and a single tear formed at the outer corner of his left eye.

Dr. Angelo released the store manager's hand and held up the book. "Interesting cover."

Jessica glanced between the two men, not sure what had just happened.

The Manager spoke slowly. "Yes, it's quite...stunning. Don't you think?" He shook his head as if to clear his mind, then spoke much slower than before, "Jessica, we'll be setting you up in the store in a few minutes. I'll come back and get you then."

She glanced up at Dr. Angelo, then back toward Wally, "Great, thank you so much for your help."

Wally looked back at Michael, "I don't know who you are, and I'm not sure I want to know, but thank you just the same," With that he turned and walked slowly toward the retail floor.

Tzadkiel felt a nudge on his shoulder, and turned to look. The angel next to him pointed into the air.

The two looked up into the early morning sky to see a brilliant flaming object that their angelic eyes could just make out.

"Falk!"

"Yes. A long way to go yet."

A tall man paced in front of the store waiting for it to open. He had blonde hair with a flat top. A dark overcoat covered his large frame, not unusual attire for a fall day in Toronto. His silver-rimmed sunglasses glinted in the morning sunlight as he checked his watch. "They should be open by now!"

Finally, a clerk came to the front of the store. The store's name "World's Biggest Bookstore" in huge red letters adorned the front of the building.

The clerk fumbled with his keys searching for the one that would open the door. Then, having found the right one he inserted it into the door's lock. With a twist and a quick yank the door was free, the clerk bent down to unlock the upper and lower deadbolts found on the edge of the still closed left-hand door.

The man in the overcoat would not wait, he pushed past the clerk, just about knocking him over.

"Excuse me!" exclaimed the clerk sarcastically, but the large man ignored him.

Once inside, the man's eyes scanned the store until he saw what he was looking for. He made his way to a display table, where several large posters announced the arrival of a new book, the cover bearing burning wings, like some angelic meteorite. And the title, "Beginnings," but there were no books on the table. He looked behind the poster just to be sure. The poster's date clearly said September 30, 2011, but there were no books!

"Excuse me," the man said to a female clerk, "isn't this book supposed to be here today?"

"Yes, sir, they're here, I saw them in the back. We usually bring them out when the book signing starts, which is about twenty-five minutes from now." She began walking toward the rear of the store.

The man followed like a lion fish follows his prey, "Is there any way I can purchase the book now? I'm in a bit of a hurry."

The clerk continued to walk, her ponytail bounced in time with her cadence, mocking him. Her tone was almost robotic, "I'm sorry, sir, you'll have to wait for the book signing to start. You can get the book signed at the same time."

He wanted so much to slash the young woman's neck and take what he came to get, this girl wasn't even chosen, who would care? But he knew there was an angel in that back room, he could feel him, and if the rumors about the author's companion were true it would not be worth his efforts to try and steal what he wanted. Any outbreak like that would start something he wasn't prepared to finish, at least not yet. "Look, miss, I don't want to get the book signed, I just want to purchase it and be on my way."

The clerk stopped just shy of the stock room door and turned to face the customer. She peered up at him and said, "I'm sorry, sir, but you're just going to have to wait a few more minutes. Besides, you'll get to meet the author, you know?" The all-too-pleased-with-herself clerk backed through the stock room door.

The man moved his head out of the way as the door returned and swung toward him. "Maybe that is not such a bad idea," he said under his breath.

———————

Falk's eyes burned blue. His face a scowl as twenty or so dragons rushed toward him. He pulled up, paused mid-decent, almost completely extinguishing the flames that covered him. He held his shield in his right hand, out away from his body.

The beasts raged closer, they would stop him if they could. Falk watched the mass hurling toward him. His upper lip quivered, showing his teeth, his jaw flexed against the sides of his helmet, teeth clenched.

Get to the perimeter guard. He would not have said it, if it were not possible. I must find a way. He drew in a deep breath, then let it out through pursed lips. He reached, left-handed, for his sword. It burst into deep blue flames. The angel stared at it, "I'm going to make it through. My Elohim, help me." His eyes shifted back to the enemies ahead.

Falk's wings lifted him higher in the air, the momentum allowed his body to pivot up, feet higher than his head, then he shot forward with massive thrusts of his wings. In thirty seconds his head and torso were engulfed in flames once again. He pulled the shield back to his chest.

At fifty yards from the dragons he held his sword out ahead of his body and shifted his wings, allowing his body to pivot like a cork screw. A spiraling blur piercing the sky. He sliced through four of the opponents with body parts scattering in all directions, sizzling and popping in their twitching disintegration dance as they toppled through the air.

Falk felt a large thud and found himself hurling end over end. Yellow sulfurous vapor enveloped the messenger as he struggled to free his weapon. His sword was caught in the side of a beast and he could not free it. The two-hundred-foot dragon tumbled backward several hundred yards through the air, the little angel attached. He refused to release the sword amid the beasts blistering multi-octave shrieks.

Falk worked the weapon back and forth, causing the dragon to scream louder until all at once the beast fell silent. Falk gave one last tug on his sword and it was finally free. Falk watched the corpse of the dragon tumble through the air. The ground beneath was only about fifty miles away and no enemies blocked his path. His wings raised to thrust him forward.

Severe pain, his right wing refused to move. He turned to his right just as the dragon that held him began to shake him back and forth. He felt his muscles tear. Pain surged from the end of the wing and down his right arm. The dragon's mouth enveloped the entire wing. Time slowed, and the messenger began to see his own molten fluids vaporize in the air around him just before he felt a pop. Then he was free. He tried to fly forward, but something was wrong.

He turned toward the big dragon again in time to see him spit out the wing, feathers tumbled through the air. The dragon spit several times, each time more feathers emerged.

Falk turned to glance over his shoulder, his right wing was gone. His left wing flapped, futilely trying to control his fall, but it was no use.

Molten fluid gushed from his back into the air leaving a dense smokey trail. In the distance his smoking appendage spun in the air like a samara fruit, only this wing bore no seed as cargo. This wing crackled and popped as it evaporated into a fragrant white cloud. The brief second Falk watched his limb spinning in the air seemed like hours. Then he felt it. The dragon spun around and smashed his tail into the messenger's mid-section. The swatted Falk toppled toward the other dragons.

———————

Tzadkiel shouted, "Falk is in trouble, get three others and follow me!" He leapt into the air, followed closely by four large warriors.

———————

The line had progressed slowly and the man in the overcoat fidgeted, with an occasional glance toward the signing table. He kept a wary eye on the large man who stood beside the seated author. He wiped his brow and bit the inside of his right cheek.

The man spoke quietly to himself, "It is just a signature, not a big deal. I am no threat, this day."

"Excuse me?" The woman in front of him turned and looked at the man as she said. "Are you an author?"

"No, no. Not me. I'm no writer."

"Oh, I thought you said something about not being a threat."

"Sorry, I am just a little nervous."

"Nervous? A big man like you? Did you play football or something?"

He looked down at the woman. She was pretty. Probably around five foot seven inches in height and around thirty years old, maybe a little younger. Her face reminded him of his first wife. She had died so long ago, so long that he'd almost forgotten her face.

"No, I don't play. Life is too short."

"I see, well I'm next in line." The woman turned to face the table just as the person in front of her stepped aside. She spoke briefly with Jessica as the two large men stared at each other. Dr. Angelo clenched his jaw as the woman thanked Jessica and turned to leave.

The man in the overcoat spoke first. "Michael, it's been a long time."

"Yes it has, when did you get out?"

"Not long ago."

"Carrying out the traitors orders again?"

"We all carry out orders, don't we?"

Jessica interrupted the two giants, "You two know each other?"

"Yes, Jessica, this is..."

"Remiel" The stranger interrupted. "My name is Remiel, I am pleased to make your acquaintance."

"What?" She smiled at the stranger and motioned for him to come closer.

He bent forward, his eyes staring at the Captain.

She whispered, "Aren't you an Archangel?"

Michael's chin lifted and his scowl tracked Remiel's movements.

"Yes, as a matter of fact, I am," He laughed and stood up straight once again, "Not exactly like these school girls that seem to be watching out for you." He focused fully on Jessica, "I look forward to reading your book. Many are waiting to see what it is you are writing about. Would you mind signing this one for me?"

"Of course," Jessica opened the cover of the book and wrote, "To Remiel, with love. You're an inspiration to many." Then she signed the book and handed it back to him.

Michael reached over and placed his hand on Jessica's shoulder as Remiel opened the book to read the inscription. Jessica looked at her companion to ask what was happening as her vision began to shift. She began to smell something rotten, like the smell of death.

Michael's gaze remained on Remiel and he motioned for her to look at the man in line.

She turned back, her hand over her nose. Now much taller, the angel before her was shrouded in a dark fog that distorted her view. He wore tarnished armor that was dented, and dull. Parts of it had obvious repairs. Rows of dark, uneven chainmaille could be seen between the metallic plates and his enormous wings looked like a mirage covered in sinuous dark vapor, there was a hint of purple. His hair hung down past his chest, dark and dingy, a tangled mess. His face, a blur that revealed many faces spinning to the left. Face after face, there must have been at least a dozen. Then one face settled in place, it was gaunt, with sunken cheeks and eyes. His irises burned with a smoldering yellow-orange color. Each pupil, a smokey abyss.

Michael removed his hand from Jessica's back and her sight returned to normal. The man glanced up from the book.

"I take it you will continue writing these books?"

"Yes."

"You will be receiving another scroll soon?"

She glanced over to Michael, then back, "I suppose so, yes."

"That is what we thought." He leaned toward her, motioning for her to meet him half way. His eyes remained fixed on the archangel, "Let me fill you in. Falk, your carrier pigeon can be stopped you know."

Michael's attention sharpened, something Remiel noticed, his eyes flicked back toward Jessica though now his face bore the hint of a sickly grin.

Jessica responded, "What are you saying?"

"There is a surprise for him this time. He will not make it to Earth, not with that scroll anyway." He turned, and walked toward the front of the store.

Jessica sat motionless, stunned. "Michael, what happened to him, and who is Falk?"

The archangel's eyes continued to track the man, "That is Remiel and he is one of the fallen."

"He fell during the war in Paradise?"

"No, he led many legions of angels in the war to rid Paradise of the followers of Satan."

"Then I don't understand, when did he fall?"

"During the second angelic falling away, he was with them."

Remiel approached the check-out clerk at the front of the store, and Michael watched as the woman who had been ahead of him in line approached him. She laughed, as the two spoke and placed a hand on his arm. A wide grin covered Remiel's face and once he'd paid for his book the two moved together toward the front door.

Still smiling, Remiel paused in the doorway, turned toward Michael and winked. Then laughed again and walked out of the store with the woman.

———————

Twenty five miles to go, the five angels roared through the air. The messenger, having been tossed around like some rag doll was in the grip of the largest dragon. Tzadkiel let out two staccato chirps, very loud. Then two more.

———————

The largest dragon's four wings held him almost motionless in the air. Falk, still holding his sword and shield looked over his left shoulder toward his captor.

"What's the little messenger to do?" The big brute laughed, he clearly enjoyed this.

Something caught Falk's attention, a chirping sound. Then he heard it again and his eyes moved to see what it was. That's when he saw them, Tzadkiel and several others climbing steadily toward him.

A thought struck him, something he never would have thought. He needed a diversion, and he knew just what to do. Falk threw his sword into the air and caught it with his right hand. Then in a fluid movement the sword flashed through the air, over his left shoulder, severing his other wing. Molten fluid filled the air with smoke.

―――――――

"No!" Tzadkiel saw it. Time slowed to a crawl and he yelled again, his wings grabbed at the air and pushed him as fast as they could. His whole being moved in a steady undulating rhythm, as he worked to reach Falk.

―――――――

Falk, his eyes closed from the pain, shifted his sword to a two-handed grip. The smoke from his severed wing filled the air, obscuring the vision of all. The flaming sword came down on the hand that held him. It jerked, but Falk continued to hack away at it, until he felt himself drop from its grip.

If the hand was severed or the dragon let go, he did not know, but he was free and in the confusion of the moment the dragons did not notice as their prey tumbled toward the ground, and by the time they did, Tzadkiel and the others were upon them.

———————

Falks right cheek spasmed from the pain rushing through his body. Somehow, even without his wings, he managed to get into a head down position in an effort to gain as much speed as possible.

———————

Tzadkiel and the others blocked the dragons from following the plummeting messenger.

———————

Falk gained speed. His cheek continued to twitch, ooze flowed from his wing stumps and from under his breastplate. Smoke trailed behind him. As he neared the ground he sheathed his sword and covered his face with his arms and shield.

———————

Belle swayed back and forth, her head bobbed and danced above her shoulders. She washed her breakfast dishes to the sound of ABBA that filled the house.

Then she felt it. A tremor, sharp and quick. The water in the sink sloshed back and forth, then found its level.

She looked out the kitchen window, "An Earthquake? Up here?"

———

About 45 yards from Jessica's house the dust began to settle and several of the guardians flew toward the impact crater. Malkiel was the first into the pit and the first to see Falk half buried in the dirt. He pushed some of the debris aside.

One of the angels on the rim of the crater called out. "How is he?"

"Not good. I need help."

———

As the door of the bookstore closed, another man approached Michael from behind.

"Captain, there has been a development in Colorado."

Michael leaned down to Jessica and excused himself, turned and walked several steps away from the signing table, "What is it?"

"Sir, Falk has been injured and we cannot get him back to Paradise at this time. The enemy is too strong."

Jessica signed the book for the last person in line.

Michael asked, "How bad are his injuries?"

The man lowered his head and turned away.

Jessica overheard a little of what was being said, so she stood and turned to join Michael.

Michael looked toward the man and lowered his voice, "How bad it is?"

The man continued to look down, "His wings are gone, sir, he fell to the ground. He is broken up and unconscious."

Jessica responded, "His wings are what?"

The man replied, "The enemy tried to stop Falk from getting through, and in the fight his wings were cut off."

Jessica looked at the smaller man, "Where is he now?"

"Less than 50 yards from your home, ma'am, just inside the perimeter guard. He is protected."

Michael asked, "And the package?"

The man responded, "The package is intact."

Jessica blurted out, almost without thinking, "Take him into the house." She turned to Michael, "Have them take him into the house. There is an extra bedroom downstairs, I'll call Belle and tell her to expect them."

Michael looked at Jessica, "Are you sure?"

"Yes, of course I'm sure, it's the least I can do."

Michael turned back to the messenger, "Have them take him to the house and get reinforcements from Jeremiel."

"It shall be done." The man walked toward a row of book shelves and disappeared as he turned down one of the rows.

Jessica sat down and rifled through her purse. "This is the Falk, Remiel spoke of?" She found her cell phone and hit the speed dial for Belle's phone.

Michael nodded, his eyes closed, listening. Half a minute passed before he became alert to Jessica delicately telling Belle the situation, while saying as little as possible.

Jessica clicked a button on the side of the phone and put it back in her purse, "We're all set, she knows they're coming and is getting the room ready."

"Good, thank you."

Chapter 3
The Depths of the Earth

Anarkum found the cave's hidden entrance. Inside it split into several tunnels, then those split up into more tunnels, until after only a couple hundred yards the many paths formed a sort of labyrinth of passageways. There were so many paths that it would be very easy to get lost, bones of animals and men sparsely littered the tunnels and testified to this fact. But the main pathways wound through the tunnels and past large room-like openings and corridors. Anarkum paused at the entrance to one of the rooms. It was large, very large, and the giant men inside reminded him of his former life. It occurred to him, as he peered into the room, that the bloodlines of the Watchers were much like these passageways. There were many, and it would be easy to get lost if one tried to follow the reasoning behind each one's path through time. He knew that the goal for each generation was to improve them, that is to say, to try to come up with a generation that could blend in with the images of the Creator.

Anarkum was among the first generation of the serpent seed and there had been many generations since that time. The breeding of each blood-line had been specific and painstaking. When a line had come to a dead end, like many of the caves in this mountain, it was quickly abandoned in favor of other directions. This process whittled down the total number of bloodlines from two-hundred to the current thirteen. The number, while small, was strong and each had different strengths. The members of these family lines never married outside of the prescription outlined for them. The idea of marrying for love, was anathema to them. They might divorce after their requisite children were born, and then marry for love, but those secondary unions would never produce offspring that would be in leadership roles. Those roles were reserved for those of pure lineage. Thus the lines of the serpents remained alive, active, and in power around the world.

He could not afford to stay, though he was keenly interested in the enhancements this group had received, but his father had summoned him, so he moved on.

The cave continued into the mountain several hundred yards before the descent began. The steepness of the path was more than enough to deter all but the most ardent adventurer. As he descended, he entered into what men called, "utter darkness," even though to him, with his much more comprehensive sensory abilities, it was far from dark.

In fact the last man to wander this far into the mountain, more than a mile and a half down, had been consumed in fire. He had probably run into the one thing he never would have expected so far under the jagged mountains. Anarkum laughed and thought, *he'd probably been burned up so fast that he didn't feel much, if anything. It makes no difference if he felt anything or not, he's gone now anyway. That had been more than a thousand years ago and now not even a footprint remained.*

Anarkum moved along the path much faster than he could when he had a mortal body. This wispy vaporous existence felt more natural than the hard packaging he once knew. Instead of seeing with two eyes, he now had a sense of his surroundings with higher clarity than eyes would allow. Indeed, reality was something better viewed without eyes. At least not those fleshy orbs that absorbed the leftover light that was reflected and thereby rejected by the surfaces they bounced off of. Those "organs," while useful for a certain amount of discernment, paled in comparison to the vision he enjoyed now.

Mankind broke down the electromagnetic spectrum into categories. Visible light, infrared, ultraviolet, radio wave and microwave frequencies. There were more, but that didn't matter in this muted world. He could "view" all of these and much more of the spectrum in his current state. It made him feel good knowing that his perceptions were far beyond those of the one's who were supposedly made in the image of God. *If that were even true*, he mused to himself.

As much as he'd gained after death, he knew his father's kind could see, or perceive, much more. Anarkum had always been very different from his father, maybe because his mother was from the line of Adam. That in itself made him feel tainted, somehow. He had never really looked like his father, at least not his father's true form. That is to say, the form his father was created with. In fact, he bore little similarity to even the manlike form his father had adopted prior to his birth. Anarkum's hair was always red, actually more orange, while his father's hair was white, almost. And Anarkum's eyes were green compared to his father's blue eyes. None of this would have mattered now, in this age. Lots of people have red hair, and lots of people have, what they call, blond hair. But back then, the lighter appearance had real significance. Back then hair color ranged from a deep rich black to dark brown. The lighter colors didn't come in until the gene pool began to weaken, eye color was a dead giveaway. Everyone back then had darker, less frail eyes.

The underground pathway he followed glowed an eerie infrared as he continued downward. The air pressure here was twice that of the surface and the temperature, over one hundred and forty degrees. The smell of gold, silver, and copper had been in the air for quite some time now, and as he moved, the smell of burnt sulphur grew more and more distinct.

He did not mind the smell, not anymore. He had grown used to it over the millennia. This cave had almost no circulation so the burning smell was natural, as was the steam. The cave walls were saturated with moisture that seeped through from the surrounding water table and with the fires below, steam was a natural consequence.

Two miles below sea level, the jagged mountains soared above him, he heard the sounds of massive metal chains clashing against one another up ahead and he hesitated at the last bend, surely his presence was already known. He still had the same overall shape of his former self, but he would never have the physical body he'd had before the rupture. His father didn't like to see him so thin, so transparent, but there was nothing he could do about that. He stood a little over twelve feet tall, and rose to his full height as he rounded the last corner.

Jessica pressed once more, "Are you sure?"

"Yes, yes, everything is fine," said Belle. She continued, "Several men brought him in and I showed them his room downstairs. Oh, and a few women were here, they said they received word about the messenger and came by to see what they could do to help."

Jessica was surprised, "Women?"

"Yes, and oh my gosh, you should have seen them, there must be some sort of height requirement where Dr. Angelo works, they're all so tall, and gorgeous. Oh my gosh, and polite, they are so polite, except the messenger, he doesn't seem as tall, but I really couldn't tell you if he's polite or not."

Jessica squinted her eyes, "Slow down, Belle!"

"Sorry, I'm just excited. What were you saying?"

"I was thinking you should grab some of your things and move to my bedroom for the night, for proprieties sake."

Belle twisted a strand of hair around her finger, "Yeah, I was wondering about that. Actually, there are three of those guys... what's his name?"

"Who's name?"

"You know, the messenger?"

"The injured one?"

"Yes, what other one is there?"

"Falk."

"What?"

"Falk, F-A-L-K, Falk. That's his name."

Belle moved on in the conversation as though everything were normal, "Yeah, ok, Falk. Strange name. Anyway, three of Falk's coworkers are down there with him now. Sorry, I never really got his name in all the confusion."

"That's fine. Listen, Belle, just tell me if you'd rather stay at a hotel tonight? It's not a problem, and there's that one just outside Woodland Park."

"Oh, no, I'll be fine. Really."

Jessica could hear the smile in Belle's voice. As with most things in her life, she was taking this in stride.

"I'll be back in Denver a little after two tomorrow afternoon. So, I should be back to the house before five."

Belle asked, "Ok, how did the signing go?"

"It was fine, a low turnout, but fine. Got to meet some interesting people, to say the least."

"You'll have to tell me about it when you get here."

"I will, you take care tonight and I'll see you tomorrow evening."

"Sounds good, and don't worry, OK? Everything will be alright."

"Ok, I'll see you tomorrow."

The Demon turned the corner and walked into the massive underground chamber. The expanse of floor was covered with scratches and claw marks. The floor of the cave was nearly flat, dark granite and the scratches formed a large map of the ancient Persian region, complete with mountain ranges and other geographic forms. The ancient map had been further divided to show the modern dividing lines of the nations. Other markings indicated where various people or spirit groups were and whether they were stationary or moving. Swirl marks were all over the map, places where water had been used to clean an area so updates could be made. Piled along the edges of the cavern were large chunks of rock, their light color was out of place in this deep cave, they were surely used for writing and had been brought here by those his father still led.

Azazel, the great strategist of old, sat at the far edge of the huge dark cavern, hidden from sight in the darkness. "Son, I'm glad you're here."

Anarkum could make out an outline of his father but no details, even with his heightened vision, "Please, Father, will you allow me to see you this time?"

Azazel exhaled loudly. The sound of clashing metal echoed through the chamber followed by large scraping sounds, metal on rock. A wheezing breath, gasping, then the shadow of a massive creature, two horns protruded from the front of the lower jaw, four from the outside edges of his the brow line, two on either side, and one above the snout. His eyes glowed orange-red in the darkness, their color flickered from the center and moved outward toward darkness.

Rarely would Azazel allow his son to see him. It had been at least a century since Anarkum had fully seen his father and he still could not make out any details that would tell him visually how his father was doing.

"Father, I still cannot see you properly."

Anarkum heard a deep gurgling inhale followed by low rumbling, "Very well." The sounds of scales scraping against one another rose higher and higher, then flames shot out from the darkness as two fiery breaths lit the edges of the cavern all around in a dim light.

Azazel stood, though crouched in the tall chamber that was easily eighty feet high, he had not been able to stand fully erect for the entirety of his sentence, and his arms and legs were bound by huge chains forged by hands much larger than Anarkum could imagine. He had been here for over 4000 years, in this dark, dank, and for his father, cramped cavern. The only light in this place came from the heat of the cave and the dragon's fiery breath. The great father of the mighty and terrible king, who's kingdom was enveloped by the sea so long ago.

Azazel, known for his cunning and guile, remained the leader of the dark armies of the Persian region, and he'd kept outsiders at bay for untold centuries.

The rows of heavy scales on the seraphim serpent glistened in the dim light of this place. His deep green color was only hinted at when he lit the cavern ablaze with his roaring breath, which had ignited portions of his wings and body at the same time, not that it mattered.

"Father, you look gaunt." The thick hide of the dragon appeared to drape over the bones of the beast like an ill-fitting garment. Every bone on his back clearly outlined, the skin hung loosely beneath the huge body, swaying back and forth, with a sound not dissimilar to that of chainmaille, when he moved. "What has happened to you?"

"Darkness. My kind gains strength from light, and my time here has been long." He paused to look into his son's face. "Son, I will be fine, I cannot die, and I will be released soon."

"How do you know?"

"The Creator told me I would be here for a season. And the end of the season is at hand."

"Why do you trust what *He* says? He's your enemy!"

"He never lies."

"I hope you are right, I don't trust Him."

"Why is that?"

"If He is as powerful as you say, why does He let you continue to rule this region? He allows us to tinker with His image like pawns in a game. Why does he wait? Why not be done with us?" Anarkum thought for a moment. "I do not think He is all you make him out to be, power must be proven and He is unwilling or more likely, unable to prove anything."

"Be careful son, your words have gotten you into trouble before."

Anarkum gave his father a dead-pan look, then changed the subject. "I saw the new crop on my way here, they look good."

"Yes they do, aside from a few temperament issues, very good, but they are not the latest."

"Really?"

"Yes, we made several key enhancements in recent years, properties that eluded us for so long, we had almost given up on them. Those you saw, we once called fours, but not now."

"So I'm a one, right?"

"Right, you are a one."

"Canan had the twos?"

"No, Sodom had the twos, briefly."

"Sodom?"

"Yes, that's right, and Canan had threes, and those threes migrated to the new world, they were chased out of the so called 'promise land.' Eventually, the followers of the Creator followed the threes to the Americas and hunted them down. They wanted no trace left on Earth."

Anarkum turned away from his father. "So those hunters became the Native Americans."

"There is nothing 'native' about them. They traveled there to hunt your kind. It was genocide."

"That's why there are so many decalog carvings across America. The conspiracy theorists were right all along."

"They're right about that, but not right about everything, of course. There are so many theories that the truth gets buried in the absurd, which is the intent. We label the truth as ludicrous, and the sheep follow what we say over the truth. It's amazing what a little name calling can do to keep the truth hidden."

Anarkum laughed and turned back to face Azazel, "And now you have what you call fours, what makes these so much better?"

"With each group we've been able to change things in their structure. Things that make them harder to spot. Our aim, of course, is to 'normalize' them.

"This last batch is smaller, and can walk around in the cities unnoticed, if you do not know what to look for. Not all of them are small, but enough are that they can be hidden amongst men."

"And the ones I saw earlier?"

"They were bred to be big and strong, much like the first generation, your generation. We have similar children around the world. They are battle-ready with uniforms, appropriately-sized weapons, and they are fully trained. They stand over two-and-a-half times the height of a normal man, and weigh easily four times as much. If they were to fight a gorilla, bear, or lion, they would tear them in half with little effort. That is, if you could find an animal stupid enough to face one of them.

"You will see them soon, but enough of that, let me tell you why I sent for you. I have received word that a woman in North America is writing a series of books from the Antediluvian Period, our first time."

"From my days in the flesh, why the concern?"

"Her first book has already been released, Remiel was sent to acquire a copy."

"And? Does this book of hers threaten our plans?"

"She has touched on truths that led some among us to believe she is getting closer to the truth than any in her culture before her. We believe her next book might expose us."

"You think they will see your strategy when they read it?"

"Our method for breeding with mankind, and the animals of this world, has changed for the most part," Azazel paused, "we do not want them to see any similarities with our conduct in the past. In order for us to corrupt the images of Elohim again, we have to do it without them knowing it has been done several times already."

"I see, so you do not want them to see the pattern. I am sure you have a plan."

"Of course."

"And you have called me here, what is my part?"

———————

Belle eased down the stairs to check on the visitors. While she did not want to be nosey, her curiosity would not allow her to stay upstairs. She opened the door at the bottom of the steps and walked over to the bookcase, listening. The basement den was equipped with a couch and loveseat, a large wooden coffee table, and a prominent bookcase/entertainment center. The couch and bookcase faced each other along the two longest walls. Between the door and the bookcase was a window and just past the bookcase was a sliding glass door. This door served as the main walk-out basement door, though there was another exterior door in Belle's bedroom, down the hall. The sliding glass door was near the corner of the room and on the adjacent wall was the only other window. Directly opposite the sliding door was the room where the injured man had been brought. She could not remember his name, mostly because it sounded strange to her.

She stood in front of the bookshelf as though looking for something to read, however, her attention was on that door, or more accurately the room beyond it. It was quiet, though she could hear muffled voices and what sounded like singing. She thought perhaps her mind was playing tricks on her.

She pulled a random book from the bookcase and eased over to the sitting area. *The couch or loveseat?* She thought for a moment. *If I choose the loveseat my back will be to the door, but it's closer to the door. Or I could sit on the couch and be less conspicuous if they come out of the room.* She decided on a compromise, and plopped down on the right hand side of he couch, the end closest to the door.

Belle looked at the book in her left hand, without noticing the title. Her thumb ran down the pages and the light that spilled in from the sliding glass door caught her attention. She looked outside and saw a deer, a large buck ten or fifteen yards past the door. Smaller than the deer in Maryland, his rack was a good ten-pointer. He was busy with the wild strawberries that grew along the ground, they were tiny, but intensely sweet.

The knob on the bedroom door turned and out walked the woman Belle believed to be in charge. She was tall, probably over six feet, with long, wavy, light blonde hair, and a fair complexion. She moved in a way that seemed effortless and graceful as she turned to silently pull the door closed.

She let go of the door knob and looked up with a smile for Belle, then turned and walked around the loveseat, "I hope I am not disturbing you."

Belle smiled, "Oh no, not at all. Please sit down. Your name is Ariel, right? I'm terrible with names."

The woman wore a pale patchwork-style turtleneck sweater with a sleeveless jacket, jeans, and nice upscale wide calf boots. They resembled riding boots except the soles had an aggressive lug pattern. Serious, yet stylish, Belle thought. She couldn't help but think how pretty this woman was.

"Yes Belle, I am Ariel. I wanted to say thank you, you have been a wonderful host. It was generous for you to allow us to bring Falk here."

Ariel's eyes expressed a kindness Belle had never experienced before, more than beauty, her genuine thankfulness penetrated to her depths. Likewise, her accent was distinct, but Belle could not place it, it sounded similar to Dr. Angelo's, but at the same time it was so foreign as if to be from some other world, though she knew that was impossible. Belle asked, "Is he going to be alright? Do you need to take him to the hospital?"

"Oh no, he will be fine. I was wondering though if you would mind if I stayed the night, Falk has a couple of injuries that need special attention. I could sleep on the couch, so I can be right close by."

"Oh no, I don't mind at all, you can use my room, it's right down the hall. I'm sure Jessica wouldn't mind."

"Do you need to speak with her, just to be sure?"

"No, no, she won't mind, it's not a problem at all."

Chapter 4

Crumpled Messenger

It was sometime after four-thirty in the afternoon when Belle heard the garage door begin to open, followed by the sound of the burly pickup pulling into the driveway, and then into the garage. Jessica was back.

Belle opened the kitchen door to the garage as Jessica pulled the key from the ignition and opened her door.

Belle called out, "Hey there stranger, how was your flight?"

Jessica slid down out of the truck, then turned and reached for the back door handle, "Uneventful, which is always good."

"Do you need help?"

"No, I just have one bag. I'll get it." Jessica pulled the large bag from the back seat. It was overstuffed as usual, but there were casters on the bottom. It landed with a loud thump and Jessica pulled the bag toward the kitchen door.

Belle held the door open, "I'm amazed those wheels survive, you always pack too much, Jess."

Jessica lifted the bag up over the step and onto the hardwood floor. "Ha, says you. How are things here?"

"Well, you missed meeting Ariel. She was taking care of Falk last night."

Jess heaved the bag into the air, so as not to scratch the wood floor, and walked past the kitchen and den, "She stayed over night?"

Belle followed along, "Yep, she said he had a couple of wounds that needed dressing for the first twelve hours or so. I told her it would be no problem to stay."

"I see. That's good."

"She left about an hour ago."

Jess stopped at the office area, just past the steps that led down to the basement and dropped her keys on the desk. "I'm glad she stayed, where did she sleep?"

"I made my bed for her, but I think she spent the night on the couch. My bed was untouched."

"Have you been down to see him?"

"Not yet, I was about to go down to see if he needs anything."

Jessica tugged her bag over the carpet to the end of the hall and through her bedroom doorway. "Ok, give me a minute and I'll come down with you."

The injured messenger, now in human form, laid quietly on the bed facing the wall. Even in this human form, he noticed how thin the air in this Earth realm was.

Jessica followed Belle across the basement den to the room where the messenger lay injured.

The two stood in the doorway for a long moment, then Belle's questioning eyes made their way to Jess, who turned to her and shrugged her shoulders.

Belle's soft voice interrupted the silence, "Falk?"

"Yes, ma'am?" The young man turned with a groan toward the sound of the voice. As he turned, he noticed a look resembling anguish wash over Belle's face as she approached.

"Oh no! Your eyes look terrible!"

He looked down, as if he might be able to see them.

She took a couple of steps toward him, squinting, "The whites of your eyes, they're so red, do they hurt?"

He spoke in a broken whisper. "I believe my entire body hurts ma'am."

"I've never seen anything like that, it hurts me to just see them." She turned to Jessica and motioned for her to come closer. "Jessica look at his eyes."

"Yeah, I see them," Jessica moved into the room but stopped short, "Falk, I'm Jessica and this is Belle, you're welcome here for as long as you need."

"Thank you, I am glad to meet you both. Your delivery is behind the door, Jessica."

"What?" Jessica turned back and swung the door partially closed, revealing a long bundle propped in the corner.

Falk's voice rasped, "Take it."

She moved forward and lifted the bundle, "It feels heavier than the first one."

"Yes, this one does carry more weight, you are right."

"No, that's not what I meant."

Belle broke in, "We'll go, we didn't mean to disturb you. You need your rest."

Falk thought for a moment. *There is no shalom for my kind yet.* "No, please stay." His face winced as he completed his roll to fully face them. "I would like some company, if you do not mind."

Belle eased a couple of steps closer and looked toward her friend. Jessica motioned toward the chair at the desk. Belle looked back to the young man. Her concern fully manifest now. As she approached, she pulled the chair next to the bed and sat down. "Is there anything I can get you? Something to drink, or eat?"

His voice remained low, "I would like some water."

His eyes floated in their sockets as his eyelids blinked in rapid succession, she thought the pain must be horrendous. "Would you like something to eat?"

He made a concentrated effort to open his eyes fully, "No, thank you."

Jessica walked over to the bed. "Falk, I'll leave you with Belle, you're in good hands."

Jessica, bundle in hand, left the room.

"Ok." Belle paused for a moment, trying to think of something to say. "What happened to you, how were you injured?"

"I fell." His eye lids drifted about halfway open.

She shook her head slowly, "It must have been quite a fall."

"It was, ma'am." His eyes closed. He no longer had the strength to keep them open. "My being here has changed things, there is purpose in this."

That comment struck her as odd. "But you're injured, how could there be a purpose in that?"

"Purpose is always with us," he spoke through a groan, "I am sorry, I thought having company would be a good thing..." his voice trailed off, then with effort he continued, "I need to close my eyes for a while."

"That's quite alright," she smiled beneath her sad eyes and stood to leave.

"I'll close the door if you would like some privacy."

"Yes, please."

She left the room and quietly pulled the door closed behind her.

Belle walked across the basement's den, toward the stairs. Something caught her eye and she turned toward the coffee table. The book she had gotten the night before was laying there, she picked it up and read the title aloud, "'*This Present Darkness*,' Mr. Peretti," she spoke to the book as if it were the author, "I had no idea this was the book I had last night." She returned it to it's rightful position on the shelf, right next to its sequel. She glanced back toward Falk's door. There was a glow beneath it. "The sun is awfully bright for this time of day, I hope he can get some sleep."

Belle closed the basement door quietly and eased up the stairs. As she neared the top of the steps she saw Jessica standing at her desk, a long leather pouch lying on top of the desk, in front of her. Belle could see that something was on her mind.

Belle interrupted Jessica's silence, "What's wrong?"

Jessica turned, "What?"

Belle walked around her and leaned against the desk, "Are you alright?"

"Yes, there's just something about the new scroll, I'm not sure what it is."

Belle looked at the long pouch on the desk. "Wait, this is what Falk delivered? The scroll?"

"Uh huh."

Belle's hand eased closer to the pouch, "May I?"

"Sure, be my guest."

The young lady pulled the tube out of its enclosure, then placed it down on top of the desk.

Remiel approached from the south. This had been his territory, though that had been thousands of years ago, but nevertheless, he was glad to be back. He did not care much for Canada, not that anything was wrong with the country, but this was home. It had changed much during his incarceration, but he was back now.

He continued his flight path and as he passed Cripple Creek he shot toward the ground. He leveled off below the tree line to the smell of gold in the air. Men had apparently discovered the gold in these mountains, and had been harvesting it for many years.

Hundreds of years of experience came back to him now, his body and wings twisted and ducked through the trees with great speed. His target lay ahead, the headquarters was now occupied by a contingent of enemy forces and he would know soon enough what had become of the little messenger.

The thought occurred to him that he did not know who was in charge now. Whoever it was, wouldn't necessarily be glad he was back.

He had to take time to consider what to do next, and to find his bearings.

He pulled up short as he crossed the highway and saw beneath him a large pasture which held twenty or thirty horses as well as upwards of 150 elk who were on their yearly migration to their birthing grounds.

Remiel, face spinning, dropped into the field among the elk in the darkness. They scattered in all directions. One of the big bulls eyed the angel. Remiel stared back, his face froze in the form of a wolf, fangs bared. The elk ran off with a jolt. Then the angel's face began spinning again amidst deep throated, course laughter.

A dozen or so of the fleeing elk moved toward a being who stood motionless, statue-like, among the trees. Katriel, leader of the perimeter guard, had taken up position here an hour earlier at the behest of the Creator's Spirit. One of the elk cows walked right up to his outstretched hand.

The angel drew the cow closer to himself and spoke with a gentle tone, "Do not be afraid little one, he will not harm you tonight." He lowered his head to hers, their foreheads met and she groaned her appreciation.

He lifted his head and looked back toward the dark angel in the field who had stopped and looked in his direction.

Remiel stopped and stared toward the edge of the field, probably two hundred yards away. A cluster of elk cows gathered together, and several more were moving in that direction. He figured it could be an enemy, the wildlife were drawn to them like insects to flames.

Toward the north a dark flame rose among the trees—a spiritual flame, not of the Earth realm—looked to be his destination.

His wings stretched out and with several beats he rose into the air and toward the north, in a matter of seconds he descended upon a small clearing where a small dragon stood watch.

The seraphim, who was close to twenty-five feet long, looked at the approaching cherubim, then turned back to the fire and breathed his hot breath on it once more, sending flames higher into the sky.

Remiel touched down and walked toward the flames but stood opposite the dragon.

"Welcome home Remiel, your territory has been in good hands."

"It is good to see you again my old friend."

"You approached from the south? I heard you were in Canada."

"I had business with Kokabiel."

"Ahh, in Peru. So he was released as well, that is good."

"He was released not long after I was and Azazel had a message for him."

The dragon paused, looked down at the fire and breathed new flames to replenish the old, "I was in Peru a few months ago, to see Kasdeya. He's had a breakthrough. The mixture he's come up with aborts their children with very few side effects, other than the pain, but it is effective. Things are going according to plan."

"Good! So he's still at it, just like the old days. Should be easy to get past the regulators in the land of Amaruka."

The dragon showed his agreement with a grunt. "Have you heard anything of his sentence, when he's coming back?"

"Should be anytime now. From the look of things this land would be better off having its power back."

"Either way, it's good to have you back, Remiel. I know we doubted you when you first joined us, but that's all in the past now."

Remiel looked over at the dragon, "Thanks."

The dragon laughed, "I'm gonna have to get used to that face of yours, or those faces."

They both had a good laugh. Remiel broke his laughter short, "I find it gives me... options."

"I suppose so, it certainly keeps your intentions hidden."

"Yes, it does."

The two sat and stared at the fire for a few minutes before the dragon broke the silence, "I suppose you heard about the commotion with the messenger."

Remiel raised his head, "The last I heard, his interception was imminent. Speaking of which, where is Falk being held?"

"I thought you knew...."

"Knew what? You did get him didn't you?" Remiel's face's stopped, bearing the resemblance of a man.

Those spinning faces made the dragon feel uneasy, but now that the faces had stopped spinning, he felt worse! "First of all, I wasn't part of that group; I had nothing to do with it. Second, no they didn't stop him."

Remiel rose to his feet, "What?"

"He was badly injured, but he slipped through, with help. So, the Mozes woman has the scroll, or probably has it by now."

The dark Cherubim's face began its cyclonic motion once again, a dozen faces came and went each passing in the blink of an eye, "How did he get through?"

"I'm not clear on the details, but I do know he can no longer fly. I believe his wings were cut off."

"OK," Jessica reached over to grab her legal pad and a No. 2 pencil, "I'm going to get started, and see what this one is all about."

Belle started toward the kitchen, "While you're doing that, I'll make dinner."

"I'm not that hungry, Belle."

"OK, I'll make something light, then."

Chapter 5
The Festering Will

Jessica rolled the scroll open on the desk and began reading the ancient writing. Piecing together words and thoughts from the ancient angular Hebrew text, the look of which had been corrupted during the Babylonian captivity so long ago. She thought that this was surely how it was intended to look. She began as she had with the first scroll. The real task was enabling the mindset of the original writer to carry through to the modern reader.

And so she began again...

A giant eagle soared above the vast garden and watched a streak of light that wove a path through the trees. The garden bird increased her speed in an attempt to keep pace with the runner below. She knew her efforts were in vain, but she tried anyway. The light outpaced her and pulled farther and farther ahead until finally the great raptor tucked her wings and dove toward the ground. She began to make up the distance when the light emerged from the trees and into a great plain. Woman came to a stop.

A sound caught Woman's attention and her head snapped to the right. Around two hundred yards away, three cheetah's emerged from the trees. They had not seen her yet. She glanced at the wind, its iridescent colors danced and swirled across the landscape. The air moved past her and toward the cats. She knew it would only be moments until they caught wind of her. She waited.

Just then a giant eagle shot past her, slowing with the spread of its wings. It rose higher into the air and circled around.

She looked back toward the cats, now staring at her. The grass around her tipped and grew in her direction. She chirped, exactly as a cheetah would, beckoning them to run with her. In the distance she heard the reply and all at once the woman and the cheetah's started out across the plain, angled to intersect with each other's path.

The eagle joined in, flying just above the woman and in a matter of seconds the three cheetahs, the woman, and the eagle were moving across the plain together. A half-mile ahead, was a herd of antelope, grazing peacefully. An antelope buck turned to see the approaching runners, then turned back to take another mouthful of the sweet grass. The four ran through the herd, the members of which, felt no fear because there was nothing to be afraid of. The eagle flew just a couple of feet above the woman's head, about ten feet above the ground.

To the first woman, running was a pleasure that could last as long as she desired. She loved the feeling of the wind in her hair, the sight of the animals, the trees, and the contours of the Earth. She loved the complexities of the air, how it flowed around everything, producing vortexes of vibrant color; and she loved the colors of the spirit—how they coursed in and through everything, giving life. She spread her arms as though they were wings, wind slipped between her fingers. It had a denseness to it, almost as though it would be heavy, if she could somehow scoop it up.

Normally the cheetahs would not be able to run this long, now thirty minutes, as they would tire and need to rest, but they were running with Woman, who's light added to their strength and endurance.

They all ran and then a wide smile erupted across Woman's face. She saw her husband up ahead, he was several miles away but she could see him quite clearly. He was on the far side of a large lake. She chirped again, to thank the cheetahs for joining her, then she bolted ahead, faster than even they could hope to travel. The eagle, too low to dive, gave up her pursuit and circled around, to find a warm vortex of air so that her assent would be easier.

Straight across the water she ran to join her beloved.

Her kind saw no shadows, she was the light to the world around her. Day or night made no difference because she outshone the sun, it paled in comparison to her. Indeed, the sun was there to provide sustenance to the Earth, but she caused the garden and the creatures around her to prosper. She, like her husband, was an ambassador of another realm. The Kingdom of her Maker flowed in, around, through and out from her.

Satan watched. Before the war he had been ordered to watch, and here he was doing it. The irony of it all forced a chuckle out from the red dragon's lungs.

He was among the largest of the fallen seraphim. His compatriots who stayed in the Crypsis, those who had stayed in the dark, remained small and malnourished. Satan, because of his assignment, was of course not only on the Earth where the seraphim grew larger, but he was assigned to the images of the Creator. Being in such proximity to the light that clothed these creatures allowed him to grow to enormous proportions.

Only one, that he knew of, was larger than he, but that dragon was now two. Somehow, in the war, one of the seraphim had been split in half, but instead of going into destruction, each half healed as they were thrown to the Earth like lightning. And as if that were not strange enough, one half turned out to be female and the other male.

The female half fell into the sea, and she became a great sea serpent, able to find heat along the steep slopes off the world's coasts, out past where the water and land meet. She found that heat from the subterranean pillars of fire could be felt in these regions, perhaps because the crust of the Earth was thinner here. But this heat enabled Leviathan to grow to a vast size.

The male half, on the other hand, was not as large. But he was still quite big, and always angry. He was the one that had to be steered, because he destroyed anything in his way. Without thought Behemoth trampled everything underfoot.

It appeared that the female half came away from the split with all of the intelligence. Satan knew it could not be true, but it seemed that way.

He looked down and wondered if he himself were both male and female.

Satan was only slightly smaller than she and he was cloaked in an ashen murk. The darkness surrounded him and hid his armored hide, which in turn hid his rippling musculature. This dragon had faired well after the angelic fall since he had taken up this simple assignment. An assignment he had given himself.

He wondered through the years what exactly he might find, following these simple-minded fools through this garden. They surely had no idea that there was anything else besides this lushness. Indeed, the garden was surrounded by wilderness. Especially to the east, the region trampled down by Behemoth, called Duidain.

These simpleton creatures were made to bring order wherever they stepped, and the stupid thing was, they had no idea of their influence. One thing was certain, Satan's self assignment would lead to their fall from the good graces of the Creator, sooner or later. There would be a revealing, but he had to wait.

Indeed, there was something about this man, that begged to be discovered, some secret. And Satan was determined to find out what it was. *"Was I supposed to figure it out? Did the Creator plan this?"* He shook his head as though annoyed, *"Who cares what I'm supposed to do."* He muttered to himself, *"We're here, and we have changed His plan, for better or worse. He's going to have to work around us now."*

Woman spoke in a whisper, "Satan is following us again."
Adam took her hand, "I know."

She tried not to look behind them, and toward the dragon, but she stole a glance. "He has grown larger since last I saw him."

Adam wasn't sure, "You think so?"

"Oh yes, and his countenance continues to grow darker. I'm finding it increasingly difficult to see him, but he is clearly larger."

"I do not help them anymore, since Michael warned us to be cautious around them." Adam turned away from his wife, "I cannot imagine what would cause such a creature to fight against the Creator." He turned back, "And we helped them! I get so angry when I think about that."

Woman reached out to take Adam's hand, "So do I, but we must put that behind us now. Maybe if we give him no attention, he will go away."

"Why does he continue to follow us? I do not understand."

"He was healed long ago. Why would he not leave as the others did?"

"I suppose it does not matter. He will stop soon, we are almost to the meeting place. He always keeps back farther when we are with Elohim."

There were times when the big serpent defied detection, but today he did not try. He sought to unnerve them. Maybe something significant would come of it.

Just then the pair walked past one of the Earth serpents. Satan saw the beauty in this creature immediately. It stood upright, about the same height as the man. His hind legs were long, sleek, and muscular; useful for a quick sprint. His fore limbs were shorter, quite short in fact. His tale, used mostly for balance was also subtle and dexterous. Yes, this creature was a masterpiece. He had wings tucked close to his back, they appeared to be similar to his own, except that this creature had but two.

Satan's eyes shifted back to the second light, the light of the woman, who now walked toward the little serpent, when he heard the woman's melodic voice.

"Greetings Ebal!"

The dragon shook his head, "Ebal? What kind of a name is that?"

Ebal stopped and turned toward Woman. "Greetings Woman, how nice to see you again." His voice was smooth, graceful.

Woman continued, "Where is your Ela?"

"She is tending to our little ones, I am gathering food to take to her."

"Oh my, I would love to come and see the babies."

"Of course, would you like to come now? I am just about ready to head back to them."

"I cannot go now. We are on our way to meet Elohim for our evening walk."

Satan watched the little serpent closely. Something was there, under the surface. He was sure the woman did not see it. She would never expect it. The serpent spoke with cunning, leading the conversation, directing it. He told her enough to draw her in, but he knew she would not be able to go with him now. Everyone knows that Elohim walks with them every evening.

Satan turned from the conversation before him to ponder the scene he had just witnessed. Where had this "Ebal" learned such a skill, certainly not from Man. They were too naive, too trusting. The angel was intrigued. "Maybe I need to get to know this little creature."

The fallen angel turned back just in time to see the conversation end and the two part company. Ebal walked to the edge of the clearing then began a fast trot though the thick trees, unknowingly, he ran directly toward the big angelic seraphim.

Ebal trotted a couple hundred yards. His pace slowed when up ahead he saw a huge dark area in front of him, or maybe more like a murk in the trees. He slowed to a walk. The darkness had shape and cast a shadow.

"A shadow with a shadow? How can this be?"

He stopped, eyes squinted, and moved behind one of the large oak trees, he moved so the tree was between himself and the dark figure ahead.

A voice erupted from the murk, "Ebal is your name, is it not?"

"Ye...yes. Yes, that is my name."

"You spoke with woman just now, did you not?" The sound was deep and gravelly.

Ebal poked his head out, "Who are you?"

"I am one who admires your skill."

"What are you talking about? Come out of the shadows so I can see you."

"How you spoke with her, leading that exchange where you wanted it to go."

"I do not know what you mean."

"Sure you do, you know exactly what I mean. You knew she could not come back with you, everyone knows Elohim walks with them every evening. You invited her because you knew she would not come."

"I had forgotten the time of day, it had slipped my mind."

"No, it had not."

"You are wrong. I did not mislead her. She *is* welcome anytime. Come out of the shadows or I will not speak to you anymore."

Satan crept from behind the trees. His claws sunk into the soft grass-covered ground making no sound. The fog-like mist clung to and swirled around him making his outline difficult to see. He emerged from the trees by half his body length, more or less, but no doubt about it, he was huge. Ebal stood, stunned.

One of the larger oaks snapped off at the base and crashed to the ground as the dark creature pushed against it.

Ebal saw Satan's eyes, like orange-red flames escaping from vertically slit pupils in the center of each. The red glow illuminated the vapors that surrounded them.

The little serpent's voice slipped from his mouth, almost without thinking, "Come out of the shadows."

Satan let out a menacing laugh, smoke belched from his mouth with each horrible pulse. Then he spoke. "I AM THE SHADOW, and I have been watching you."

Ebal dropped his fruit and ran toward the brush. When he had cleared the hedge line the light before him faded. The shadow had shifted, his path now blocked.

Ebal cried out, "What do you want with me?"

"You have a relationship with Woman that I can use."

"Use? What do you mean? I do not know what you are talking about. Let me pass."

"You do not understand. I did not intend to keep you, I just want to talk to you."

"Your appearance is... I do not want to talk with you."

"My appearance? I cannot control how I am made anymore than you can."

"I suppose not, but you are talking in riddles that hurt my head. I cannot follow what you are saying."

"Do not test me little serpent. You know far more than you are letting on. Stop playing dumb, you are an intelligent creature. You can help me with the woman."

Ebal began picking up the fallen fruit, "Help? Why do you need my help? You look like you would have no need for one such as I, how could I possibly help you?"

Satan sunk to the ground, his face level with Ebal's body. "You and I share many things in common."

"How? How am I like you?"

"We are both serpents. I am just a different kind than you are."

"You must be mistaken, there is only one kind of serpent. You must be a lizard or something else."

"I am called a seraphim serpent."

"I have never heard of that before. Where were you created?"

"Far from here."

Ebal looked to the east, "Outside the garden? Are you from Duidain? That is a hostile wasteland. Are you the monster that roams there?"

Satan shook his head, "Beyond this garden and past the borders of Eden to the west, beyond this world, and I've come to help Mankind, but they do not allow my approach and I cannot help them if they will not speak with me."

"What sort of help?"

"I'll tell you later, when you decide you can trust me. And after I have shown you a few things about this world."

"And if I decide not to trust you?"

"Then I will not trouble you with this sorted business." Satan moved into the clearing, the murky shadow all but disappeared. He reared up onto this hind legs and the little serpent watched this magnificent creature whose muscles rippled underneath overlapping layers of metallic armor-like scales.

Ebal gasped, transfixed, as the fallen angel spread his six wings, crouched, looked to the sky and with a powerful thrust of his legs and wings rose into the air, the rhythmic beat of his wings pulsed the air as he rushed away.

Ebal stood and stared, mouth agape until the shadow creature was but a dot amongst the trees.

Chapter 6
Clash of Monsters

Satan hovered a few hundred feet above the ground approximately 750 miles east of Eden province in the region of Duidain. One look across the immense landscape told him the rumors were true, this Behemoth had made what was once a lush forest into a wasteland. Not a single tree remained whole as far as his eyes could see. Many of the trees were upended and the remainder were broken off or torn apart where they stood. He settled in a slow decent to the ground, his feet touched down, first one and then the other, as if in slow motion, elegant.

Just then he heard movement behind him, the ground shook. Billowing dust moved toward him. Behemoth was a massive creature, much larger than the Commander remembered, and he wondered how he had not seen him before now. Satan moved out from among the broken trees and into a clearing to get a better look at the approaching monster.

Behemoth, who's size surprised Satan, was easily five or six times the mass of the Commander, and like a giant boar, he approached with unbridled fury. His head tossed back and forth, bursts of flame and black smoke shot from his nose and mouth. Iron-like claws tore into the Earth sending clouds of dust and dirt high into the air. All at once a violent multi-octave scream escaped the creature, the massive head still whipping to and fro.

Satan raised his hand in greeting, however, the beast did not stop, he did not slow down, but instead barreled toward Satan with an intensity that shook the Commander's confidence. Satan lept straight up, his six wings grabbed at the air and yanked him higher still. Satan watched the monster scream past, beneath him, and studied his terrifying form.

The head of the monster, massive and thick, was covered in the remains of iron-like scales, remnants really, most of his exposed skin was heavy and tough with a calloused look about it. His boney forehead protruded well past his cheekbones. The beast's long, curved and twisted horns jutted out from above his tiny eyes and worked their way along the sides of the skull, then jutted out beyond and in front of Behemoth. His lower-jaw tusks, while not as long as the horns, were none-the-less sharp as swords. Along the central ridge of his head, neck, and spine stood a tall flowing stream of dark brown hair. His sides, like his head, were adorned with remnants of metallic scales from his former life, though now hair pushed out between the remaining individual scales, many of which had fallen off and many more were loose and dangling. The striations of his heavily muscled body and legs appeared as heavy rope, bound together and tightly draped with a thick outer hide.

Behemoth had given a final burst of speed, in an attempt to gore this intruder but ended up smashing into the broken stump of a cedar tree, sending massive chunks of wood, dust, and splinters everywhere.

The great beast spun around and searched for his prey amid the blinding cloud of debris. Then, out of nowhere, the Commander dropped onto the much larger Behemoth's back. A split second passed before the enraged colossus realized what had happened, but then, with renewed vigor, he shot across the clearing with the invader in tow.

Satan grasped for the monster's hair and held onto the sides of the great beast with his legs. He had heard reports that this Behemoth was more on the deranged side, but now he knew it for sure. Straddling the beast, the Commander spread his wings in a effort to slow the brute's charge, but the resistance only seemed to anger the monster even more and if anything, the pair's speed increased. Satan, his hands still grasping the colossus, swung his right leg back behind and around the huge monstrosity and slammed both feet into the ground, his tail searched for something, anything to get ahold of, his wings grabbed wildly at the air, uncontrolled.

Satan pushed his feet into the ground with all of his might, dust and dirt flew everywhere until neither dragon nor monster could see anything, yet still they continued forward.

All at once the sound of a tectonic collision silenced all other sounds, and just like that, Behemoth came to a halt. Satan, still grasping the beast's hair, whipped forward past the brute. He flipped mid-air, tucked his wings close to his body, his hands still holding clumps of hair now separated from the beast. Unable to see, the

Commander hit the ground hard, back-side first, then tumbled forward, arms out.

Mid-air, Satan heard another of the big brute's screams as he then met the ground again, this time on his chest and long neck, nearly flipping. Satan's body finally settled to the ground and he found himself between two massive oaks, mostly uninjured.

The two creatures breathed heavily, still blinded by the dust that now filled their lungs. The relative quiet was interrupted by a burst of fiery breath shot into the air from Behemoth's wide-set nostrils and seconds later, as the air cleared, Satan could see why they had stopped. The beasts horns had pierced and were now lodged in an oak log over three hundred feet long and at least twenty feet in diameter and this log was buried beneath many other equally large timbers.

Satan rose to his feet and stumbled toward the monster. He grabbed one of Behemoth's massive horns with his left hand to steady himself and peered beneath it into an eye that seemed too small for this beast. The eye was wild and uncertain, it flicked back and forth, unruly. The orange flames of the iris jerked open and closed around the black center.

Satan whispered in his graveled tone, "Shhhh, listen to me friend. I am not here to fight you. You are half of the former guardian Celestrel. You remember the war, do you not?"

That got Behemoth's attention, the visible strain in his mighty body relaxed, slightly.

"Ah, so you do remember. Now we are making progress." Satan slithered back enough for the monster to see most of his body. The Commander's scales absorbed most of the light and a dense, foreboding vapor swirled out from him like fingers. "I know, I look somewhat different than you remember." Satan coughed out a hoarse laugh and writhed closer, "But then, you are much different as well. Do you remember how you came to be in this form?"

The creature looked down, blinked, then looked back toward the dragon. He calmed a bit more.

"You do not remember." Satan lowered his head to again peer into the now softened eye. "Just before the end of the war," Satan glanced away, "you were cut in half." The Commander paused. Unsure if the creature understood, he looked back into the eye. "Your two halves healed in the light of Paradise, in the light of the Creator, in ways we could never have imagined." He paused, "That is to say, your two halves healed separately. You now exist in two bodies, two very different bodies. You are now male and your other half, Leviathan, is female." The eye of Behemoth remained motionless and over a period of several seconds the Commander came to realize that this monster either could not, or would not, understand what he was being told. Satan's head rose higher and he looked back at the logs that served as a prison, "Let us do something about these trees, shall we?"

Behemoth began to move his head back and forth, his movements severely limited, while Satan slithered to the far side of the wood pile and began moving the trees to one side. Once the log that held the monster was uncovered Behemoth raised his head, the impaled tree still fastened firmly in place rose as well.

The Commander leaped onto the wood beam and slammed it back into the ground. Then he leaned forward, his hands grasped the beasts horns, and peered down at his prisoner. Behemoth snorted huge fireballs into the air, his eyes again filled with rage.

The Commander, steadied by his tail, waved his right hand back and forth to clear the air of the fire and smoke. Then he lowered his head slowly as he spoke, "Now, Behemoth, I will help to remove this log which holds you, but I expect you to remain calm. I did not come here for confrontation, I came here to reason with you. After all, we *are* brothers."

Behemoth's muscles once again relaxed from their tense posture. Satan marveled at how this one had grown so powerful. Surely he could never be defeated. The Commander stepped backward, his movements smooth, elegant.

Satan grabbed the log with both hands and wrapped his tail around one of the broken oak stumps about thirty yards away and said, "Pull back."

Behemoth's heavily muscled legs began to push backwards.

Satan's body responded in kind, his tail grew taught and swelled with it's own muscular contraction.

Behemoth's claws sunk into the ground, his long, thick tail searched for something to grab.

The Commander's head flung back, teeth now exposed from the strain. Then he felt the true power of the monster, it was as though Behemoth had only been pushing with half of his strength, or maybe less. But now Satan's whole being lunged forward. The Commander's feet sunk into the ground as he felt the stump behind him, his tail still grasping it, lurch forward unable to anchor the dragon.

Great pillars of fire poured from the Behemoth's nostrils as he gave a final lunge backward, the stump Satan held launched free from the ground. Satan's eyes opened with the release of tension to see the stump, now a projectile, overhead on its half-mile journey through the air.

When Behemoth felt the Commander's resistance release he collapsed. Satan let go of the tree and found the lower portion of his legs buried in the hard ground. He stepped up out of the Earth and eyed the stubborn tree that still imprisoned his friend.

He had an idea. With a wink to the big brute before him, he inhaled deeply and breathed out a long column of flame, lighting up the center of the log.

After a few minutes the dull expression of the monster changed and he again breathed a column of fire from his nostrils, only now the fire resembled that of a blow torch. His eyes squinted and his jaw clenched, another set of torch flames erupted toward the sky, his horns and brow ridge now a brilliant orange. The log burned along the horns, from the inside out, and loosened. Behemoth peered toward the Commander. His eyes took on the formerly frenzied look.

Satan gave the brute a sideways glance as the head of the monster and the log turned away from him slowly.

With great effort the beast's head snapped back toward Satan. The log, which was loosely connected to Behemoth's horns, became a flaming projectile with a final flick of the beast's head.

The Commander dodged the main portion of the log but the end caught his outstretched hand and buried it into his chest, knocking him backward. His wings alone kept him upright.

The rage the Commander felt was met by the madness of the crazed beast who again charged toward him, this time with red-hot horns. Satan took to the air and the furious Behemoth watched helplessly as his prey climbed out of reach. The monster pawed the ground, erratically he lunged forward time and again, his body rippled and flexed in a gigantic show of strength. Fire erupted in short, pulsating bursts from his nostrils and that sickly scream filled the atmosphere.

Satan looked at the beast, breathed a long sigh, shook his head, and flew north to the hill country.

Behemoth followed along for nearly an hour, snorting and trampling everything in his way.

Then the monster's head jerked to the left. Something to the west caught his attention, but what it was he did not know. His pace slowed, then he stopped. The beast snorted, rage began to build once again, and all at once he flung himself into a full-on charge westward.

Chapter 7
Challenge

In the future, mountains would tower to vast heights with high cliffs and broken, jagged boulders as though they had been wrenched upward in some horrific battle between the Earth's crusty plates. However, in the beginning, those kinds of mountains did not exist. In those days, mountains were more like what we would think of as rolling hills. Even though they could climb to heights of around 9,000 feet, they had a much more gentle look about them than they would in the future. These hills were areas of the Earth's crust where there were fewer heavy elements.

The Earth's crust covers and seals a deep layer of water, but the crust does not float very well, and the places where the crust was the most dense sunk down into the underlying waters and came to rest on solid ground beneath those waters. The places where the top crust and bottom crust met were called the pillars of fire.

They were called pillars because the low-lying portions of crust became the support for the crust above. And the reference to fire came from the fact that these pillars glowed red some ten miles beneath the world's surface, in water pressurized by the weight of the top crust.

———————

Satan flew north for several hours and came to rest at the top of a hill that rose to a height of around 8,500 feet. Unlike the surrounding hills, this one had a bare top, except for a thin covering of green grass.

Satan sat with his tail curled around his feet, his scales drank in the light that was all around like a thousand ravenous throats, refusing to reflect the light, they kept most all of it to themselves. From a distance he appeared as a void in the surrounding brightness—that is, most of him appeared as a shadow but the parts that could be seen were dingy, hard, and cold. However, his metallic tail spikes, now dark grey and weathered, glinted in the sunlight. He stared, with flaming orange and yellow eyes, at the sun, with thoughts of a garden and the two creatures the Creator had placed so much confidence in.

The problem was that the pair were in the best of all circumstances. They were in the one place on Earth where everything was perfect, they did not see the rest of the world, the fallen angels had seen to it that most of the remainder of the Earth looked nothing like the larger province of Eden, and certainly not like the garden that stood in the east part of the province that held Man and his counterpart in its bosom.

Just the thought of those two welled up the heat inside him. His underbelly and throat glowed a soft orange-red, but he contained his emotion, only allowing a small trail of fiery smoke to escape his lips. He looked up toward the doorway which led to Paradise, he knew where it should be, though he could not see it from the surface of Earth.

"I am an outcast, because I would not bow to those creatures of yours. You dress them up in light, those clay idols, to look like you and then expect me to bow to them, when they should be bowing to me! They are DIRT, or dust, or whatever this filthy planet is made of.

"This one you call Adam, this Man, is the color of the mud you made him from, there's no disguising it. He is made of Earth, he is the Earth, INCARNATE!

"You placed him into a perfect garden, which is in the best province on this dirt ball and he does everything you tell him to do. Does he think for himself? No!

"You claim to give him free will, you claimed to give all of us free will, then when we used it, in a way you do not like, you exiled us from our home! You forced us out!

"Will you force your Adam out as well? Of course not, you've given him no choice at all. He does not see that he is in a cage that you call a 'garden.' Sure, it is a nice cage, a lovely cage, but it is a cage all the same!

"What would happen if he were to break your one rule, that one rule you gave him? The one concerning the fruit, the seed?

"Indeed, what if he were to figure out the riddle of your rule? What if he were to see what you had hidden in those words? If his eyes were opened to what you really meant?

"Of course you have him encased inside that wall, with guards ever watching, lest he should strike his foot against a stone. You protect his every footstep. You keep him from danger, because you know he would turn on you as quick as lightning! He would see that the knowledge you keep from him would set him free of your nice, soft, tyrannical grip! That knowledge would set him free.

"As I am free."

A crackling sound caught his attention, he turned. A thin column of fire stretched from just above the grass straight up into the sky, through the clouds. It swelled in thickness, like a heartbeat, an invasion of the Creator's presence, here where the dragon thought he would be alone with his thoughts.

To anyone else it might have sounded like thunder, indeed it was thunder, but to Satan it had tonal inflection, cadence, and meaning, "I see you are considering Man and Woman."

Satan's head bowed, not out of reverence but because the weight of the voice would allow for no other posture. He pressed against it, hands on the ground, neck straining, head turned from the flames, silent.

The Creator continued, "Michael and his choir will be recalled to Paradise in two days, the garden will be unprotected from the setting of the sun, until the setting of the sun on the following day."

Satan sneered, "What is that to me? Why would you tell me this? Are you trying to trick me, somehow?"

"You boast alone on the top of a hill. Where are your brave words now? You think you can sway my plans? Do you not see what you have already started, the seed that must grow to maturity?"

Satan fought harder against the weight that held him bowed low, yet his head would not rise. Frustrated, he snarled, "You talk in riddles, speak plain!"

Satan's head bobbed upward, the crackling had turned to silence, the weight now gone. He jerked back to see where the flames had been. Nothing. In the blink of an eye, the Creator's flames had vanished though the scent of Paradise remained until a light breeze carried it away.

Satan's hand reached up and rubbed the back of his neck as he turned in the direction of the garden. "I must prepare."

Chapter 8

Cold in Paradise

At first, Katriel did not understand the words that flowed into his heart. The command was clear, but never did he expect to receive a call bidding him to depart from his station as guardian to the Earth creature, Adam.

He looked over at his fellow guardian, Tzadkiel, and saw the same confusion on his friend's face. The big angel returned his gaze as Katriel looked as though he had something to say.

Just then their attention was diverted upward to see Michael soar past the two of them on a direct path to Adam. With that, Katriel and Tzadkiel rose into the air, along with many other guardians who had heard the same message, and followed close behind.

From several miles up, Tzadkiel looked back to see tens of thousands of angels evacuate the Garden of Eden in a steady progression. Then, as the last of the guardians rose from the interior of the garden, the perimeter guards began to rise as well.

Adam and all the male animals in the garden were in the north and west section of the garden, while Woman, and all the female animals were in the south and east portion.

Adam, clothed in a light brighter than the angels, looked all around as wave after wave of guardians ascended away from his home. The lights streamed upward into the darkness of the early morning sky. He knew most of these angels by name, but had somehow not realized how many thousands had been in and around the garden.

Just then he felt a presence behind him and turned in time to see Michael, the angelic captain land a few steps away. Adam walked toward him as the angel bowed.

Adam greeted his friend, "Michael, as always, it is good to see you, though this morning it is especially good."

"Greetings Adam, I come with news."

"I should think so." Adam motioned toward the skies.

"As you can see, the angelic guardians have been recalled to Paradise."

"All, at the same time?"

"Yes."

Adam searched Michael's angelic eyes and could see there was more to be said, that Michael was troubled. "What is it?"

Michael looked toward the center of the garden, then up at the last of the departing angelic choir, the guardians stationed around the two central trees, the tree of knowledge and the tree of life.

He looked back into Adam's eyes, "We will be gone for one day."

Adam smiled, "One day is not long."

Michael continued, "This will be a day unlike any you have experienced before."

"How so?"

"Do you remember what the Creator said concerning the tree of knowledge?"

Now it was Adam's turn to look toward the garden's center, "Yes, we are not to eat of it."

Michael prodded, "And you remember the consequence of disobedience?"

Adam turned back to his friend, "Death. Yes, of course, I remember. What do you suppose the 'knowledge of good and evil' is, have you thought about it?

Michael ignored the question and thought back to the first sin, when the Commander pointed his finger at the one who made him, the one who loved him. The cost had been so high, "To disobey is sin, and sin has a way of sweeping in those around you who are not prepared for its enticements. It can capture those around you, those you care for, and plunge them into its sticky embrace, making their choices that much harder."

Adam leaned toward the archangel, "I do not know why you are telling me all this. I know this. In fact, just two days ago the Creator told me about redemption."

"What did He say?"

"I did not understand it."

Michael pressed the man, "What did He say?"

Adam thought for a moment. "He said something about sin, that it can be redeemed, but only by one that is without sin. Only by one who is perfect, and then that one must decide, freely, and He stressed that point, that it has to be done freely. This one must lay down his life for the one that sinned."

Michael reasserted, "Sin has a cost, and that cost is death, do you understand?"

Adam shrugged his shoulders, "No, I do not understand, I have no conception of death. How can something die? How can one pay for another? What if the sinner sins again, can the person who paid their debt, if that person paid with their life... can that person die for them again?"

Michael looked up into the sky again, "I do not know, I know only what I am told, or have experienced." He smiled and placed his hand on Adams shoulder, "How about you stay clear of this thing called sin, I do not think you want to find out through experience."

Adam's smiled returned, "I do believe you are right, I do not want to know first hand."

Michael looked into Adam's eyes, "I have a message for you, from the throne. It contains essential truths you must remember."

Adam furrowed his brow, "What is it?"

Michael cleared his throat, "Adam, love Woman in such a way that you set her apart. Care for her. You must be willing to wash her, and clean her with the words of Elohim in order that you might equip her to stand before yourself and her Creator. You must be prepared to step in and cleanse her, if need be. For only in your purity do you have the ability to cleanse and sanctify."

Adam shook his head, "That sounds very similar to what the Creator told me."

Michael continued, "There is a price that must be paid for cleansing, and it will be paid." He paused and looked directly into Adam's eyes, "Would you be prepared to pay that price, for her?"

Adam, his mouth now slightly open, waited a few seconds to be sure Michael had finished. "I am not sure I know what you mean, cleanse her from what?"

Michael looked away and wiped his eye, "I do not know. As I said, you must remember what I have told you. Will you do that? Will you remember?"

"Yes, of course, but..."

The Archangel motioned for Adam to stop, "I can say no more, I must return to Paradise now."

Adam looked down, "Very well, I will see you tomorrow." Adam worked up a smile and embraced his friend.

When the two parted, Michael unfurled his wings and said, "We shall return tomorrow evening."

Michael leapt into the air and his massive wings pulled him with powerful lunges into the sky. Adam watched the archangel until he could no longer be seen, then he closed his eyes and felt something strange in the pit of his stomach, there was a sort of pain in the angel's departure.

He decided to seek out Woman, surely her experience would be similar to his and perhaps this would be a good time to enjoy one another's company.

Adam turned and walked toward the center of the garden with a great multitude of every sort of animal behind him.

———

Gabriel hugged Woman and ascended slowly into the evening sky. When Gabriel was almost out of view she saw another, familiar angel, ascend from the northwest.

"Michael must have come from talking to Adam." She looked toward the center of the garden, the place between the two great trees, the place she and her husband would meet from time to time. "I would like to see Adam, if he is feeling the same way, perhaps he will go to our meeting place while the angels are gone."

Thus she began the long walk toward the center of the garden.

Ebal pointed again, "Do you see that? That is the last one. He is the mightiest of them."

Satan grimaced, "The mightiest, is that what you said?"

Ebal kept his eyes trained on the archangel, "Yes, that is what I have heard." He turned toward Satan, "Have you heard something to the contrary?"

Satan glanced at Ebal, then back into the sky, "What does it matter? The opportune time has come. You have an opportunity to better your position and replace Adam and his wife. You and your children can rule the world in their place."

Ebal flew to the top of the wall and looked into the garden, "I am afraid the Creator will be terribly angry with me. Besides, I wouldn't know the words to say."

"I can speak through you, if you will agree to it."

"What will you say?"

"Leave that to me, little serpent. I will ensure your future for you. Will you agree to it?"

Woman walked through a grove of fig trees whose trunks, if you could call them that, resembled clusters of huge worms or lizard tails twisted together. Many of the roots wound and writhed on top of the ground for some distance before plunging into the soil. Each trunk had the appearance of fifty or more thin vertical members tangled and knotted up. Then after rising from the ground to a certain height, maybe twenty feet, the various tails took off at odd angles. Some of the gnarled members doubled back, the rest continued on. The trees, the Woman thought, looked like a tangle of serpents. The leaves of these trees were enormous, easily as large as one of Adam's hands, maybe larger. All together they formed a thick canopy overhead.

Under this canopy, where grass did not grow due to the lack of sunlight, Woman's garment of light shown under the trees and grass began to grow around her feet as she walked, to a distance of about thirty yards round about her. Fruit began to form overhead, the same as with any other tree in the garden, when she or Adam were present.

As she continued on, Woman took care not to trip over the coils and spines of the roots that covered the ground. Many of the lower limbs had roots of their own that dangled down, like fingers in search of ground, they formed a sort of curtain that sunk into the Earth.

This was not her usual route to the center of the garden and these trees had grown in strange ways since last she'd seen them. She had a strange feeling in her stomach, something she could not explain.

In the distance she saw glimpses of a much taller tree, not something she could focus on, with the fig tree canopy being so thick and the roots under her feet. She found herself next to the straight center wall of the garden and let her hand drift against it as she walked. Normally, one of the angels would assist her when she passed through areas that offered so many opportunities to stumble. She missed the companionship of her winged friends.

As she continued on, the fig trees looked more and more twisted and she wondered what caused them to be like this. She thought perhaps she and Adam should tend to this part of the garden more.

Woman came to the opening in the central wall. It ended just past where the grove of trees gave way to a grass-covered clearing that was several miles across with only two trees standing in the center, several hundred yards from each other.

The two trees were strikingly different and the first tree she came to was the Tree of Life. This tree was maybe a mile in height, but the radius of its canopy was easily three times that. It provided shade while not being so thick that it completely cut off the light from shining through. It was a cool canopy that allowed grass and small plants to grow beneath it.

As for the other tree, Woman had a difficult time seeing the top of the Tree of Knowledge, as it was easily three miles tall, possibly taller. It's trunk was several hundred yards across at the base. She new it would continue to grow because even at its current size, it was still in its infancy. This tree was so tall and thin that most of the shade it provided was from its trunk, which all but eclipsed the sun.

Compared to the tangled grove of fig trees behind her, this solitary tree was comforting to look at. It had leaves similar to the carob tree and fruit like that produced by vines. It was a majestic example of strength.

She continued to look at the tree, and as her eyes moved back down she saw movement in its lower branches. She began to walk around it to get a better view and realized that the movement was on the garden's center wall, on the opposite side of the tree from her.

Ebal saw Woman's eyes lock onto him, but then again, he could not be sure. She looked toward him but her eyes questioned what she saw. She began to walk around the tree. Ebal hung silent, the claws on his wings fastened over the top ledge. Now motionless, he hung like some sort of gargoyle, statue like.

His actions hid his fear of what might take place next. He was promised an elevated position in the garden, that by bringing the woman and then the man down, his position would elevate automatically. He was also promised that the words that came from his mouth would not be his own, Satan would speak through him, as long as Ebal agreed to the arrangement.

He was positive now, Woman saw him. Then the unthinkable happened.

———————

Woman called out, "Ebal!"

Ebal tried to remain still but then his eyes drifted down and to the left. He hoped she would not notice and at the same time his eyes continued their painfully slow excursion until they met Woman's.

She called out again, "Ebal! What are you doing up there?"

He tried to move his head, but it was locked in place. He opened his mouth to say something but his voice had turned into a high pitched squealing groan. Then he thought, *I agree! Speak through me, Satan!*

A certain tingling feeling washed over the serpent ending with his face flush with warmth. Then a smile spread across his face.

Woman called out again, "Ebal, I know you can hear me, what are you doing up there?"

Ebal's head jerked toward the sound of the voice, "I am watching you, looking at this tree, of course!" Then with another quick jerk he released himself from the wall and with a few heavy wing flaps dropped to the ground some ten yards from her, his body facing the tree. Then with a sideways glance he peered over at Woman.

Turning back to the tree, he said, "You are staring with great intent at this tree."

She walked toward him, "I am amazed at how it has grown, it is taller than the other trees in the garden, It might be the tallest one in the world."

Ebal stepped closer to the tree, "How would you know if it were the tallest? You are confined in this garden."

She thought for a moment, "The Creator is protecting us from the fallen ones."

"I may be mistaken but I thought I had seen the guardians leave."

"Yes, they left for a day. They will return tomorrow."

"So the Creator is protecting you, and yet He removed your guardians, what do you suppose will happen in their absence?"

"I do not know, what do you mean?"

"It doesn't matter, listen, I have had a question on my mind for some time now, I was wondering..." His voice trailed off.

"What were you wondering? I will answer it if I can."

"It would be such a shame if it were true, and mind you, I was not there when the command was given, but did the Creator say, 'You must not eat from any tree in the garden?'"

"Oh no, we *are* to eat the fruit from the trees in the garden. All except for this one, this tree in the midst of the garden we are not to eat from, nor even touch it."

Ebal smiled, "I wonder what the all powerful Creator is afraid of?"

"What do you mean?"

Ebal looked down at the ground and pursed his lips, "He made this tree, placed it before you, then said you should not eat of it."

"Right, because if we do, we will die."

Ebal shook his head. "Die? That is not true. You shall surely *not* die. Can you not see what He is doing?"

"You are confusing me, you said we will not die when the Creator was very clear on this matter."

"And you believe He is trying to protect you. These walls hold you in, they do not keep anything out." Ebal remembered the monster he had seen beyond the walls and tried to stop his mouth, but Satan had full control. Ebal's voice continued, "He removed the angels from their posts, how does that protect you? He knows you will not climb the walls to your freedom. You believe you are free when you are locked up!

"Do you not know that there is a whole world out there? Maybe there are taller trees than this one, but you cannot know. Why? Because you stay in the garden, because you blindly follow. You could be so much more than you are, but you stay in your cage."

Woman put her hand to her forehead, the world Ebal described fit her situation, but his point of view made the Creator, her Creator appear cruel, in the most underhanded of ways.

Ebal continued, "Perhaps He is trying to keep you from the ones that can help you to be more."

"But He created us, He knows what is best for us. He made us with purpose."

"He made you as pets and placed you inside this cage so He can come and pet you once a day. Can you not see why you are not to eat from this tree? He placed it here as a cruel joke! He knows the truth about this tree."

"What truth?"

"This truth," Ebal jumped into the air and flew to the nearest clump of fruit from the tall tree. He grabbed the base of the grape-like cluster and snapped it back on itself, breaking the entire clump free from the branch, and sending a half-dozen leaves twirling in the air. He descended back to the ground, this time right next to Woman. "This is the truth you are missing," He held the fruit out to her as she reeled back. "When you eat of this fruit you will become more, you will be like Him, you will be like the Creator!

"When you eat of it your eyes will be opened and you will see the truth. You will no longer need to follow along as one with no eyes. When you eat of this fruit, you shall be like Elohim. And like Him, you will know and judge what is good and what is evil."

Expressionless, Woman watched the leaves of the tree drift to the ground at her feet and replied, "I cannot touch that fruit."

Ebal leaned toward her, the cluster of fruit held in front of his face. "Look at me, I am not dead. How could it be any different for you? Are you not made to have dominion? You are made higher than I, if I can touch it and not die, you will not die."

Ebal turned from her and spoke into the air, "Unless you are beneath me."

Woman turned her back to the serpent. Thoughts raced through her head.

He said we would be like the Creator, and Elohim's counterpart will be like Him.

But Elohim said not to eat from that tree, He said we would die.

But Ebal is not dead.

Woman reached down and took hold of one of the tiny leaves.

Adam's voice broke into Woman's consciousness. "Like Elohim?"

Woman looked toward the sound of her counterpart, "Adam! I am glad you are..."

The serpent interrupted her, "See, there is nothing to be afraid of."

She scowled, "I am not the one holding the fruit."

"This my dear is fruit, not some evil elixir. It is harmless," he held it out to her, "See?" The serpent stepped toward her.

Woman backed away once again. "I am not going to touch it."

The serpent teased her, "You act like it will bite you. Besides, you already touched the leaf, and you are not dead."

Adam whispered to his bride, "Did he say we would be like Elohim?"

Woman looked into Adam's eyes, "Yes, he did."

Adam thought as he spoke, "Is it not true that Elohim's counterpart will be like Him? In the same way you are like me?"

Her eyes shifted to his lips, "Yes, I suppose so."

His eyes caught hers, "Elohim's bride will be taken out of Him, right?"

"Yes, as I was taken out of you." She took hold of his hand.

Adam's eyes grew stern, "We were taken out of Him, were we not? All of creation was..."

Woman glanced back toward the fruit in Ebal's hands, "...but Elohim said *not* to eat it."

Adam shook his head, "Yes, you are right. I do not claim to understand, maybe this fruit will make us into the counterpart sooner, Elohim would not have to wait any longer."

Woman looked away, thinking out loud, "So if we eat the fruit, we will be like Him, so we will be changed into His counterpart?"

Adam nodded his head with a scowl distorting his face, "Yes, maybe, but I cannot be sure."

Woman took in a long breath, held it briefly, then took a step toward Ebal and motioned for some of the fruit.

Raguel, the Archangel of Justice, flew toward the throne room. He soared over the grass field, arms outstretched under his broad black wings. The trees surrounding the field and throne room moved in rhythm. Their leaves, fluttered in a way no wind could account for and produced harmonic shimmering sounds while also reflecting light in a visual and auditory chorus of song.

The palace had grown larger in the season following the six days of creation. As he neared the entrance a cold wind spun him around and knocked him backward in the air. Raguel caught the air, circled round, and flew back in his previous direction.

The trees fell silent and a great clamor rose from inside the building. Something must have happened, but what could happen here, in Paradise? The angel touched down just outside the doors and pushed through without a sound.

———

The ground beneath Man shuttered. All around him, darkness mingled with light. He looked at the base of the tree and noticed, for the first time, darkness, in the form of shadows in front of him. Where he once cast light, now he cast darkness. His eyes continued downward, slowly. Flesh, he saw the flesh that covered his feet. His skin looked like the skin of the creatures all around him. For a moment he did not comprehend what he saw.

Woman gasped.

He looked up and saw her without the garment of light that had always surrounded her. She stood naked, staring at him with panic in her expression. He felt dizzy.

The ground shook once more. The man looked up into the trees. The colors of the leaves faded before his eyes.

He spoke to the air around him, "What is happening?" The green faded and the veins in the leaves turned to a reddish color while the fleshy parts changed to a golden yellow.

A single leaf fell from the tree.

Adam picked it up and peered at it before turning it over, utterly confused.

Another leaf fell.

Woman knelt down to pick it up.

Several more fell and Adam's eyes pulled free from the leaf in his hand. He peered past Woman, leaves fell as far as he could see. "What is happening?" The leaf in his hand fell to the ground.

Woman caught another leaf as it toppled through the air. "I do not know."

Adam peered at his wife, this time realizing what he was seeing, then back at himself, "We are naked!"

Woman's hands aimlessly groped her body, "What happened to our covering?"

Adam looked at his wife, "Did we die? Are we dead?"

"I do not know!" Woman exclaimed.

Adam held the remainder of the fruit out in front of him. "The leaves, why do they fall?" With furrowed brow he peered at the remaining round orbs. "What have we done?" He turned his hand over releasing the fruit, his offense held firm. He shook his hand, releasing the sticky grip of the fruit, and it fell to the ground.

Adam grabbed his wife's hand and the two ran through the clearing and into the surrounding fig trees.

The Earth trembled beneath them once again, this time the shaking was more intense and toppled both of them to the ground. Leaves fell in mass over them, partially covering them.

Adam rose to his feet again, "The trees are dying!"

Woman grabbed some of the leaves. "These can cover us, look." She held up an armful of leaves over her breasts and glanced toward her husband. Adam shook his head and her glance was met with questioning anger.

He closed his eyes, and faced the sky.

Woman questioned her husband, "Adam, can you not see that we can fix this?"

His head pivoted back down and he opened his eyes slowly, she had never seen this foreboding look before. It scared her. She saw an idea pass over him and he turned to face the watershed divide. They could not see it through the thick grove of fig trees, but it was there, the place of Adam's creation.

She broke his concentration if only for a moment, "Adam?"

Adam's mind raced, he could not bear to listen anymore. *The place where it all began, where I began, I must get back to that place. The answers are there.*

Adam ran.

Woman shouted, "Where are you going?"

No response.

She sat down under one of the fig trees, among the contorted roots. Leaves continued to fall around her. She caught one and ran her hand over it. She held it as though it was something precious.

"Why did I listen to Ebal?" She sat and stared at the leaf, or maybe she stared past it, in silence.

———

Jessica looked up from the note pad and scroll, leaned back in her chair, and looked at the clock on her computer's display, two o'clock in the morning. "People will not accept these books as the truth of what happened."

She heard a familiar voice behind her. "They are not intended to."

She swung around in her chair to see Michael leaning against the wall, "What do you mean?"

He pulled out one of the dining room chairs and sat down to face her. "These books are not intended to be a new Torah, or a new Bible."

Jessica placed her pen on the desk, "So, you're saying that they're not what happened?"

"I am not saying that, I am saying that you were charged with writing three novels, not scripture."

She thought for a moment. "Ok, so I'm not writing the absolute truth."

"Did you think you were? Why would your assignment involve novels, if the Creator wanted you to write scripture?"

"So what am I doing this for? I mean, if I'm not presenting the truth, then what is all this for. And why would the enemy be against me? For Pete's sake, there's an injured messenger downstairs! Why does someone care enough about novels for all this to be happening?"

"Your mission is to write these books. In doing so, you are planting seeds into the culture that have been lost. Some who read these books will feel those ideas resonate within them. That resonation will help to change how they see the world."

"Some? So not everyone will accept them?"

"Of course not. Choice is never pushed aside."

"So, some will never, or maybe *could* never, accept the books, that's what you're saying?"

"Correct, in fact there is a controversy stirring right now over your first book."

"What do you mean? What are people saying?"

"It is of no importance."

"How can you say that? What if it's important to me?"

"Because you did not write the book for the praise of men. As I said before, when I collected the first scroll, there will always be those that side with the enemy, as well as those who will never take sides. You cannot give those people a second thought, they are not given to you."

"But if I could just talk to them, maybe I could convince them."

"Do not allow yourself to be pulled away from the mission the Creator has given you, the enemy is the master of delay and to step aside from your calling to convince a few outspoken skeptics would play right into the enemy's schemes. You must trust in the one who called you. And you must be able to believe that the Creator's voice of approval is all you need."

"I have seen that about your kind." She paused. "I admire it."

Michael let out a deep breath, "Not all of my kind have held to these ideals. Sometimes the right thing to do is also the hardest thing, to stand in the middle of a buffeting wind of adversity. To remain, when loud voices all around demand that you shrink back. It is then that you must prepare yourself. Those are the times when you must be strong and your belief must rise above those voices. You must allow the spirit of the Creator to be louder inside of you than those voices that are outside of you. Only then can you endure to the end."

"I know you are right, I trust your words. You have become a good friend, someone I can listen to and know you will only ever speak truth to me." She stood and pushed her chair into it's place. "I'm going to turn in so I can hit it fresh in the morning." She looked down and moved her mouse to a corner of the screen to start the screen saver, then glanced over at Michael. "Goodnight."

With that, Jessica walked to her bedroom and eased the door closed behind her.

Michael smiled.

Chapter 9

Desperation

The captain stood on the scribe's balcony and looked out over the field they had once used as a parade field. So much had happened since those days. He heard footsteps behind him and turned to look over his shoulder at the sound of a familiar voice.

"Michael! It is always good to see you my friend!" Metatron moved toward the archangel and the two grasped each others forearms forming a sort of embraced handshake.

"You sent for me?"

"Yes, yes. Please come inside. I can see from your countenance that you have come from the throne room. You must be on your way back to Earth, that is good. You have been doing a splendid job protecting the daughter of Moses. I see that she has published the book, all is going according to plan, of course."

"Is this why you summoned me?"

"No, no. There is another matter." The scribe motioned for Michael to come closer. "There have been a number of seraphim leaving the region of Persia and moving toward the America's."

"The Prince over Persia has released troops? That is unheard of!"

Metatron turned to face the old parade field once more, "Yes, but it is true, and you should be prepared."

Michael thought out loud, "So with the release of the book they have uncovered Jessica's assignment...."

Metatron continued his sentence, "...and they are determined to stop her. Anarkum is on his way, as are others from across the globe."

Michael's eyes stared off into the distance, finding nothing to rest on. "It has begun again. As it did with Hook."

Metatron spoke without turning, "This time you can succeed. She is different."

Michael moved next to his king, "Will we succeed? I do not want to lose another one, not this one."

Metatron looked at the archangel, "I know, she has become precious to you. You are beginning to see her heart, and why she was chosen."

Michael stood motionless for a moment, then turned to look over the grass field once again, his jaw clenched.

Metatron looked back toward the field, "The next steps are yours to plan."

The archangel's eyes glanced in Metatron's direction then back to the field below. "I will speak to Uriel. Perhaps he can spare some troops."

"Help will come, I will see to it myself." Metatron paused, "There is one more thing, Anarkum will take Hook's grandson."

"I HATE WATER!" Anarkum exclaimed as he stood at the base of a cliff surrounded on three sides by the waters of the Mediterranean Sea. He could think of no worse spot than one such as this. He hated the sea, hated rivers, lakes, and streams; He hated water!

He stood there on the most northeastern spot in Cyprus, hour after hour, waiting. The ferry from Turkey had been bad, possibly worse than this, since it was quite a long and bumpy ride. He'd chosen to spend the trip away from the other passengers. It was not that he thought they would dislike his company, but more to the point, that he could not stand being with these children of Man. Unless of course he was in possession of one of them.

He had paced fore and aft, the entire trip, restless. The people he could not stand, inside the boat, and that horrible water all around.

A few were "chosen" and he could not stand to be around that crowd, ever! They were insufferable! The white glow that emanated from their torsos, some quite bright but most flickered rather dim. Even so, they were easy to spot.

On the whole, the majority of people radiated a sort of darkness, the opposite of the light of the "chosen few," as they liked to refer to themselves. To him they were arrogant idiots, following the ultimate arrogant idiot.

The one they followed was the one that had pulled Anarkum and a legion of his cohorts out of a man on an island, and spewed them into a herd of pigs. As though making some sort of statement about their original bodies being unclean. Then, when those same swine cast themselves into the sea, that one stood idly by and watched them all drown. It was the same as at the time of the great rupture.

He paused at the stern of the ferry, and looked all around at the sea, then continued his vigil, pacing, like a crazed dog, worried.

He hated water, absolutely hated it.

His father had repeatedly assured him that the world would never be flooded again, that the Creator had promised, but Anarkum did not trust the Creator. The incident with the pigs showed that He didn't mind drowning them again, and again.

He hated water.

———————

He waited close to five hours, bored and impatient, when finally the sea to his left began to heave upward. A form could be seen beneath the water. Anisotropic reflections from sunlight on scales magnified by the refraction of the sea. As the immense body neared the surface, the water above it shook violently, frothing. Then a deep growling roar made the outcrop of land vibrate. Fear arose in the demon, or maybe it was dread. Either way, it was something he had not felt for a long time. Now, the long forgotten feeling threatened to choke him, like coils wound around his throat, tightening ever so slowly.

All at once the head of the beast rose from the water, sending a torrent of spray in all directions. It moved toward the rocky cliffs that separated the land from the sea, piling coil upon coil onto the barely submerged land just in front of the demon.

In the many millennia of his existence, Anarkum had not actually met this "Leviathan" before and the soothing voice was not what he would have expected from a serpent of the magnitude before him. Then, after she had heard the message from Azazel, her words were poised and steady, "There will be no death by my hand."

Anarkum began to boil, "When did you gain a conscience?" Then unbeknownst to him, his ghostly properties began to condense into a sort of body, similar to a man but thinner, less dense.

If she noticed his change of state, Leviathan gave no indication of it. Perhaps she had something to do with it. "You wish me to do your part? I will not. You are the death broker, I will turn the whole world against this 'Jessica'. It will collapse around her, encompassing her in coils that restrict her movement, then her vision, then her very breath. I will lead this woman to the brink of death, but I will not push her over. When I'm through with her she will decide on her own to walk away from the Divine path, of her own accord, more or less." He had to admit, the gentleness by which she discussed this woman's demise intrigued him.

Anarkum, with his back to a cliff, stared at the 1,800-foot, coiled and writhing creature for a long moment, "I will do what must be done. My heart is not so soft as that of the great and terrible sea python."

Leviathan's head turned away as the tail of the creature cracked, whip-like. Anarkum sailed backward into the cliff, his face grimaced with pain as he fell to his knees. Pain shot up his thighs, and down his shins.

Leviathan's tail pushed the demon tight against the cliff, then shoved him up against the rocks, his feet unable to touch the ground. The massive coils wound tighter on themselves, thousands of metallic scales ratcheted over one another raising a cacophony of sound. The snake's massive head swiveled back to the demon. She could have swallowed Anarkum with little effort, at least in this more solid form, but instead her tongue flicked mere inches from the unclean spirit's face.

"You would do well not to test me, demon."

Anarkum gasped as the grotesque smell of stagnation and rot filled the air with every word from the great serpent's mouth. He tried to breathe as little as possible. "I only meant that you seem less...fearless, than I had anticipated. Obviously, first impressions can be misleading." It had been so long since he had felt sensations like this, yet here he was, struggling to breathe.

"For the sake of your father," the serpent pushed the demon harder against the cliff. Anarkum's right cheek began to spasm as he struggled in vain to maintain his composure. The serpent spoke slowly. "I will turn my attention to this woman." She turned her head away to face the waves that slapped against the cliffs, sending spray high into the air. "Where is she now?"

The demon wheezed out a slow but perceptible answer, "A small town...North America...Divide...Colorado."

Her head reared back, she thought for an instant, then turned back to the demon. "Divide? Interesting," the serpent released Anarkum, who toppled back down to his knees. "I am familiar with that region, in fact one of the captives is returning there now."

The demon rose to his feet, rubbing his neck, "Which one was released?"

"Oh, you will have fun with him. I will let you discover who it is on your own."

Adam ran as fast as he could, jumping rivers and streams. Face soaked with salty tears, he scanned the garden around him. As far as

he could see, leaves drifted to the ground. Something within him
drove him forward. He pressed on, surely there would be an end to
this madness, somewhere. He moved fast, and covered the distance to
the watershed divide in just over an hour, easily forty miles. He leapt
over the divide's surrounding moat and continued through the trees,
without breaking his stride, toward the top.

Just then a tree reached out and snagged his arm as he flew by, the
surface of his muscle ripped open. He pressed on but slowed when he
reached the grass-covered hill top. Just inside the tree line he gazed
out at the place of his creation. The place where it all began, for him at
least.

———

The massive Leviathan uncoiled back into the water. Anarkum
watched and marveled at her size and obvious strength. She did not
appear withered up like the land dragons and he wondered if the
hoards of angels under her command looked as good. Surely, she held
some secret under the waves.

———

Now motionless, Adam surveyed all that was given to him. He
peered out over the garden and the surrounding countryside. Once
green, everything had become muted, pale. The Earth shook once
again.

He reached up with his left hand, aimlessly, to a dampened pain
on the outside of his right bicep, blood seeped from the wound.
Something stabbed his finger. He held his arm out and looked at the
cut. There was something in it. He reached over and pulled a five inch

thorn from his flesh, held it up in front of his face, then looked up into the trees, bewildered. He had no memory of the trees having thorns. The Earth quaked once again.

The dam of his emotions broke and he whispered through uncontrolled tears, "What have I done?" He dropped the thorn. "The beginning of my eighth year is marked by my death."

Up ahead a sound cut through his consciousness, something crashing about. He ventured forward toward the sound. One of the smaller trees moved and shook. Up ahead he could make out a patch of tawny fur, stained with blood. Adam moved into the clearing to see a stag, his antlers caught, bucking wildly in a panic. The big bull's head, covered with blood, was host to dozens of the tree's thorns, most of which were buried deep in the deer's flesh.

Adam's first instinct was to help. He rushed toward the bull and grabbed one of the big antlers just as the stag broke free. Several limbs crashed to the ground and the sudden jerking motion pulled the man off balance. He tripped, lurching toward the bull. The stag jerked backward as well, then stopped and peered at the man. Adam righted himself, and moved toward the deer, as he would have done on any other day. But then something happened that Adam would have never expected, the deer backed further away and lowered his antlers, he looked past them at the man.

Adam did not understand, something was wrong, "What are you doing?"

The bull charged and Adam caught the antlers. The bull's brow tines piercing each of his palms. Adam yelled once again, "What are you doing?"

The stag did not answer, but kept pushing until he had the man up against the very tree that had a moment earlier held him captive. Adam pushed with all his might, muscles rippled, veins bulged, teeth bared, but the stronger bull pushed the man flat against the tree with a deep grunt, eyes wild. The bull's rack caged the man, the tines pierced his hands completely through. Then all at once, with a great thrust the bull pushed Adam upward along the rough bark. Adam strained against the pain while the bark cut into his back. His head thrust back, into the thorns, several broke off under the muscles of his forehead. A guttural snarl escaped through clenched teeth as the tree's bark tore deep gashes into the meat of his back.

Adam roared, "STOP!"

The bull pulled up, backed away and Adam fell to the ground, pain surged through his feet and legs. He thrust forward and the limbs he had fallen on came with him, their long spikes empaled both of his feet. The bloody beast backed further away, head cocked to one side. The man and the beast stared at one another, frozen. Then, as if startled, the big animal turned and disappeared into the woods.

"How could we...," Adam's voice trailed off. Blood and sweat trickled down his face. He worked the limb free from his feet and sat alone among the lifeless barren trees. A fog rolled in. His eyes wet, he brushed his nose with his forearm. His expression washed away.

The Earth shuddered once more. Sobs replaced the peace that had once filled the garden, while the grass around him faded to a light brown. Among the tears the man muttered to himself, "it's all dead...dead."

―――――――――

Ebal watched the woman. In a daze, she sat among the serpentine roots of one of the larger fig trees. Her expression blank, a single tear rolled down her left cheek. Her eyes drifted up, at nothing. She pulled her knees up and rested her arms on top of them, then lowered her head to her forearms and cried.

Ebal wasn't sure what he should do, he drifted closer to her, knowing he should at least apologize. He opened his mouth to speak but what came out was more like a bark or cough. His left hand grasped his throat.

Woman looked at him.

He looked down at the fruit in his right hand. His eyes grew wide and he threw the wretched food behind him, moving silently backward toward the edge of the clearing unsure of what was happening to the world.

Woman wiped the tears from her eyes. Her left hand fell to the ground and she felt the leaves under her palm. She picked one up and looked intently at the pores in the surface of the leaf. She pulled at its flesh. The softer parts tore away from the ridges. She picked the flesh clean, then picked up another and began the process over again, fascinated with the structure of each leaf. Her mind found a measure of comfort in this mindless business.

After she had stripped several of the leaves she held up the naked remainder and picked off the side ridges, leaving only the single middle strands.

She began splitting the stems, revealing the fibrous interior. Eyeing the fibers she began twirling them in her fingers. Her interest returned to the leaves and she held one up, and pushed an intact stem through it's flesh. Then she fed the twirled fibers through. The end of the fibers had a bit of the stem intact and would not pull through the leaf's flesh easily which gave her an idea. She lifted another leaf, pushed the stem through it's flesh and fed the fibers through the second leaf. She looped the fibers and tied the end.

"I can fix this!" She began scooping leaves from all around her and busily repeated the process, sewing together the leaves.

Adam remained in a heap, silent. He could not think, no reason remained in him, only bitter dejection. Cool air washed over him. His body felt strange. He sat up. The cool breeze blew past again, coming from behind him. He turned to see a mist, then rose to his feet, *The Creator will be coming.* He looked around to regain his bearing. *I have left Woman to bear this pain alone and Elohim will be coming! I have to get back before His arrival.*

He limped a few steps. The pain in his feet had decreased a small measure, but he knew he had to get back. He took off the same way he had come. A thorny tree caught his other arm, maybe the same tree as before, he did not stop.

Satan watched Adam rise to his feet and take off toward the center of the garden, a wide grin across his face.

Raguel stood in the doorway of the throne room, blank expression, shoulders slumped. His skin, for the first time, cold. He searched for Metatron, but could not find him. The four giant seraphim-hayoth creatures around the throne snapped and lashed out at one another. Hurling insults back and forth. The chaos was foreign to his eyes, at least in this place.

The cacophony of millions of angels surrounding the throne, whose praises for the Creator could be heard throughout Paradise, were now but a low, soft drone. Chant-like.

Raguel squinted, "What is happening?" A figure knelt before the throne. "Metatron!"

The big archangel leapt into the air and in several minutes came to rest some fifty yards shy of the scribe. He stood, staring into Elohim's purple-blue flames, they now flowed downward, and washed over Metatron, enveloping him. The scribe's back rose and fell, his sobs could be heard over the roar of the flames.

Raguel glanced to the stadium seats.

Empty.

He stepped to the side, to look past the throne, then stepped again.

Empty.

There had been two figures up there, directly in the middle of the multiplied millions of seats, now nothing. The archangel moved forward toward the scribe.

A searing pain shot through him as his foot proceeded into the flames. He jerked back, scorched, and his flesh healed quickly.

Adam ran as fast as he could, though now the way looked different, the trees continued to loose their leaves, but now they appeared angry, maybe it was their naked limbs. He could no longer sense their praise to the Creator, perhaps they were already dead. His pace slowed as he looked at them, his chest heaved with an uncontrolled shutter, even as his lips quivered. He was too tired, his life had drained out. He had lost the ability to express anything.

"...but do not eat of the tree of the knowledge of good and evil, for in the day you eat of it, you shall certainly die."

That phrase repeated itself over and over in his mind. It mocked him. It was laughing, jeering, a sickening laugh. His stomach hurt as though it carried some heavy thing.

He closed his eyes in a effort to see the throne, to find some comfort. He could not see it. Come to think of it he could no longer see the cherubim, seraphim serpents, nor the ophanim orbs that hovered throughout the garden. Then he remembered that he could not hear the intentions or "voice" of the stag that had been caught in the thorny tree.

"I must be dying. I am loosing my ability to see and hear! Woman? I must get back to her. If we are going to die, we are going to die together!" He sprinted with new found energy toward his wife.

Woman stood, covered in leaves she had stitched together, she'd used some of her own hair as a loop to hold it up around her neck. She had pulled the loop over her head when Adam approached.

"Adam!" She held a second garment up for him to see." Look what I've made from the leaves."

He grimaced, "What is it?"

"A covering! So we are not naked any more. I hope it is long enough, you are so tall. I had to guess at the length." She walked over to her husband, who stood and stared at her, bewildered. She held the apron up by the loop of hair.

He continued to stare at her, then raised his eyebrows. Clearly she wanted him to do something, but he had no idea what. "Adam, let me put this over your head. Bend down a little."

He grunted awkwardly and bent at the waist just enough for her to loop the hair-strap over his head. When he straightened back up the apron covered him fairly well. The two stood there looking at each other, the aprons hanging loosely in front of them.

Woman's face contorted into a grimace, "They could use some improvement."

Adam's face turned red, he felt a heat rising inside him. He was angry without knowing why, exactly. *She is trying to undo what we have done. She is trying to fix this.*

He looked down at his own garment and pulled the sides around his waste, "Maybe one more loop of hair would do it. We can use mine."

Woman looked at her husband's wounds as he spoke, "Adam, you look terrible! What happened to you?"

Startled, he looked up.

"What is this?" She reached for his bloody arm, but he turned away, his back toward her, blood still seeped from the long gash.

She looked at her husband's face, "What happened to you?"

Just then Adam heard a distant roaring sound, then felt a sudden wind. His head swiveled toward the sound, "Elohim is coming."

"Where?"

"I do not see Him. But I hear Him." Adam and Woman moved behind one of the large fig trees.

Woman clutched the tree. "My heart is pounding. I cannot breathe. Husband, I think I am dying. I can no longer see the Creator on His throne." She shook her head, her eyes, swollen.

111

He peered around the tree's truck, "I am dying as well. I cannot see the throne either, nor the guardians."

Woman reached over and took Adam's hand, "I am glad you came back before the end."

"I am too." He leaned toward her and kissed her. Her lips felt cold and her breathing fast, much like his. He squeezed her hand slightly. Adam heard the sound of his wife crying, softly. His own emotions again broke open and all of mankind felt the anguish of regret, the kind you wish with all that you are, you could take back.

But you know you cannot.

Distant thunder peeled toward them. Clear and distinct it spoke, "Adam, where are you?"

Woman whispered, "The Creator is here."

Adam's heart broke yet again, he closed his eyes. *How do I face Elohim? I cannot stand before Him now, not now.*

He clutched his stomach and sunk to the ground. "The Creator told us this would happen." He leaned over, one hand against the tree. Back arched, his stomach wretched in a violent dry heave, then another, and another. Saliva drooled to the ground and mingled with tears, sweat, and blood. His entire body ached. Woman held him around his torso, her cheek against his back. His blood stained her face.

He righted himself. "I feel like my body is turning inside out. 'surely die', is what He said, right? He said we would 'surely die?'"

Again the thunder rolled gently over them. "Adam, where are you?"

"Elohim?"

"Yes, Adam," The voice was all around them, but their eyes could not see Him.

Adam wiped his nose with the back of his hand, "I hide from you because I am naked." Tears again flowed down his face.

An outer layer of skin began to form over the dermal surface of the man and his wife. Since the covering of light had left the two, the Creator provided them with a new, fleshy, protective layer of skin.

"Who made you know that you were naked? Have you eaten from the tree of which I commanded you not to eat?"

Woman crouched next to her husband. Her apron failed to cover her now and Adam stared, in all his agony, transfixed on her form. For a moment his eyes cleared, though his breathing increased.

The man tore his gaze from his wife and looked down at the ground as though searching for something. Panic rose through his being, then words blurted out, "The woman, it was the woman you gave to me, she gave me of the tree and I ate." Realizing what he'd just done, Adam buried his head in his hands. His face squinted as though some deep pain tore at him.

Woman backed away from her love, her eyes wide. She looked up into the air, all around.

The sky again erupted in thunder, "Woman, what is this you have done?"

Her jaw dropped as she looked back at her husband, incredulous. Out of the corner of her eye she saw Ebal, peering out from behind another of the fig trees. She pointed at him, "It was the serpent! He deceived me and I ate."

Ebal felt the crushing weight of the Creator's stare. The pillar of fire was clearly before him, but now Ebal could not speak. He felt hatred for the woman, his friend betrayed him. He stood and hissed, his tongue flicked the air.

The Creator spoke again, "Serpent, because you have done this, you are cursed more than all livestock and more than every beast of the field."

Ebal's legs gave out and he flopped to his belly.

"On your belly you and your kind are to go and eat dust of the ground all the days of your life."

Six cherubim approached the serpent. His head reared up and looked at each of them. In perfect unison they unsheathed their swords. Terror filled his mind as they surrounded him, he wanted to scream, but all that came out were hoarse coughs. All at once the cherubim lunged toward him, each taking hold of one of his six limbs. They stretched him out flat on his belly, the serpent's bellows and coughs turned into screeching wails that made the man and woman wince. In perfect unison the six swords came down, severing the limbs of the serpent. The wounds healed instantly in the presence of Elohim, and Ebal laid screeching, his body twisting and buckling, unable to move. Unnoticed by the serpent, his pelvis and shoulders began to dissolve while ribs grew from every vertebrae. The angels moved off to find each of the serpents kind, in order to carry out the mandate of the Creator on each of them.

———————

Satan watched from a distance, a chuckle erupted with a tuft of smoke when the angels exacted Ebal's punishment. He knew that by wounding the man, he had wounded the Creator, and driving a wedge between the two made it all that much better. Some thought he was mad, that going after Man was a lost cause, but he knew differently and now his knowledge had paid off. He knew from the day Adam was created that the great Elohim had a soft spot for these creatures. A soft spot that had now been successfully exploited. He had severed the tie and had caused mankind to fall away. Now to really stab at the heart of Elohim, he would have to make Man love Satan, in place of Elohim. He would prove the Creator was wrong—that He had erred —and any creature that errs cannot be a God.

––––––––––

The Creator's gaze shifted to Satan, pushing him to the ground. The Creator spoke, "And I put enmity between you and the woman and between your seed and her seed. And her seed shall crush your head and you shall crush his heal." His gaze moved off again and He continued to speak to the man and his wife, but Satan could not think, could not reason. All he could do was lay there, he hated the Creator and he hated the Creator's power. Then a thought centered itself inside of the dragon's vast intellect. A thought that consisted of one word, a word he had not considered before and certainly never thought could be applied to his kind. The word ran through his mind again and again until, finally, he whispered it.

"Seed."

Chapter 10
Arrival

It was a little before two o'clock in the morning when a taxi pulled up to the Safeway grocery store on the edge of town. He'd finally made it to Woodland Park, Colorado and the town was every bit as horrible as he had first imagined it would be. The air was crisp and cool and the stars shone bright on this cloudless night. The peacefulness in this place disgusted him.

"Soon enough," he thought to himself, "I'll get this place stirred up."

The taxi driver that he possessed would never know how he had ended up so far from Denver. The whiskey-induced stupor had plunged the driver so far from consciousness that he'd been easy to control. No pesky interruptions from the host. Anarkum had considered killing him, as would be normal when he left a host but then he decided not to, saying to himself, "This one will cause enough problems on his own."

Anarkum sat and thought about waiting for morning to arrive. Many people would come and go from this place and maybe he could find his next host before the driver awoke.

Just then a small black SUV drove up. Anarkum watched with little interest until a tall young man unfolded himself from the smallish vehicle. It was a mildly amusing sight until something else caught his attention.

"Red hair. I haven't seen a good head of red hair in a long time."

The kid straightened his black apron and put his store hat on as he walked toward the building. Anarkum felt compelled to follow and pulled himself free from the unconscious driver. The cabby groaned as the last bits of the demon departed.

Anarkum caught up with the young man then matched his speed, remaining a few feet behind him. The young man stopped at the store entrance and began tapping his car keys against the glass.

Anarkum drifted around the young man in an attempt to figure out what he was doing. The tapping continued for a minute, a long minute.

Finally, someone inside the store arrived and unlocked the deadbolt, letting the young man in. The kid thanked the woman as she closed the door behind him. She smiled and locked the door.

Anarkum slid through the glass and continued his pursuit. The young man pushed one of the shopping carts and let it drift into the open area just past the doors then he turned to the right and walked into an area marked "Employees Only." The demon watched as the young man punched the buttons on some sort of device on the wall and walked back toward the cart. He waved at a couple of the night stock workers and pushed the cart past the checkout stations, he paused at several of the food shelves to check the packaging of the baked goods.

"Let's see," the young man rubbed his eyes and rummaged through packages of cinnamon rolls, "It's the twenty-sixth. OK, so I need all the one's with yesterday's date."

The demon watched the young man put several containers in the cart and continue down the row. He did this same thing several times on his way to the opposite end of the store.

He rounded the last isle and Anarkum glanced at the stock workers refilling shelves with packages of food before he too rounded the last isle and saw someone he had not expected to see. A tall dark cherubim stood next to the bakery counter staring at him.

"Remiel!" The demon shot across the store.

"Anarkum? You're a good bit outside your territory."

"Heh, yeah, my father sent me here."

"How is Azazel? Was he released?"

"He's about the same, and no, he's still locked up in those mountains."

"I remember the Creator spoke of his sins more than the rest of us, that's too bad. Did he send you here because of the book?"

"Yep, the Mozes woman."

"Have you seen the angelic covering yet?"

"Not yet, I just pulled in, but with you here, we should have no trouble."

"I wouldn't say that. Michael is with her."

"Yeah, that's what Father said. But we have Leviathan."

"How did you manage that?"

"My father, of course."

"Well my boy, your father knows how to stack a death, I mean deck."

The two laughed.

Remiel motioned to Anarkum, his chainmaille rustled, "What are you doing here?"

"I told you, my father sent me."

"No, I mean here, in this store."

"Oh, that kid, something about him intrigued me."

"Maybe the red hair, and his height?"

Anarkum laughed. "He's not as tall as we were, and he's skinny."

"He's tall for a man of this era."

"Maybe I should just kill him."

"That's one way to become less intrigued. Eh, leave him alive, maybe you can use him."

"Maybe. What's he doing in there?"

"I only know of one way to find out. Follow me."

The two moved to the rear of the bakery and found the young man looking onto a vat of hot grease. A wheeled, vertical rack of fifteen wire mesh trays each with two dozen pieces of flat circular dough stood beside him.

Remiel leaned over toward Anarkum. "Donuts."

"What?"

"He's making donuts."

Anarkum watched, "What is donuts?"

The man used a wooden stick, it looked almost like a drum stick, to flip each donut in the hot oil.

"Fried bread, they put sweet stuff on top. Nasty, if you ask me."

"You've tried it?"

"Sure, it pained me terribly."

The young man pulled the wire mesh with the cooked donuts from the hot grease, letting the excess oil drip back into the big fryer. Then he moved the screen over to a tray that was covered with wax paper and tilted the mesh just enough to let the donuts slide off.

Remiel sat down on the center table, it was a work table that measured six feet by four feet and resembled a thick butcher block cutting board.

Anarkum turned to the former archangel, "What are *you* doing here tonight?"

"I was flying over and saw you cross the parking lot, I came in through the side wall. Actually, I wasn't sure who you were. This *is* my territory after all."

"I see."

Anarkum began looking around the bakery, drifting around the work table. Behind him he heard a mechanical whirling. Surprised, he turned, a dispenser shot a paper towel out. Anarkum looked back at Remiel.

"What the heck?" The young man spoke, startled by the dispenser. "Geez, that thing scared the crap outta me!" He finished the tray he was working on by dipping the last two donuts into a tub of melted chocolate frosting and walked over to the sink, washed some chocolate off of his fingers and tore the paper towel off. There was an audible click as the machine reset itself. He stood there drying his hands and stared at the machine. He waved his hand in front of it again, and once more it spit out a paper towel. He tore it off and finished wiping his hands, then tossed the paper towels into a large trash can on his way back to the donuts. He glanced back toward the dispenser one last time, shook his head, and got back to work.

Remiel mused, "Maybe it saw you."

"How? It can't see me, can it?"

"Right, and you're still in front of it."

Anarkum's countenance went blank.

Remiel prodded the demon, "You can't stay there forever. Come on, let's get out of here." Remiel stood up from the table and walked toward the front of the store, not bothering to avoid obstacles. He slipped through them, sending energy ripples through everything he touched.

The demon exhaled loudly, looked at the towel dispenser and followed the cherubim. The machine whirled to life once more.

"What the heck!" The startled young man looked over at the machine once again. "What is wrong with that thing?"

––––––––––

Jessica stood on the back deck clutching a brown mug of hot coffee.

She sensed a familiar presence nearby and heard Michael's voice, "What is that look for?"

She glanced over at the archangel and sat the cup on the railing, still holding it. "What do you mean?"

Michael slowly appeared to her right, at the opposite end of the deck, "I have seen that look before, you are pondering something. Can I help, or would you prefer to be left alone with your thoughts?"

She looked into her mug for a short moment, then glanced back to her angelic friend, "You already know what I'm thinking?"

"Of course, but ask anyway."

"Alright," She turned around and backed up against the railing, "Why would God put an evil tree in the garden?"

Michael's voice was soothing, "The tree was not evil."

"Come to think of it, why would God *make* an evil tree? Can good create evil?"

He spoke again, "The tree was not evil."

"The tree in the garden, the 'knowledge of good and evil,' tree?"

His words slowed to a metered cadence, "The - tree - was - not - evil."

"Why do you keep saying that? Of course it was evil, they weren't allowed to eat its fruit."

"There are many of those trees in Paradise, it is not an evil tree. In fact, that very tree is in Paradise right now."

"But wait a second, why would He say not to eat from it if there was nothing wrong with it?"

"I am telling you, there was nothing wrong with it. What does it say that the Creator gave a boundary, which was abided by for a number of years, then when the boundary was violated the boundary itself was, and still is, blamed? It was not the tree that was evil, it was the act of judging the boundary. Now this is my perspective, but when Man judged the boundary and decided to do the thing that was forbidden, he judged the Creator, by judging the boundary."

"So they judged God?"

"Correct, your kind did in essence the same thing Lucifer had done in the throne room, the day he pointed his finger at the one who had given him life and declared judgement over the Creator. Then he convinced your kind to act like him, instead of being like the one who created you. In that moment, your kind was acting in the image of Satan, not Elohim. It was the act of bearing the image of Satan, or agreeing with sin."

He leaned with his hands on the deck rail and looked toward the woods, "Do you know what sin really is?"

"Yes, I was taught that sin is 'missing the mark.' It's an archery term, used for when an archer misses the center of the target."

Michael glanced back toward Jessica and then turned again to the forest. "Yes, that is true, in the most elementary sense, but it is more than that. There is an essence to it. That definition does not tell the whole story.

"To define something, such as sin, so narrowly, is to lose the real defining nature of the thing. You lose the reality within the definition."

Jessica raised the cup to her mouth, "So help me to understand." She took a sip.

Michael continued, "Lucifer originated sin and the weight of sin that has followed rides on that singular act. It took root and spread its branches far and wide. The consequences of his lack of self governance has rippled through time and space. Only Paradise itself is immune from its effects, and that is true only because Lucifer and all who agreed with him were expelled from Paradise.

"In order to understand sin you must first understand self government. You must understand what true self government is.

"Self government is an act of the will. It is when a created being, a creature, places herself into the will of the one that created her. This is true self government—governing or restricting one's self as originally intended."

He looked at Jessica and began walking slowly toward her, "Imagine that sin had never happened. Sin is, as I have just said, the act of willfully operating outside the will of the Creator. It is a state where an individual does not govern, or restrict, their own desires or behaviors.

"Sin is when a person says, in their own heart, 'I do not believe the Almighty knows what is right for me. I will decide what is right for me, regardless of any consequences.'

"It is not just a matter of an archer missing the mark, or missing a target by some mistake or miscalculation. It is more like the Creator made an archer that never misses the mark, until one day that same archer decides that to miss the mark is better than to hit it. He decides to shoot whatever he wants."

Jessica looked confused, so he tried again. "It is like a person saying something like this, 'I do not believe the Creator is worthy of being trusted with my life. Since I cannot trust him, I must take matters unto myself and exclude Him. I must therefore stand in defiance of the one who made me."

His voice became louder, "It is like saying, 'If sin had never existed before, I would now start it myself. But, since sin has already begun, I am glad it exists, and I hereby sign on as one in agreement with it."

Michael stopped in front of Jessica, their eyes locked together, "It is standing with pride in the camp of the enemy and proclaiming Satan to be right. It is to judge the Creator as the one that is wrong."

Nick stood in the back of the bakery, he'd finished all the early bread baking and the donuts, and aimlessly cleaned the large central work table.

The morning clerk had arrived and was at the front of the bakery, at the counter, putting the fresh bread into bags. Then she attached a label to each bag.

Nick looked at the clock to see that it was almost time. He would leave at 8:00 a.m. for his "lunch" break.

He looked out past the bakery counter and saw the usuals in for their breakfast donuts, bagels, and pastries. Most wore business attire, probably picking up treats for their offices. Then, someone he'd never seen before walked toward the bagels. A short blonde, very cute. Her walk was confident and she wore blue jeans and a sweater. Not the usual attire for the morning crowd here. Usually, if they weren't wearing business clothes they were women who looked like they'd just rolled out of bed, they were lucky if their hair was combed. Heck, some even wore slippers. No, this one was different.

"Nick?"

He could have sworn he'd heard his name.

"Hey Nick!"

He turned to see Cara, the morning clerk looking at him.

The older woman laughed at him. "Yeah she *is* cute, huh? I thought you were leaving at eight."

"Oh, I didn't even notice the time." He reached around his back to untie his apron.

Cara laughed as she looked back toward the blonde and shook her head. "No, I guess you didn't."

Nick hung his apron onto a hook next to the clock and walked toward the store floor. A man on a mission.

Cara laughed again, "You never go out that way! Not avoiding people like normal today?"

He smiled at her, "Nope, not today."

Nick walked right over to the young woman, "Excuse me miss, are you finding everything ok?"

"Well I'm not finding any blueberry bagels."

"I'm sorry ma'am, looks like we're out for the day."

"Do you have more in the back?"

"No ma'am, we only bake a certain number per day. Looks like someone came in and cleaned us out. Have you tried the cheddar and jalapeño bagels?"

"Jalapeño peppers? Oh, I don't know about that, I'm not really into spicy food. I mean really spicy, a little hot is ok."

"If you'd like I can let you try a sample."

"Sure, that would be great."

Nick opened the glass door on the bagel display, pulled what looked like a plastic tissue from a dispenser and used it to remove two bagels, a cheddar jalapeño and a plain cheddar. "Ma'am, if you'll follow me, I'll cut this for you."

She smiled at him, "Alrighty."

Nick walked behind the counter, Cara smiled and shook her head as she continued to bag the morning bread.

The young woman watched him cut the two bagels, then noticed his name badge. "Your name is Nick?"

"Yes ma'am!" He placed a piece of the first bagel on a paper towel then began to cut the second bagel. "Now here is your first bite of a cheddar and jalapeño bagel and I'm cutting another without the jalapeño just in case."

"Thank you, Nick." She reached for the first morsel. "My name is Belle, and it's very nice to meet you." She held the bite size piece in front of her mouth, looked up at him and raised her eyebrows before sliding the bread into her mouth.

Nick watched her chew, she seemed pleased with the selection. Then all at once her eyes grew wide and she began to fan her mouth, breathing in and out through pursed lips.

A look of concern took over Nick's face, "Too hot?"

She nodded her head quickly and he slid her the other sample. She picked it up without a care for grace or semblance of dignity and shoved it into her mouth. She chewed fast and after a few seconds relaxed and shook her head. She swallowed with a big gulp. "That was hot!"

"Normally they're a big seller, I didn't think they were that hot."

"Well you must be used to it then."

"Sorry about that, Belle."

She looked down, "I forgive you," she glanced back up with a wide smile, "this time."

She stood motionless for a moment, then as though a thought struck her upside the head, pulled her cell phone from her pocket. "I lost all track of time, I need to get going, thanks so much for your help, Nick. I appreciate it."

You're welcome, I need to get going too, I'm supposed to be on my lunch break."

"At 8:15 in the morning?"

"Yep, I get here at 2 a.m."

"Oh, that's just gross. Well, I won't keep you, I just need to get some bagels and get back to work."

"Ok, well I hope to see you again, sometime."

"I'm sure you will, I know where you work."

They both laughed and parted ways.

Remiel and Anarkum watched from the side. The angel leaned closer to the demon and motioned for him to listen. Then he spoke without taking his eyes off of the woman, "Do you know who that girl is?"

Anarkum shook his head.

Remiel adjusted his stance, waves of energy rippled through the surrounding shelves and bread. "That, my dear friend, is Ms. Mozes' assistant."

Anarkum laughed under his breath, "Now that *is* interesting. Perhaps, I can use him after all."

Chapter 11
City of Enoch

"Awan, wake up, we must go!"

A hand nudged her shoulder. She tried to wake but her eyes refused.

Another nudge, "Awan, you must awaken."

Her eyes flicked open just a bit longer, "Why, where are we going? Where were you today?"

"Something has happened, we must go."

She yawned and attempted to speak, "What happened, where are we going? Is this another of your tricks?"

Cain lowered his voice, "No, this is not a trick, I will explain later, please hurry."

Awan sat up and ran her fingers through her long dark hair. "Alright, do I need to gather some things? How long will we be gone?"

"No, just wear what you have on, we need to go now." His eyes, illuminated by the full moon, urged her on. She had never seen him look like this.

"Alright, give me a hand."

He helped her to her feet. "Do not make a sound, Father and Mother must not hear us."

She rolled her eyes at him and whispered, "Alright."

Cain reached for his sister's hand and the two hurried from their family's cave toward the edge of the river and followed it south for about an hour until they came to the Cave of Treasures. Once there they moved out across a large plain, and even at their current pace it still took several hours to cross, neither said a word. Cain pushed forward, with Awan in tow, consumed with navigating the tall brush until they approached the largest of the four prime rivers, the Old Euphrates.

A vision flashed into Cain's mind of his brother, Abel, walking along a path in front of him.

His hand relaxed and Awan pulled free. "I am not walking another step until you tell me where we are going, and why. Are you going to tell me what has happened? Why did we have to leave in the middle of the night, without telling anyone where we were going?"

———————

Cain closed his eyes and the vision continued. This time he saw his walking stick strike his brother across the back of the head.

———————

Cain looked up at Awan, "Abel is gone."

Awan's head jerked back slightly, "What do you mean gone? Where would he go?"

———————

The vision jumped forward, Abel on the ground, bloodied, with one of his eyes swollen shut. He is pleading with his older brother, "Stop! I do not know why you are doing this, but either stop or end my life now!" His eyes glanced in the direction of some stones next to the path.

The plea is met with laughter.

———————

Cain stared at the ground, "I mean he is gone, he is not coming back."

"And you did not tell Father about this?"

———————

Cain sees the large bloody rock fall to the ground, dirt and grass stick to it.

Abel is silent.

Cain looked away. "No, Father would blame me, and it is not my fault."

"Why would he blame you if Abel left?"

"I had to get out of there. I needed you with me." He reached out and took both of her hands and pulled her close. "I am concerned for you."

"What? You are concerned for me? Why?"

"Because, I knew you would be heartbroken for Azura."

"What are you talking about?"

"Because Father and Mother bore two sons each with a sister. With Abel being gone, where does that leave you and Azura?"

"I do not see how this relates to Abel. Wait, are you talking about marriage?"

"Yes, of course!"

"Not of course, we are talking about Abel leaving. What does that have to do with marriage?"

Cain looked at her. "I knew you would treat Azura preferentially, that you would put her before yourself. So, I chose for you."

Awan shook her head, "You mean to marry me? That was to be Father and Mother's decision."

He grabbed her shoulders, "They would have given me Azura."

Her tension eased and she felt like she was talking her brother through one of his fits of emotion. Her head slumped to one side, "How do you know?"

His voice softened to a whisper, "I just know."

"And now? They will come looking for us, then they will decide for us anyway."

Cain's head jutted toward her, "Not if we marry first."

"How? We need Father and Mother here, to make the marriage binding."

"Why? How did they get married?"

"What do you mean?"

"I mean, there was no one else. They made vows to each other and consummated the vows."

Awan stepped back, "You want to marry me, now?"

"Yes, now, before they find us and force me to marry Azura, and in turn force you into seclusion."

Awan's heart felt like it would burst out of her chest, so much had happened in the last few hours. *I do not want to be without lineage. Cain is right, there is no other way, with Abel being gone.* "Alright, I will do this with you."

Cain and Awan stood under the moon and vowed their lives to each other.

––––––––––

Cain's wife woke first, the sun had not yet risen, though it was about to. She rose to her feet and stared at the horizon, where the darkness of night was just a bit lighter. The air tingled with a prickly stillness that almost hurt. She rubbed her arms and looked up into the sky. The clouds above her churned and bore a light in them that she knew was not the moon. There was a glow in the center that at first looked to spread out a little ways, then it began to get brighter. Then, as fast as lightning the fire came down from the sky. The force of the impact threw Awan back and she toppled to the ground, face first.

When Awan came to, she saw only white, and heard about as much, a single high pitched tone that would not allow any other sound past it. She rose to a kneeling position, and allowed her eyes and ears to clear.

After a little while she heard the sound of flames crackling and a buzzing that gave voice to the feeling she had felt on her skin earlier. She stood and turned to see Cain, standing, fists clenched, arms straight to his sides. He stared straight into the column of flames. Then she looked past him, at the column. It radiated a great mass of fire and smoke, or maybe it was steam. She was so afraid. She had seen Elohim's pillar of fire before but only from a distance.

Then, like millions of water falls intertwined with millions of thunder peels and crackling splinters of air, the Creator spoke. "Cain, where is your brother Abel?"

Cain squinted. "How is it that you do not know? Am I responsible to keep track of my brother's whereabouts now?"

The deafening voice erupted once more, "Abel's blood cries out to me from the Earth."

Cain pointed a finger at the flames, "It was Your fault!"

Awan became dizzy, then collapsed into a heap.

When she awoke Cain sat on the ground next to her, holding his head. Blood seeped between his fingers and for a moment she thought he must be sleeping, he was so still. Then his eyes opened and he looked at her. He seemed relieved and pulled his hand away from his face. He looked at it for a few seconds then held it out to her. "See what He did to me?"

She gasped, "You are bleeding..."

"Yes, Elohim blames me for Abel."

"Why?"

Cain turned away, "He said Abel is dead."

Awan sat up. "What?"

He turned back to her, "Abel is dead and He blames me."

"Abel is dead?"

He glanced down to the ground, "Yes, and I don't know what I'm going to do."

Awan broke down. Her body erupted with uncontrolled sobbing.

Cain looked at his wife, "Did you not hear what I said? The Creator blames me!"

Awan rose to her feet. "Our brother is dead! We must go back." She began walking back the way they had come.

Cain rose to his feet, shoulders slumped, "We cannot go back."

She did not stop. "What? Why not? We must go back, I want to be with Father and Mother!"

Cain's voice broke, "We cannot go back."

Something in his voice stopped her. She turned toward him, "Why can we not go back, Husband?"

"Because I have been marked."

She began walking slowly toward him, "Marked?"

"Yes, the Creator marked me."

"And how does that keep you from going back?"

Cain's eyes became like glass, there was something he did not want to tell her.

She thought for a moment. "You said the Creator blames you. Wait, you said the Creator blames you? And our brother is dead? What did you do?"

Cain looked away.

She stormed back to him and yanked his shoulder, forcing him to face her. "Cain, do not look away."

Cain's shame turned to rage and he turned faster than she had expected. She felt the impact of his palm against her chest. She stumbled back, tripped, and fell to the ground.

The same finger that had pointed at the Creator now pointed at her, "Do not think you can force me to do anything, daughter of Eve!"

The weight of her brother's deception began to make itself known, "You have killed our brother. You lied to me. What happens if I do not go with you, will you kill me like you killed Abel?"

Cain looked down at his right hand, it trembled in a way he could not contain, "We are already one flesh, you must stay with me."

"You said Abel had left, you tricked me into this union."

"But it is still a union. You agreed with your whole body. That cannot be undone. Besides, if you go back, there is no other husband for you."

She refused to look up at him. Her anger was palpable, and she felt like a fool.

Cain continued, "Abel said you were his, that I had to marry Azura, but I wanted to marry you."

"So you killed him like some animal?"

"A man came to me and told me that Father and Mother hated me, so I would have to marry Azura. That since they loved him, he would get to marry you. He said the only way to prevent that from happening would be to kill Abel."

"A man? What man? There are no other men, besides our family."

Cain turned to face his wife, "I don't know who he was or where he came from. I have gone over all that in my head, I do not know who he was but he was real, and he knew many things about me. Anyway, he told me that Father and Mother have never loved me like they loved Abel. Abel always bowed to their wishes and I am not like that, usually. Of course they loved him, and they hate me."

Awan crossed her arms. "And what did you suppose would happen to Azura?"

"The man said she would be cast off."

"Cast off?"

"Yes, sent away without a husband."

"And you believe Father and Mother would treat Azura that way?"

"All I know is what the man told me."

"And for the sake of what this unknown man told you, you killed Abel, thinking it would doom Azura to a life alone?"

"Yes! I mean no! That was not why I killed him."

"Then why?"

"The story is long."

"We have plenty of time."

Cain refused to look into Awan's eyes, instead he looked down, then turned away again. "Father came to me three days ago, he told me to go with Abel. He said that he wanted Abel and I to present offerings to the Creator. Of course, Abel brought the first of this year's lambs. Then, he came to get me. He said he would wait for me if I were going. I went to one of the baskets of fruit, the fruit looked fine to me and I was in a hurry, so I put an arm load in my apron and walked with him to the alter that Father built.

Awan interrupted, "Did Father go with you?"

Cain glanced at his wife, "No."

"Go on."

"Abel walked ahead, eager as always. Once he was at the alter he butchered the lamb. I pushed him to one side, since my sacrifice was ready and his would take a while. I certainly did not want to be there all day."

Awan shook her head.

Cain continued, "Abel said he would wait until I had finished so I told him he could not use the alter. I knew he would try to rush me."

Awan interrupted again, "And what did he do?"

"He started piling up rocks, next to the alter, that were laying around. His makeshift alter was really small, I had to laugh. Anyway, I finished with my offering and asked the Creator to accept it." Cain paused.

"And? Did Elohim accept your offering?"

"No, nothing happened at all. After a while I took a peach and ate it. Abel put his lamb on that pathetic pile of rocks and started to pray." Cain paused.

Awan prodded him, "And what happened?"

Cain looked up into the morning sky, "The flame from Paradise fell on it." Cain stood silent for a moment, looked back the way they came, then he lowered his voice, "Abel did not say a word. Nothing, not a word. But I knew he was happy about it, I mean happy that his was accepted and mine was not."

Awan interrupted, "Maybe he was pleased that his offering had been accepted, maybe it had nothing to do with you."

"You can say that, but you were not there. You were not humiliated, I was. He just walked away. I was so angry and he would not talk about it, then I remembered what the stranger said about him, and you. Father and Mother loved him more than they loved me and now Elohim loved him more too!

'He was so arrogant, I could not take it anymore, I always hated that about him. He always did everything right, he always got what he wanted. Well, not this time."

Awan plucked a flower next to her and held it out in front of her face, "That is all I am, some *thing* to take from Abel?"

Cain's voice rose once more, "No, I wanted you to be my woman, my wife!"

"And you knocked me down."

"I am sorry about that, you should not have pulled on me."

She held her tongue, his volatility was not far from the surface and she did not want to set him off again.

Cain looked at her and sighed, then turned and walked back toward the river, away from her and the family she wanted to go back to.

To go with her new husband or return to her parents, that was the question she had to answer. She sat and thought for a long time, until he had almost disappeared from sight. When she stood, something inside told her she would always regret this decision, but she looked back with longing eyes toward home, then turned back and followed her husband.

———————

Their relationship was more like duty and obligation than a marriage. For her, she did her duty for her husband, and in time bore him many sons and daughters. Her children reintroduced her to love as an essential ingredient of life. What she had lost on the first morning of her marriage she would never be able to get back, it was a lie after all. She poured herself into her children and worked very hard to keep them from the anger their father seemed so prone to.

———————

And Cain did not make offerings to the Creator that had rejected him. Neither did he teach his offspring to follow in the ways of Adam and Eve. Instead they treated each day equally. For them there was no Sabbath and no Jubilee.

Their lineage continued to grow, first children, then grandchildren, great grandchildren, and so on until the couple's family became a small town. Cain decided to name the town after his first born son, Enoch.

As for the town, it started out humbly enough, the original lean-to shelters evolved into small homes built up from long sticks bound to uprights with braided vines. At some point they began covering their homes in mud, which provided more privacy and better shelter from the sun, wind, and rain. But, of course, after every rain their homes were in need of repair, a fresh coat of mud.

While Cain kept busy with building and planning their new city, he also directed Awan, and later his children in the ways of agriculture. The Earth, as it turned out, would no longer produce anything productive for the once excellent farmer. Having swallowed Abels blood, it held Cain in contemptuous resentment. So the work was left to the others, under Cain's direction and as such they were able to put together vast orchards that contained identical trees, whose fruit could be harvested at the same time. This made for efficient harvests. His farming efficiency made life much easier and with the help of the generations that followed him, the work proved satisfying. Their community continued to grow and no one was in need.

A development such as this did not escape notice. The eyes of many dragons had taken notice of this place called Enoch. Unlike the other, smaller group of men, these did not acknowledge the Creator, most did not know of Him at all. The dragon's leader had whispered into the ear of this man, and altered his life. The power of suggestion, in the garden he thought it was true, but now he knew for sure. Cain must have wanted to believe the lie. Mankind so easily believed lies. Such minds would prove a fertile ground for the planting of ideas. Ideas that would surely get him what he wanted and lead to the population of the world bearing the image of *his* kind.

Chapter 12
Years of Invention

The angels were told to watch and to learn. In so doing, many of the angels came to understand by experience, what they had been told at the beginning, that by learning about creation, they were learning about the Creator. Whether they were sent to study a star or a quark, large or small, the portion of creation they were sent to learn about would show them things profound and amazing concerning the one that made them. These were the things they were to teach mankind. It would be a continual revealing of the one that had created them.

Man and angel were designed to work together. Angels would provide insight into ideas and principals that would shape Man's reality—give him technological progress—and allow Man's creative spark to shine. This progress would allow societies to improve, reduce workloads, and make life in community much more beneficial to all.

The most common way for the angels to teach men was by the use of dreams. A man would have a dream—given to him by an angel as prescribed by the Creator—that would point him in a direction. Then the angel might bring about a synchronicity of events. For example, once, the teaching angel prompted a son of Kenan, who was seven at the time, to take a piece of wood out of the fire and run around with it, sending smoke all over the place. The children enjoyed this little game and soon were running and playing in the smoke. But then in a moment of inattention little Kenan ran into his father, bumping the wood out of his grasp and into the vessel of molten iron, sending carbon through the liquid metal.

After Enosh's anger subsided, and upon working with the hot metal, he noticed it was different than the iron he'd made before. This was more flexible, less likely to crack. Then with a bit of refinement of the process he was able to come up with a good formulation for what would later be called steel. Steel could be made thinner and lighter while maintaining the strength of the bulkier iron.

These times of teaching and learning came to be known as the "years of invention." Not everyone had them, but when they occurred, Man's technological improvements were felt throughout society.

Seth, Adam's son, had been taught the processes of refining and working several types of metal during his years of invention. The tools he made, really just simple hand tools, had greatly helped his generation in the process of planting and harvesting. But it was his plow that had made the most difference. The tying together of invention with animal labor had changed everything, providing a way to plant so much more. This innovation led to an abundance of food, to the extent that the excess could be used for bartering. This allowed for families to specialize in certain crops, breeding for still higher yields that would benefit an entire community.

Seth's son, Enosh, during his years of invention, had been introduced to the workings of steel, or more accurately, he was introduced to a way of moving air quickly to heat iron hot enough that steel could be formed, with a small amount of wood blackened by fire. The material proved far superior to the iron and bronze his father made, as it resisted wear and held an edge much longer than either of the previous materials. He used this metal to replace the bronze axes, hoes, and other small work implements his father had made.

Kenan, Enosh's son had figured out that steel would remain strong even when hammered into thin, flexible sheets. He and his father worked with the steel trying to find a way to cut wood and using a flexible sheet with a wooden handle on either end, they made the first hand saw, or hand blade, since it had a smooth edge like all the other cutting implements. It proved to be less of an advancement than they had expected until one idea was given to Kenan in a dream.

The idea was to change the edge of the blade so that it had alternating teeth, that's when the saw came into its own. The tool greatly increased their ability to process tall timbers, allowing them to quickly cut the trees into more manageable sizes for building.

During Mahalael's years of invention or "years," as they came to be called, he was directed to look back at what Seth had accomplished. Seth's plow held a key to what would be his contribution to the good of their growing society, and Mahalael's angelic instructor encouraged him to think about the timber problem. Processing timber, even with a saw, was such a tedious process that Mahalael was sure there had to be a better way, a way to harness the strength of animals in order to ease the work load. They had plenty of animals capable of pulling heavy loads, and although they were very strong they were also difficult to manage. However, the donkey and ox seemed like good candidates.

He worked tirelessly on the large beams needed to yoke together the animals. His first machine brought together four donkeys. The smaller of the favorable candidates. This choice allowed the machine to be smaller, meaning less work to prove his concept was sound.

He formed the beams to radiate out from a central pivoting axel and the sprawling ends were held together with more beams. The central axle proved to be a major hurdle in the making of the first of these machines, its precision was something Mahalael struggled with for some time. Though he had devised many smaller machines in the past, none of them had placed this much of a demand on his abilities. He spent many months on the design and several months in the construction of his invention.

Mahalael stood, hands on hips, when his son Jarod emerged from their small home, having just finished his chores. He looked at his father and wondered if something had gone wrong.

Jarod, Mahalael's 19 year old son, called out from about thirty yards away, "Did it break again Father?"

Mahalael turned his head slowly, a wide grin on his face, "The machine works."

Jarod smiled and ran to his father, "Are you sure?"

"Yes, watch this." Mahalael positioned himself where one of the four donkeys would be and pulled one of the the straps over his shoulders. He began to walk, with a good bit of effort, to pull the central axle in a circle. The axle turned a wheel twenty yards away by way of a thick band of woven flax. This wheel pushed an arm up and then down. The young man watched, entranced as a saw moved up and down on the arm.

Jarod broke away from the saw and turned to his father, "Can it cut wood?"

Mahalael stopped to catch his breath, "Not yet, but soon, I hope."

"What would happen if I put wood there when you turn it?"

I am not strong enough to turn the axle with wood there, I tried. That is why I am building this big wheel."

"I do not understand. Are more men going to push?"

"No, donkeys will push, or pull that is."

"How will you convince them to do that?"

Mahalael picked up one of the harnesses. "You think they will be stubborn?"

Jarod laughed, "I know they will."

Mahalael laughed and tossed the harness to his son. "Help me put together three more of these harnesses and maybe we can test with animals tomorrow."

Michael whispered behind her, "What does Jarod mean? What does Mahalael mean?"

Jessica looked up from the scroll, "I don't know, they're names."

Michael continued, "Do you think their meanings matter?"

She realized from the sound of the cushion that Michael was behind her, on either the couch or loveseat, "I don't know, should they?"

He sat transfixed, "Why do you doubt the words of the letter given to you by the Creator?"

"I don't, what do you mean?"

"You look at it as though there are words in there that have no application."

Jessica placed her pencil on her yellow pad and swiveled in her chair to see the back of Michael's head, "I don't know what you're talking about. I believe all the words in the scroll are there for a reason."

"So you believe there is a different meaning if the word 'and' is there as opposed to the word 'or'?"

She nodded, "Of course."

"How about the word, Jarod."

Her brow furrowed, "It's a name, Mahalael's son."

"And?"

"And what? What are you getting at?"

"Do you believe Jarod was given his name for a purpose?"

"I don't know, it was just his name."

"Do you know what it means?"

"No."

"Why not?"

"I don't make it a practice to know the meaning of names."

"But you just said that every word in the letter is there on purpose."

"Wait, these names are here on purpose? Their meanings are here on purpose. Wouldn't that imply that God gave them names?"

"It is possible that when they were born, or perhaps before they were born, their parents were given names for them? Maybe they felt drawn to the name, possibly years before the child was born.

"What if the parents mess up and give a child the wrong name?"

"Have you ever noticed that sometimes the Creator changes people's names?"

Sure, you mean like when he changed Abram's name to Abraham, or Saul's name to Paul?"

"Why do you suppose He did that."

"I'm not sure."

"Perhaps the meaning of names is important to Him."

"So what does Jarod mean?"

"It is the Hebrew verb yaradh, which means, 'shall come down.' His name was a prophesy."

"So you're saying that his name foretold something?"

"Right."

"Something that would happen during his lifetime, maybe?"

"Maybe."

"So something, or someone came down during his lifetime?"

"Possibly."

Jessica rose to her feet and walked around the stairs. "So what came down?"

Chapter 13
Infrared Sensor

It was three-thirty in the morning and Nick stood in the grocery store restroom looking into the mirror. Dark circles under his eyes told part of his story, he would have been tired from his schedule alone. With his school schedule during the day and these nights in the bakery, he had to find sleep when he could, and he was not getting much. But there was more. His cheerful exterior belied the tension that brooded in his belly. He waved his hands in front of the faucet, the motion sent water flowing over his hands.

Nick...

He blinked once, looked back and forth, then grimaced at what must have been his imagination.

Nick...

He backed away from the mirror and turned to his left, toward the bathroom door. It remained closed.

"Nick..."

The voice sounded closer. Just then the faucet to the left of the one he was using turned on, but no one was there.

Then, next to his ear he heard it again, "Nick..."

The young man jumped back, startled. His right hand clutched his shirt, in an attempt to steady his heart.

"Nick, I know who you are..."

He stumbled back into one of the stalls, the door slammed open, and into the wall. He slammed it shut, and slid the latch closed.

"Yours is a family of quitters..."

"Shut up!" Nick yelled.

The voice did not stop. "Your grandfather quit, at the end of a rope."

"Leave me alone!"

"Your father quit as well, couldn't stand the strain of living with his father's demise."

Nick covered his ears, beads of sweat flowed down his brow.

"And now, here you are, life is a tangled mess, you come from a line of quitters. Will you quit, too?"

"I don't have to listen to this!" Nick unlocked the stall door and ran for the exit.

———

One of the night stockers walked down the hall toward the restroom. He yawned as he approached the door, then, to his amazement, it shot open, spitting the tall kid from the bakery into the hallway floor and against the opposite wall.

The stocker jumped back, startled, "Hey! Are you OK?"

Nick glanced back toward the restroom as the door closed.

The stock clerk reached for Nick. "Let me help you up."

Nick pulled away, then pushed himself up using the wall in an attempt to regain his composure. His eyes had a crazed look.

Again, the stocker prodded the wild-eyed baker with his concern, "Are you OK?"

Nick looked at the man, then down at the floor. "Yes, I'm fine." He wiped his wet hands on his apron.

The stocker placed his hand on Nick's shoulder, "What happened?"

"Nothing, nothing happened." He glanced back up at the man's face. "I'm fine, I need to get back to work."

Nick shrugged the man's hand away and hurried down the hall.

The stocker shrugged and shook his head, "Strange kid. No wonder he's working the night shift."

———————

Nick walked into the bakery and glanced at the clock, without really seeing it. "What was that? Nick, get a grip already!" He walked over to the deep sink and stepped on the foot control. Water shot out of the faucet and he reached up for some liquid soap. He rubbed his hands under the water to wash and rinse them.

"Need a towel?"

The towel dispenser whirred to life behind him.

Nick's heart raced, his breath left him and he stood facing the wall. "Get a grip, Nick." He looked at the towel dispenser, one towel hung down.

Nick walked over to the dispenser and tore the towel free. "Who are you, and what do you want with me?"

Radio.

The radio is a simple device, it can snatch signals from the air and alter them in such a way that they can be perceived by Earth creatures in the form of sound waves. Then, with the twist of a knob, or push of a button, the radio can be adjusted to "pick-up" another radio station, or frequency. It does the same thing as before, only now it is tuned differently.

Just over 500 years had passed since creation began. Satan and his forces found that they possessed an ability to change their physical appearance, similar to tuning a radio to a different frequency; while in this altered state mankind would see what appeared to be men, albeit slightly different men than they were accustomed to, but men nonetheless. However, when they saw each other, they could see both the Earth version and their native forms, they could do something a radio cannot. They could perceive multiple frequencies at the same time, while making sense of both.

Seed.

The concept of the seed is among the most powerful notions in all of creation. The idea that reproduction happens because a tiny object contains every bit of information needed to produce a blended copy of an original pair is astounding. The idea that what is produced is like neither parent, while being similar to both, is equally astounding. It is a powerful concept, and the reality is that this is the engine that pushes creation forward, keeps it going. Even after the introduction of death into the world.

One seed birthed creation, and this most powerful notion is plainly seen in the world even today. The lack of recognition of this concept, says something about Man in his fallen state.

The thing about seeds is that they always produce a blend, a blend of whatever contributed to them. Sometimes the offspring is more beautiful than either of the original parents, sometimes what is produced is larger or smaller. Then there are those times when what is produced is something completely unexpected.

"And I put enmity between you and the woman and between your seed and her seed." Genesis 3:15

The Creator said it himself. The war had shifted and the Creator had made the new direction known to Satan. This notion of Satan having seed was something the Commander had not considered, that angels could reproduce.

Satan called Semyaza, Azazel, and the other generals to a meeting at the top of his obelisk, deep inside the Crypsis.

The Commander cleared his throat, "I do not suppose any of you have noticed, but the Creator has been sending his messengers to the seed of Seth, teaching them things that help them to overcome some of the burden of life in that realm of light and darkness in which he placed them. His attempts to help them are, of course, worthless. I believe the best way to ease their suffering is to kill them, but, sadly, we are not permitted to ease His pets into "death," whatever that truly means. The thing He threatened them with and yet their life continues on, unchanged, except for their change in covering. He has proven again to be impotent and His word to be without power. His affection for Man, those filthy creatures, is His weakness."

As if on cue, several of the generals broke ranks and spoke quietly amongst themselves, while a few of them peered through the darkness, searching. When there were no signs of the Creator or His messengers coming to defend the Creator's reputation, they calmed a bit.

The Commander continued, "There is something we can do, to better our plight."

The generals laughter faded into silence.

"We have all seen the value of seed. For crops, animals, and even the reproduction of Man." Satan paused for effect. "Something came to my attention, from the mouth of the Creator Himself. I do not know if you know this, but my fellow Seraphim, we have seed."

One of the dragons gasped, then looked around, embarrassed.

Semyaza spoke up, "What is this to us? Are we going to breed with each other?"

Azazel looked down at the much smaller Semyaza, and sneered.

Satan sighed, "No! Of course not. Angels cannot reproduce with each other. In this form we have no reproductive ability, we are simply not built for it."

Kokabel laughed, "I do not understand what seed has to do with anything."

Satan motioned toward the generals, "The Creator said we have seed." Then he paused, thinking they would understand.

The generals stared at him, blank.

Satan scanned their eyes, "If you have seed, it must be buried in order for it to grow."

Semyaza answered, "Yes, we know this."

The Commander tried again, "You have to bury seed or it will never germinate."

Kasdeya threw his hands in the air, "What are you talking about? Bury our seed where?"

Satan became indignant, "Did you not see me change into the likeness of Man, when I spoke with Cain? When I convinced him to kill his self-righteous brother? You must go to them and take wives, tell them whatever you have to, but our seed *will* come against the woman's seed. Our kind will have children!" Satan turned to leave.

Semyaza glanced down, his metallic scales scraped against one another with his movement, "You do not plan to participate in this endeavor," his eyes flicked up to his Commander, "Do you?"

Satan paused, "No, Semyaza, you are in charge."

Chapter 14
Unveiling

Ariel and the others stayed late into the night pouring every last bit of the assigned healing into the wounded messenger, he had regained his strength and his wounds had healed, but alas, his wings had not returned. The trio departed in silence. Falk's disappointment was evident.

Sitting on the edge of the bed, the messenger stared out the window. Angels do not sleep, but they do wait, and they do watch. The hours ticked by. Eyes closed, head back, hands wresting on his knees, palms up. His mouth moved but scarcely a sound could be heard. With his spirit he searched Paradise, though right now, he had never felt so far from the glory of his home. Without his wings and with the mass of enemy forces lurking overhead he could not return to Paradise. Apparently, he had a purpose in this place.

Falk heard Belle and Jessica begin to stir not long after the sun rose. Belle came down to check on him and commented on how much better he looked. She was amazed at the difference in his condition since the day before.

He remained in what had become his room for a couple more hours, adjusting to his new surroundings. As a messenger of Paradise, his missions were always carried out with sword and shield, flying at top speed, and fighting his way through whomever came between himself and his destination.

This was different, in this place he found himself face to face with the images of Elohim. Their culture was different than anything he was used to. He supposed this time on Earth would be good for him —though he did not know how—but he knew and trusted the Creator. He looked at the clock on the night stand, 10:21 a.m. He decided he would make the best of the situation.

Falk walked across the main room of the basement and climbed the stairs. It was the first time he had actually seen the main floor of the mountain home. He had never taken much notice of Earth surroundings before, his missions had always been direct, and had not involved contact with mankind directly. He stopped five or six steps from the top of the stairs and noticed, to the right, Belle in the kitchen, he could see her at the bar, which was a part of the kitchen. She had some sort of wires coming out of her ears, her body moved with a rhythm while her head bobbed up and down as though only loosely attached. She was cutting apples, he could smell them, and there was another smell he could not place.

His eyes scanned further to the right, dark furniture, similar to what was in the main room below, they had called them, "couch and loveseat." Only the ones up here were covered in smooth dark animal hide. There was a fire contained in glass. It was a sort of octagonal fire pit with glass sides and a metal top that looked similar to a bell, and a metal tube that led up through the ceiling, he thought the whole setup looked strange. But the fire was in a healthy rage and spinning counter clockwise in its cage.

He missed fire and found himself staring into the flickering light, although something was strange about this fire.

Jessica emerged from the hallway to Falk's left, "Hey, so you've made it up the stairs, welcome to the rest of the house." Her voice was pleasant, he turned slowly and saw her at the top of the steps. She held her hand out to him, inviting him to come with her. He took her hand and continued up the stairs.

She continued, "Listen, I was just about to go outside and mail some bills, would you like to come along, it's just to the end of the driveway?"

"Outside?" He paused briefly, and looked through the glass of the front storm door. "Yes, I would like that."

She pulled him along behind her, then pushed the glass door open and held it for him to pass. Though tall by human standards, he was a good bit shorter than Michael and had no need to stoop when passing through.

Belle called out, "I'll take the platter of fruit out to the back deck, come out there when you come back, ok?"

"Ok, will do." Jessica said as she walked outside.

Falk's movements were even more graceful than the other angels Jessica had seen, he almost seemed to float down the porch steps. Then he stopped, looked up into the trees and inhaled long and deep.

Jessica walked up the path and turned to see him following her.

"How are you feeling?"

"Better ma'am. The pain is gone now."

"How many more visits do you expect?"

"I am not sure, my time here is unlike any I have had before. There seems to be a barrier to my understanding."

"A barrier?"

"Yes ma'am, there are things we are intended to know now, and there are things we are intended to discover later. The reason I am here has not yet been revealed. At least not to me."

Jessica's eyes were kind, "I'm sure that this is frustrating for you."

Falk's expression went from pleasant to almost sad. Jessica could not help but notice that he blinked more like a bird than a man.

The pair walked up the paved path that led to the driveway, then followed the driveway to the dirt road that wound its way through the woods.

As they approached the mailbox Jessica turned to Falk, "Your name, it sounds different from the others."

"Ma'am?"

"Your name, you know, it's so different from the other angel's names, at least the ones I've heard."

"Yes ma'am, 'Falk' is more of an affect."

"Affect? What do you mean?"

"It is more like a name given, like there is a cause for it. Falk is a Falcon, ma'am. I remind some of the others of an Earth falcon, because of my smaller size and the manner of my flight, I am one of the fastest, it is an affect."

"So more like a nick name? You're known for an action?"

"Yes, ma'am. It is like that."

Jessica opened the mailbox, "So what is your real name?"

Falk froze. His head twitched to the right, toward the house.

———

Nick walked out of the bakery toward the front of the store. He walked past the cash registers, and no one spoke to him. After he punched his code in the time clock he emerged from the store and walked to his vehicle.

———

Katriel saw it first.

The leader of the perimeter guard, Katriel, was a massive angel who stood at least a foot taller than Michael. His wings held back behind him, the outer edges held firmly pressed together. This position forced the forward portion of the wings to frame the top and back of his head, when viewed from the side. The forest angels found this positioning made ground navigation of the trees easier.

A dark vapor emerged from a hole in the ground. Katriel's angelic eyes sifted through the mist to see the dingy scales of an invading imp. No larger than an average-sized modern man, these smallish creatures lacked the intelligence to plan anything, but what they lacked in forethought they more than made up for in tenacity. This one moved toward the house and while it would be unusual for this little house to be unguarded, Katriel and his group were masters of stealth. So either the intruder was unaware of the guardians, or did not care.

The huge angel shook his head and reached for his weapon. He thought, *I'll dispatch this creature back to the Crypsis.* As his hand slid to the haft of his sword, an unexpected message drifted into his ear.

"Wait."

Katriel tilted his head, his hand moved up to rest on the pommel of his sheathed sword, his eyes on the imp. His expression, resolute.

Just then, several other guards turned to see the little hard-shelled devil as it drifted just above the ground, each glanced toward Katriel who held up a hand.

Falk sniffed the air, something was not right. The odor pulled his attention back, toward the house. Whatever it was, it was beyond the home. He lifted his head, and closed his eyes. The voice he had waited for now burned within him. "Go," was all he heard from the still, small, and familiar voice. He savored the sound only briefly, then turned and ran upwind, toward the house. He traveled with such speed past the trees that when he jumped onto the roof, it seemed almost natural. When he dropped down to the back deck he had no idea that his skin had begun to shine, though it was not enough that Belle would notice. No, his decent from the roof had startled Belle, who carried a tray of fruit for the three of them. But then, without so much as an extra step to gain his balance, he jumped and pivoted over the stair-less deck's railing, down another twenty-five feet or so to the ground, and bounded straight into the woods.

Belle dropped the tray onto the table and rushed to the railing to see what was happening. The trees were in the way, but she could hear rustling and commotion. A light appeared, terribly bright, that seemingly danced among the trees. Then, the light flew to one side, toward the path that led to the fire pit. It stopped in the path. She could see the light and could see that someone was in the light, holding something. It rushed back into the trees.

Nick stood next to his vehicle, it was 10:34 a.m. and his shift had just ended. He yawned and reached into his pocket to find his keys. A cold wind blew past him as he pressed the button that unlocked his SUV's door. The hairs on his neck stood at attention against the cold. He reached out, opened the truck's door, and moved quickly into the vehicle before pulling the door shut.

———————

Falk lunged back into the trees.

Just then the dark vaporous being stopped mid-flight and began to laugh, plates of armor-like scales covered him like a dung beetle. Its laughter mocked the angel. Its face, almost flat, encased tiny red eyes and some sort of putrid fluid flowed from them. Its four broad insectoid wings beat the air in a lazy cadence.

The messenger angel, not fully in his angelic form, dove headlong into the intruder throwing the beast back into a massive fir tree. The hideous creature continued to laugh while he reached under the angel and batted him away.

The imp smiled at Falk, and tapped his chest plate with his fist and winked. "Outta'da way, stoopid Chereeb."

Falk wiped his long dark blonde hair from his face, "Who are you?"

"Maka'no deefference, I hava'now notist'a. You're wingsa left somewhere!" The imp burst out into another torrent of raucous laughter. "Yes, yes, I hav'a heerd abot'u and your fiene Gawd who leaft you in dis state!"

"What are you doing here?"

"Isacoba erran'din, Ishocoba datsa gynecic puto'n resti'n."

"What are you talking about?" Falk had never understood how or why a seraphim would want to appear in an insect form.

"Rest'a, ehhh, finalesti rest'a." He tilted his head, "Dad'ta sondest goot, maksa me'sond, goot'eh?" His body contorted into another bought of heinous laughter.

Falk did not see the humor, "Turn back now and avoid the Crypsis."

That statement sobered up the little gargoyle. "Ah! Ishoud'a lev'e na'ethe'n?"

Falk's answer was in his rigid stare.

The imp threw his arm in the air, "Den'i go," and turned to leave.

Falk watched as the imp began rising into the air. "Batsa'u sticto das gerund, maybe, I safe upun'de skii-ee. Persemaka you needsat'o traq'in up you wings, threaten me'den, Cherub."

Belle ran out the front door, and around the house. Jessica called out to her but it was no use. Belle was not listening. She had to be sure Falk was alright.

The small black SUV traveled down Highway 24 toward the turnoff for the college. Nick yawned and rubbed his eyes, these night shifts were getting to him. His first class would begin in a few minutes so he drove a little faster than he should have. He kept fiddling with the heater, warm air came from the vents but the vehicle remained cold, so he alternated holding first one hand, then the other over the heater vents. *It's like my truck refuses to heat up today,* he thought. He could still see his breath.

The perimeter guard watched through the trees, several looked to their leader for permission to help the messenger. Katriel's hand remained in the air, steady. Several angels looked at each other, then back to the scene that played out before them.

Falk watched the imp ascend up out of his reach. He looked around, expecting to see the perimeter guard in the air. But there was no movement in the trees.

He glanced back up toward the imp, his eyes drifted to the trees, head tilted. Then, in a fluid motion he ran and jumped toward a large fir, his foot found sufficient grip and the angel bound upward and toward a second fir, ripping his sword from it's sheath. He bound again, this time toward one of the larger aspens, the tree flexed and he crouched against it, his right hand on the trunk, sword in his left. The white tree sprung back and the coiled messenger sprang upward. His body glowed, masking his human form, his true self emerged, eyes burning.

The imp, startled, turned to face the raging angel moving toward him, wingless but still he soared, time slowed.

The perimeter guards watched.

Falk, arched back, both hands clutching the sword over and behind his head. His upper body and legs moved forward like the steel teeth of a bear trap, only this trap was hurling through the air, with a blade, burning a dazzling blue arc through the thin air.

The blade found its mark and smashed through the heavy plates and soft tissues that held the evil creature together.

For the imp, it was the sweet perfume of the sword's flame, searing pain, then blackness, then the Crypsis.

Victorious, and a couple hundred feet above the ground, Falk fell. Something he had not wished to do again. Rustling erupted behind him, followed by a torrent of wind. A pair of huge arms snatched him up.

"No more crash landings for you," Katriel said under his breath as he descended with the messenger. The two came to rest toward the edge of the tree line. "Well done, messenger. You would be welcome among my warriors. In all these millennia, I have never seen the likes of what you just did. Well done, indeed."

"Thank you, I did not fancy another encounter with the ground so soon."

"I suppose not."

Falk looked up at the big warrior, "Why did you not attack that beast?"

"We were told to wait. Now we know why. You have received a commissioning."

"A commissioning for what?"

"You are no longer a messenger. For a while, you have become a guardian. You served as the Creator's vengeance on this day. I salute you." Katriel held out his arm in a formal salute.

Falk dipped his head, "You honor me."

The giant angel looked past Falk, "You might want to think of what you are going to say to her."

"What? Who?"

"The woman that is now in your charge, approaches. I believe she can see us."

Falk turned to see Belle, twenty-five yards away, eyes wide, staring at him as her forward progress stopped. Her eyes were fearful, but curious.

The big angel turned toward his post. "I will leave you to it." Katriel's four giant wings unfurled once more and with one beat he was away.

––––––––––––

According to the police report, the black SUV had simply not turned with the winding road. It had driven straight off the side and plunged down the rocky slope. The reporting officer assumed that the driver had either been drunk or fallen asleep at the wheel. That was before he and another officer had climbed down to the wrecked SUV. What they found, they could not explain. The SUV had apparently struck a large boulder nose first, flipped onto its top and burned. It was still smoldering when they arrived.

Only one problem, no body.

They searched the wreckage, but found nothing.

––––––––––––

Belle stood and stared at the light, she could tell it was some sort of being, a presence, like the other's she had seen before, back in her childhood. But she'd never seen one this close, and this one was moving toward her. That's when it happened, when reality cracked. As the brightness faded she could make out a tall man-like figure with something in his left hand. The light continued to fade and the person began to decrease in size, that was when she began to see the blue flames of the sword. The man had just placed the tip of the sword in it's sheath when it, or he, came to a halt about fifteen yards from her. The light continued to fade and he shrunk down to the size and form of someone familiar.

He thrust the sword into its sheath before the transformation was complete, and pushed his dirty, tangled hair away from his face and again walked directly toward her.

Belle's eyes refused to blink. She stood frozen, her jaw relaxed, lips parted, then pursed with a deep inhale, and a heavy slow breath escaped into the cool air.

Falk spoke, "Come, you need to move inside the house." He walked past her, unsure of how to handle this moment. He knew everything had already changed, he could see it in the eyes of this woman he had grown fond of.

She turned but did not move.

Falk stopped. A heavy sigh escaped his lips. After a few seconds he turned toward Belle then looked up at the sky. Dark clouds were moving toward them. He inhaled long and deep, his eyes drifted to hers. "A storm is coming, you need to go inside."

"What just happened?" Her eyes darted back and forth, then riveted back to his.

He could see her struggle. "I did my duty. It was nothing."

"Wait a minute, what do you mean? You were glowing!"

He stared at her, his jaws clenched.

"Falk, who are... no! What are you?"

"I am a messenger."

"Don't lie to me, Falk."

His eyes began to burn. "I do not lie."

"Are you an angel, Falk?"

"Yes, a messenger."

"I need to sit down."

Falk held out his hand. "Then you need to sit down inside. Evil is stirring."

Belle stormed past him, and wondered why she should listen to someone who had hid the truth from her.

———————

A lone red-headed man walked up along the ravine. His shredded clothes were burned at the edges but the man himself was uninjured. The cold no longer effected him, though he wore no jacket. He stopped and looked back toward the truck he had abandoned. He could see two figures looking through the wreckage, *must be cops.* One was holding the back of his head as though confused, then the officer turned and looked in his direction. Nick ducked behind a large boulder and continued on, keeping the larger stones between himself and his vehicle.

Chapter 15

Seed

It was the year 513, late spring, when the lights first appeared. They were not like the stars in the Paradises, with their stationary, yet seasonal patterns. The lights moved as though controlled. The lights moved and stopped and started again with even more fluidity than a humming bird. They danced in the night sky.

Night after night the lights appeared. At first there were just three, but each night the number grew.

At first only a few residents of Enoch noticed them, but after four or five consecutive nights, more and more people emerged from their homes to see what was happening. Some even wondered out loud if the other towns could see them.

On the sixth night, a pair of lights came down and hovered less than fifteen hundred feet above the ground. They lingered motionless, silent. Eventually, the entire town emerged from their homes to see them. One little boy picked up a stone and threw it at them, but the lights held fast.

Then, just before dawn, with no warning or sound, the lights sped off, out of view.

On the ninth evening all of the town gathered outside. As if on cue, many lights appeared. More than a hundred of them came from all around. The brightest lights moved to the center of the cluster and the others began to swirl about them. They moved relative to one another as they swirled until there were eight bands of light orbiting the centrally bright mass. There was a ninth band, but it seemed less organized, more chaotic. The swirling display was centered over the closest mountain and stretched across the sky as far as the eye could see.

Some in the community expressed their view that the aerial display was a show of power, that these things were showing their mastery of the air, showing their strength. To them, it was an ominous sign.

Of course, the people were curious, but then over the sequence of nights, their curiosity turned to fear. Something or someone was up there, and while that someone clearly wanted to be seen they also did not want the people to know anything more. Why did they not reveal themselves and their intentions? Night after night the lights appeared. Something was building and the people wondered when or how the escalation would end.

Appealing to Jabal, the fourth generation of Cain and leader of the city, the group pleaded for an answer to the riddle of the lights in the sky. Was it some sort of sign? Or perhaps an omen? Jabal consulted with Cain on the matter as the two once again left their dwellings to see this strange sign in the night sky, but could not put reason to the patterns they saw in the lights.

Then, on the thirteenth night, the lights, now numbering around two hundred came together and moved in unison toward the north. Moving slowly over the course of what seemed like hours until, one at a time, they descended near the top of that closest mountain, Mount Hermon.

———————

Semyaza, the last of the lights in the sky, orbited the group of assembled angels looking for any sign of cowardice.

One of the generals called out to him, "General Semyaza! Someone approaches from the north."

The dragon spun around to see his one-time friend, Remiel, and called out to him, "I had given up on you, did you reconsider my proposal?"

"Yes, I wanted to talk to you about that." Remiel's attention turned to the mountain top. "Is this your group that will go and marry the daughters of Cain?"

"And the daughters of Seth I should think, eventually." Semyaza looked the archangel squarely in the eyes, "What have you decided?"

"I have decided to go with you, brother."

Semyaza smiled, "Descend with me, for we embark on our journey to Enoch soon."

The two drifted down toward the gathered hoard. Remiel felt a tension rise in his belly, but the craving he felt for one of the beautiful daughters of Man made him weak. He refortified his resolve as the two touched down.

Azazel rushed the two and snatched the cherubim around the waist. "What is the meaning of this? Why is this Elohim-lover here?" He peered into Remiel's eyes, "Do you mean to bring down wrath upon us again?" The dragon began to squeeze the much smaller cherubim, as the scales along his back stood up in a defensive posture and scraped against one another in a menacing, and noisy display.

Pain shot through Remiel's body, "If that were true, I would bring wrath down upon myself!"

Azazel shot a glance over to Semyaza, "Explain this! I demand to know why this one is here!"

Semyaza turned his back toward the larger challenger, "I assure you Azazel, you have nothing to fear, Remiel has decided to join our cause."

Azazel fired back, "You are so easily taken in, he is obviously lying. Why would this one, an archangel, turn from Elohim?"

Semyaza turned his head just enough to peer back at Azazel. "Indeed, why would a general turn? You could very well ask that question, and yet here you are, my friend." There was a pause, "Besides, he is smitten by one of the daughters of Cain, it seems." Semyaza's voice soothed the larger beast.

"Smitten?" Azazel looked back at the suffering cherubim, "You are smitten? You crave a woman?"

Remiel grunted out, "More than I can explain, I am afraid."

Azazel studied the angel, sniffed his chest, "Afraid? He does not speak like the enemy. They do not use such words."

Semyaza turned back toward the city they would soon visit. "Nor would they know *how* to use such words, I imagine. As you can see, we have a new ally."

Azazel released Remiel, "I will keep a watch on this one, he may be using some new strategy to bring down the host of Paradise on us once again. If he does," Azazel looked directly at Remiel, "I will dispose of him myself."

Semyaza, cleared his throat, "Attention!"

The group fell silent and a few of the smaller dragons drew closer to Semyaza as he continued to speak, "We are gathered on this mountain to reinstate our vows. I want to clarify what is at stake here. Either we are going to do this thing, or we are not. By that, I mean that we all will do it, or none of us will. If there is a penalty for this, and I am sure there will be, we must all agree to share in the consequences now."

The group fell silent.

"We all know the women in the various people groups are attractive, we have known lust for them and we now have come to know that we can fulfill that lust. But let me be clear, we have agreed to a plan that will change the course of life in this Earth realm.

We seek to fulfill our lust, yes, but we also seek to undo a great wrong that is planned for us. Our commander was told that the seed of the woman would crush the heads of our seed. We must stop this. We have the ability to render this curse null and void.

A murmur arose among the gaggle of serpents.

Semyaza let them talk for a moment then held his hand in the air to silence them. "I realize you did not understand this side of the matter that lies before us, but let me be very clear here. The war that began in Paradise has not ended. It continues here, now. We must ensure that the seed of the Woman becomes our seed. So you see, this act of lust, this taking of what we want for ourselves is also a selfless act that ensures the survival of our kind, it ensures the survival of our seed."

Kokabiel could scarcely contain his laughter enough to shout, "We are selfless in our selfishness!"

The entire group laughed uneasily.

Semyaza continued, "If successful we will change Man into a mixture of man and angel. Elohim will have no choice but to admit he was wrong. He cannot save Man once we have altered him. Only a man without mixture can reacquire what Adam gave to Lucifer, that will be impossible once their line has been mixed with ours."

Remiel looked to the side, he had not fully understood what this act would mean, he thought it was only about what he wanted, not that it was part of some grandiose scheme. He knew it was sin, but this was an undermining of Elohim. He glanced back toward Semyaza, then at Kokabiel who was already looking in his direction.

Kokabiel's hand moved to his mouth to muffle the quiet laughter that spilled out.

Semyaza continued, "Now is the time to be counted, if you are willing to do this thing, regardless of the consequences, indicate by saying 'yes.'"

Remiel, closed his eyes and said, "Yes."

And the mountain became known from that night as the Mountain of Devoted Destruction. For it was on this mountain that an agreement was made among two hundred fallen angels to take wives from among men and all would share in the curse that would surely follow.

Jabal leaned against one of the perimeter walls that surrounded the city. The wall was chest high, tall enough that with his arms crossed and resting on the top he could lay his head on his arms, and thus he leaned.

In this position he had drifted off to sleep, and at some point after that, the lights faded on the top of the mountain. Then hours passed and still no sign of the lights.

With morning came the warmth of sunlight on Jabal's face. His head rotated slowly toward the mountain and he peered at the summit. Nothing unusual.

He looked over to see if Ermiel was still next to him and was relieved to see that he was. Then he noticed his friend's gaze toward the mountain.

Jabal broke the silence, "What is it?"

Ermiel remained motionless.

Jabal thought perhaps his friend had not heard him. "Ermiel, what do you see?"

Ermiel responded without breaking his stare, though his head turned a bit toward Jabal, "Lights, on the ground now."

Jabal rotated his head back toward the mountain but could see nothing unusual. He moved closer to his friend, "Where?"

Ermiel pointed.

Jabal still saw nothing, then, a glint pulled his eyes down to the sprawling valley between the city and the mountain. He saw something, a blur of light, or lights. He lifted his head, his right hand acting as a shield against the brightness of the morning sun.

The lights were indeed on the ground and he began to count them. When he reached fifty, his heart began to pound. At one hundred he began to lose his breath, then at one hundred fifty his hands were shaking, and before he reached two hundred he turned and ran into the city yelling, "Arise! Everyone arise! Lights, as brilliant as the sun, approach on the ground!"

Many of the town folk, hundreds in fact, rushed toward the sound of Jabal's voice.

Jabal raced to his home, a small mud-brick structure with an attached tent enclosing the front. Jabal flung the front of the tent open and was met by his wife and children already dressed.

She exclaimed, "I heard you yelling outside, what is happening? Is it some omen?"

Before he could answer, his wife lunged for him and threw her arms around his neck, trembling.

Jabal wrapped his arms tightly around her and whispered in her ear, "We do not know that anything bad is going to happen. We just need to be ready for whatever will happen."

She whispered, "How can we know how to be ready?"

She pulled back to peer into his eyes, she could see his concern.

Most of the town followed Jabal and now were pushing in behind him. He turned, still holding his wife, toward the crowd. Tormon, among the largest of the men in Enoch, pushed to the front of the group and spoke above the noisy chatter. "Jabal, tell us what we should do."

Jabal held his hands in the air to settle the crowd and in the process, spotted his half brother advancing through the group. Jabal raised his voice in an attempt to override the mob, "Please, make room for Jubal."

As the crowd parted before him, Jabal's half brother Jubal spoke, "Do you want me to fetch Cain?"

"Yes, please find him," he pointed to several men in the crowd, "And take these men with you."

Jeremiel climbed higher and higher. He could see the portal that led to Paradise in the distance and pressed toward it. Having just seen his archangel, Remiel, leave with the fallen General weighed heavy on his heart. He had tried to fly toward him, to stop him, but the breath of the Creator blew him higher, away from Remiel. Mortals would not understand, but Jeremiel knew not to move against the will of the Creator. Such a move would be akin to what the Commander had done. Moving against the Creator's will would be a choice to switch sides, something he could not, or would not, imagine himself doing.

Still, Jeremiel's heart searched the wind for a word or direction until at last he heard it. "Come to the throne room."

With a clear word, Jeremiel sheathed his sword and, without looking back, shot toward the portal.

It was two o'clock in the morning, Belle could not sleep, and the confinement of the house wasn't working for her either. She needed air. She needed to breathe.

Eventually, she found herself wearing her heavy robe and faux sheepskin slippers, on the back deck, gazing up into the sky. Her breath visible in the late September air. It had not begun to snow, but the season was approaching fast.

She looked down, to the place where Falk had landed before sprinting into the woods. She thought, *There's an angel in the basement. A real angel.*

He was not some figment of her imagination, not something she made up, nor something she could dismiss. And there was another angel that she saw, a huge one!

These angels were not as pristine and tidy as she would have imagined. She had imagined angels shining so bright that details would be difficult to see. She figured they would shine as bright as the sun, at least that was a phrase she had heard in reference to them.

She did remember seeing something terribly bright in the trees, and she saw Falk take shape, but she couldn't be sure. The whole thing was confusing.

Some of the pieces fit together better, now that she knew what he really was. *He had delivered the second scroll. He had fallen. Fallen, not such a good characterization when referring to an angel. Had he, or someone like him delivered the first scroll? Did Jessica know? Did Jessica know all along, and if she did, why didn't she say anything? Why had Jessica never said a word about it?*

She must have known, she hadn't seemed surprised by what had happened in the woods, after all, Falk went out the front door with Jessica and ended up running across the roof to get to the back of the house. How could he have done that without Jessica seeing him? Why had they kept it from her?

When she was a child, Belle had seen things. Mostly round orbs that lingered near her on occasion. She thought it was normal to see such things, until she started talking about them. That's when she found out that seeing them was not normal at all. That is to say she learned not to talk about the things she saw. She eventually denied ever seeing them. In the end she dismissed the orbs and it wasn't until several years later that the realization hit her. She had not seen them for a long time. It was as if her decision had changed her ability to see.

She wondered if it were true, that people only see what they want to see, or maybe, what they allow themselves to see.

The truth was, she had seen an angel change into a man. Or at least someone she *thought* was a man.

The basement's sliding door opened beneath the deck, and she knew it must be Falk. Then she heard his voice.

"Belle?" His voice was quiet.

She called down to him, "I'm right here."

Falk spoke a bit louder, "If you would like to talk, I am able to now."

She thought for a moment. *He wants to talk now, now that I know.* Then another thought occurred to her, *If he's willing to talk now, maybe I should take him up on it.* "OK, I'll be right down."

There was no way to get to the ground from the deck, it was on the main floor, which from the back of the house looked like a second floor. In order to keep raccoons, bears, and other animals off of these mountain home decks there were no stairs to the ground level, and the upright posts were covered with a veneer of tin about four feet high and starting around three feet off the ground, making them impossible for animals to climb.

That is to say, Belle had to go through the house to get downstairs.

Belle closed the sliding glass door behind her and out of habit asked, "You couldn't sleep?"

Falk smiled, "I do not sleep."

"Oh." That caught her off guard. She motioned toward the path that led to a fire pit about fifty yards away, "How about we walk and talk?"

He joined her, "Very good."

She stuffed her hands into her robe pockets and after a few steps asked, "What was that thing you killed?"

"That was one of the fallen angels. I did not kill him."

"It looked like you killed it."

"Yes, I can see why you would say that. The truth is, nothing with life ever truly dies. I merely sent him to the Crypsis."

"The Crypsis?"

"That has been their home since their fall. It is their world."

Falk kept to Belle's slow pace and it took several steps for Belle to ask another question. "How could I see you if you are an angel, and who was the other one with you?"

"Katriel is in charge of the protectors of this property."

He continued, "I am not sure why you are able to see into the other realm, I have been told that some of your kind have the ability from the time of your birth; however, I was under the impression, in your case, that you had walked away from your gift."

The two spoke well past sunrise. Jessica made coffee and walked out onto the deck with both hands on the hot mug and was surprised to see Belle and Falk walking up the path from the forest together.

Belle looked up in Jessica's direction and waved, Jess waved in return.

As the pair approached, Jess could see that Belle was more at ease than she had been the night before.

Jessica sighed, "Looks like it was a good conversation."

Jessica walked back into the house and over to her computer, she pulled up her bank account on the web.

"Still no royalties. I'll have to call the book company again and find out what's going on." She looked back out the window, "We need to make a new budget."

She grabbed her yellow pad and pencil, then shifted her chair over to the scroll, still laid out from working on it. "Time to get working on you. What do you have for me today?"

Chapter 16
Close Encounter

The City of Enoch, with a population just shy of ten thousand men, was small by modern standards, and was laid out such that in the center was a large, open, roughly circular commons area. The commons could hold about one-third of the people that lived in the city and when a gathering was called the overflow filed into the surrounding streets that radiated out from the center.

Surrounding the center were many shops and places to eat since the center had the most traffic on any given day. The shops also lined the streets for a certain distance and then, for the most part, the streets led to the mud-brick homes of the people. The homes were separated by walls that established property lines and allowed for a bit of privacy. The short walls ended up surrounding the city, not as protection, for there was nothing to be protected from, but more as a block against the weather that would buffet the city from time to time. The merchants in the city lived either in their shops or close by. Outside the outer-most walls were crops of various kinds that formed a ring around the entire city. Outside this ring were the livestock on great open plains. The shepherds tended their flocks and herds in the expansive areas.

Several roads emerged from Enoch and connected it to other cities. Each city had a similar layout and with the connecting roads, the cities formed a network that was useful for travel, trade, and commerce. From above, the cities and interconnecting roads resembled a massive spider's web.

The lights continued to move, but were still far off. They had taken to one of the roads and continued to advance at a steady pace.

Ermiel caught his breath, "What do you think they are?"

Jabal shook his head, "I do not know."

"Do you think we are in danger?"

Jabal shrugged his shoulders, "It looks like they will not be here before midday. Perhaps Cain... I hope he will be here by then. He has seen things he refuses to talk about, so he may have seen something like this before."

The Army Ranger, or now, Army Ranger John Wilder pulled up to the local Ben Franklin's store in Woodland Park. He'd considered going to the library, but at the last minute decided to buy a book and ol' Ben's was as good a place as any to find one.

He climbed out of his Mustang, pulled on a fleece-lined denim jacket and headed for the store.

Just before midday Jabal heard movement behind him, he turned to see his half-brother, Jubal, round a corner of one of the homes, Cain in tow.

"Saba!" Jabal lunged for Cain and embraced him, then pulled away.

"Saba Cain, I am glad you are here."

Cain could hear the anxiety in Jabal's voice. "More lights?"

"Yes, over here." Jabal put his arm around Cain, to steady his shaking body, and led him to the best vantage point.

Cain squinted his eyes, "I see. Yes, they are coming this way, and quite a large number of them. What are you going to do?"

"I was about to ask you."

"Me?"

"Yes, you have seen things we have never seen."

"And you thought…?"

"I thought you may have seen something like this before."

"No, never."

"Never? Are you sure?"

"Yes, I am sure, I would remember something like this. You need to come up with a plan soon, they will be here within the hour." Cain turned to leave.

"Where are you going?"

"To wait with the crowd."

"No, you cannot, I need you here."

"Whatever for? I have no more experience with this sort of thing than you do."

"But you are older and wiser than I, please Saba, I implore you to stay with me."

Cain looked at the other men and sighed, "What are *we* going to do then?"

As Jeremiel approached the portal that led to Paradise, he joined hundreds of thousands of other angels through the entrance as well. Surely, all of them were responding to the same call.

He thought back to Remiel, and wondered why he had not been called. Jeremiel thought that perhaps the archangel was on an important mission, though he had no idea what it could be, or why he would be talking to one of the fallen ones.

It was not unusual for one to be called back and another left in an existing assignment, and since he had no idea what Remiel was doing, he knew the only course of action ahead was to follow the call. Still he could not help but wonder why so many were being pulled away from Earth all at the same time.

The Ben Franklin store had a small book section, mostly bestsellers, the kind chain stores carry. But what he was after was the other type of book they carried. John had what many would think of as "quirky" taste and enjoyed reading books by authors whose stories would not be considered "main stream." They could be late-comers to the dance, meaning their books came out after a certain craze, like vampires or zombies had tapered off. Or, books that were ahead of their time. It didn't matter, both types of books were just fine with him, and he liked reading the lesser read stuff. Sort of like walking the road less traveled, as it were.

Usually, when he took time off, he would find a destination like Hawaii, or New Zealand, and spend time seeing the sights. He enjoyed being a tourist, with the dorky clothes and a nice camera hanging from his neck. But this time was different, the sands of Afghanistan showed him things he'd not seen before and he did something he had not done before. He had come home. He needed things to be normal for once.

He rounded the corner to the book section and saw someone he had not seen since before he joined the Army. He walked up behind her, "Excuse me miss, I'm looking for a book for some light reading."

"What type of book?" She said as she turned around, and saw a familiar face covered in a wide grin.

"Johnny!" She grabbed his shoulders and held him at arms length, to get a good look at him. "I didn't know you were back!"

He shoved his hands into his jacket pockets, "Just rolled in a few days ago."

"Well boy, it's good to see you, and all in one piece. Still in the service?"

"Yep, but I'm on a long vacation."

Emily eyed him up and down, "Well, it looks like the service suits you. I'm glad for you. How long is your vacation?"

"Six weeks, I need to unwind after my last tour."

A puzzled expression covered Emily's face, "You need to unwind? Who are you and what have you done with my friend?"

"I saw some things... I'm not sure I understand."

Emily could see the emotion welling up in his eyes, and she could also see that it wasn't something he wanted to happen.

She interrupted the moment, "Did you hear I got married?"

John's demeanor changed, he smiled and said, "I did hear that, you married little Manny Garza, right?"

"Yup, yup, but he's not so little anymore, he got all growed up! And I'm Emily Garza now, don't ya know." Her eyes lit up, "Hey, and we have spawn!"

John saw how Emily had so skillfully redirected the conversation, and he appreciated it, "What? No!"

Emily beamed, "A daughter and a son, boy you've missed a lot being gone so long."

John smiled again, "I suppose I have."

"So, are you really looking for a book?"

"Yeah, as a matter of fact, I am."

A concerned look covered Emily's face. "Ok, so what were you thinking, a self help book?"

His head fell to one side, like a bolt had suddenly given way, "Is that a hint?"

"Well, I didn't want to be obvious. Is that your Dad's jacket?" She winked at him.

"What? I love this jacket! And to be honest, I was thinking more like a novel, something off the beaten path."

"Oh right, you always had a bent for the one-off's."

"Anything good?"

"Actually, we have a new one from a local author..."

"Ooooo, let me see..."

———

Jeremiel flew into the throne room, several million angels were already there and formed up. Still more flew in behind him. He continued on to his choir and touched down among his fellow thunderers. It looked like most of the members of each choir had been called back from Earth.

———————

The group of two hundred newly transformed men walked the distance between Mount Hermon and the City of Enoch. Semyaza, Azazel, and Remiel led the way. Remiel mostly because he intended to keep close to Semyaza, who was likely the only one of these serpents that did not want to slice him to bits.

Azazel broke the silence, "I see Cain has joined those who watch us."

Kokabiel laughed, "Behold, the watchers, who are watched by the very maggots who were first being watched, and yet still are watched by others."

Remiel thought, *That incessant laughing is getting on my nerves,* Then he said, "I see fear in their eyes."

"Of course you do," Azazel sneered, "They have no knowledge of such things. Cain, shielded them from knowledge to hide his own treachery. They are as witless as the beasts of the field, without the ability to understand the simplest of the universal truths."

Semyaza broke into the conversation, "We will teach them our truths, and gain their favor. In the end, they will do whatever we command, they may even worship us."

Kokabiel's laughter continued, "Can you stand to be worshiped, Remiel?"

Remiel glanced at Kokabiel and spoke under his breath, "I have no interest in that."

Semyaza quickened his pace, "Try to keep up, we will be there soon enough."

The last of the angels had come to rest in the throne room and Metatron emerged from among the four living creatures that surrounded the throne, now called "Hayyoth."

These Hayyoth had been in a state of continual change since they had taken up residency around the throne. The four seraphim serpents no longer looked as they did when they had first taken their assignments around the throne. They were much larger now, each had four wings which completely hid the lower portion of the throne when the four joined their wings together.

The changes in their bodies were more than just in size, but also in body structure as well. As though something had been hidden inside each of them all along and only now, in the presence of their Lord, did their hidden parts come to the surface.

One looked as though he was taking on the facial features and body structure of a lion, and the next, an ox, while the third, looked very much like an eagle, and the last was similar to a man.

And their song had changed as well. They still sang in unison of words, but the notes danced and intertwined with harmonics that surprised and exhilarated the senses. Each of the four sang melody and each sang harmony, in turn.

It was out from the midst of these giant creatures that Metatron walked. One who bore no pretense, though clothed in splendorous light, he walked with humility past the fiery stones and over one of the white bridges that spanned the crystal sea.

Jeremiel looked around and saw the Captain, Michael, as well as the other archangels standing at the head of their respective choirs. In fact, all of the archangels were there with the exception of Remiel.

Metatron reached the center of the steps and motioned to the archangels; who, in perfect unison, turned toward the choirs. Michael's voice trumpeted above the Hayyoth song, "Choirs! Come to attention!"

A thunderous roar filled the throne room as the order was carried out.

Then came Michael's second command, "Choirs! Shalom!"

A somewhat softer roar filled the air as each angel assumed an identical, if a bit less rigid, position.

The archangels turned to face the throne, and their Creator. Michael and Gabriel left their positions and walked up the steps, taking their rightful place, Michael to the Creator's right, and Gabriel to the left.

Metatron looked out over the angels that stood before the throne. As he began to speak, the Hayyoth went silent. He spoke as softly as a gentle breeze, yet all could hear him, for all were listening for His voice.

"Thank you all for coming."

He glanced toward each of the archangels and with each glance he smiled in a way that projected genuine love and affection. Then he looked at the place where Remiel normally stood. Though the fire in his eyes did not dim, his countenance changed.

Jeremiel had heard stories of the sadness Metatron had expressed when Mankind fell, what he saw now did not compare to those stories, but the King of Angels did show a deep sadness.

Metatron looked out over the angels, "We have invited every angel that could be spared to come to this ceremony, and here you are. We are proud of each and every one of the faithful hosts of Paradise." He paused.

Jeremiel felt a wave of love flow through the ranks.

Metatron stood motionless.

Only the fires of the Creator, the whirling emerald ring above with it's lightning, and the crackling peels of thunder could be heard. Everyone waited.

Then Metatron's eyes locked onto Jeremiel's, and he spoke once more, "Remiel has fallen."

Gasps and an uneasy tension rose in the great hall.

Jeremiel and Metatron's eyes locked onto one another. The wind of the spirit flowed through him, and he heard the words of the great Ruach ha Kodesh, the Great Spirit, speak with a feminine melody to his heart, "You saw him fall and I kept you from it. What was in his heart is not in yours. Keep your ways upright and blameless as is your custom."

Metatron spoke once more, "We have chosen a new Archangel of the Voice, and of Hope, a new carrier of the sound of Paradise." He paused briefly before continuing, "Jeremiel, would you please walk to the front to receive your commission?"

Metatron blinked and his link with Jeremiel was broken.

Jeremiel felt a slap on his folded wings, he turned and saw his old friend, Tzadkiel, smiling. The two hugged. It had been at least two Earth centuries since they had seen one another.

Tzadkiel pulled away, he thought Jeremiel might need some help so he turned him around and walked with him to the aisle, then on toward the scribe.

Jeremiel's mind struggled with what he had just learned. Remiel had fallen. That alone was enough to send his mind reeling. Now he, Jeremiel, was about to be appointed to fill Remiel's place as Archangel. He wondered how he could possibly fill Remiel's place, how could the lowly Jeremiel become an archangel?

Tzadkiel leaned into his friend as they walked, "Listen, you were chosen for this."

Jeremiel could only look at his friend, and that only for an instant.

Metatron waited while the pair walked to the front of the throne room. All told, the distance was a mile or so.

When the two reached the front of the choirs, Tzadkiel stopped his friend.

Jeremiel looked over, his brow furrowed.

Tzadkiel leaned into him and once more whispered, "Do not drop your sword."

Jeremiel smiled with the memory of the day he *had* dropped his sword and the deafening sound it had made. He had all but forgotten those times when they learned to march. Those days seemed so long ago now.

He remembered, wondering as most of the angels did, how that training would equip them for anything. Then it all became clear when they received their wings, and even more so now that they had to work together, and rely on one another. Somehow that training had done more than they could have imagined.

Jeremiel climbed the steps and stood before Metatron as Tzadkiel remained in the aisle between his choir and Gabriel's choir, between Raziel and the messenger who would one day be referred to as Falk.

The scribe spoke to the assembled angels, "Cherubim and Seraphim, today is a special day. It is a day of loss and a day of promotion. There is one thing you must all remember, whenever you conform to a way that is not your own, you lose a part of yourself. You were made with a splendor all your own, each of you is different, unique.

"Many of you have seen the metamorphosis that is possible for your kind. And while it is true that Remiel is using his ability to change, this in and of itself is not that which I now speak to you about. Indeed, many of you will be tasked to accomplish similar transformations in your dealings with the children of Adam.

"On the contrary, what I speak of is a deeper thing. When you conform your mind, or your will to the whims of anyone other than your Creator, you dampen your splendor. In the end, you blot it out completely, as Remiel has done.

"For this I am saddened."

His voice lowered, though all could still hear his every inflection, "Each of you will experience seduction, many of you have experienced it already. It is a drawing away from the true, from the real. It will undoubtedly happen many times until the final judgement. You alone determine the outcome each time the snare is set. You choose.

"All of us will face the seductions of the enemy and all of us must prepare ourselves. The fate of many rest on our actions." Metatron stood for a moment, knowing his time of temptation would come as well. When the enemy would meet him in the wilderness, in his weakness he would face the accuser, and try as he might, he could not see the outcome.

Metatron turned to face the new archangel, "Jeremiel, your Creator would speak with you."

As Jeremiel turned toward the pillar of fire, the four Hayyoth pulled their wings back and folded them revealing the sapphire blue throne-chariot, whose crystalline shape forever changes.

The swirling green whirlwind above the throne spun with a raging fury, lightning flashed this way and that. The whirlwind grew outward in all directions, it appeared to be made up of trillions of emeralds mixed with emerald dust and green cloud. Then there was the sound, the beautiful, terrible sound grew from a whirling to an all-consuming multi-octave roar.

In the midst of the commotion, the Father of all spoke with a voice, both peaceful and low, like the rumbling of thunder, "My word goes forth, and all who have ears are able to hear it. All you angels in Paradise and on Earth listen well.

"The road ahead is filled with my goodness, you must find My rest to see it. You are ready and you will be made ready. Nothing will come against you that has not already been seen and has not already been taken into account. You rest under the shadow of my wing, for my eye is always on you. Trust in Me, do not falter, do not rely on your own vision or understanding. Your vision has been given to you for the momentary, My vision sees all. Let the questions that are swarming around you settle. Do not give them voice, for they do not lead you to Love, they do not lead you to Me, for I AM Love. Find your center in Me, for when you do this, you *will* find rest. And when you have found My rest you will hear My voice.

"Victory is ahead, you will know much sorrow and you will know much pain. The Earth realm is not as I made it to be. The enemy has reveled in doubt, accusation, pride, and now lust. Man has allowed the ways of Satan to infiltrate him and his territory. Indeed, he has given the authority of all I gave him over to the enemy. And in so doing, he now lives in the encampment of the opposition, and has become blind to all that has been lost. This path must run its course. I AM the redeemer of Man," Metatron closed his eyes as he listened,

"And the path for redemption has been laid out before the chosen One.

"Man will be redeemed, the Earth realm will be reestablished in perfection, but only after the seeds of the enemy have run their course and the testimony is established before the eyes of all. All will see the results of living outside of purpose, outside of My purpose, outside of Love.

"Jeremiel, guard your heart. The fire in you is from Me, you are a splendid creature. I have made you, I will sustain you."

The winds of the whirlwind subsided and the roar of the winds decreased back to the former whirling sound. Each of the four Hayyoth slowly spread their four wings and cloaked the throne and the bottom portion of the pillar of flame.

The millions of angels broke out into praise for the Father of all.

Chapter 17
Disturbing Dream

Jessica, Belle, and Falk walked out into the garage, Jess climbing into the big red truck as though on auto-pilot. Belle shrugged it off, she figured her friend must have something on her mind, perhaps a particularly difficult section of the scroll. It had happened before, a certain phrase or syntax that almost defied translation. Jess always seemed to nail it down, and make it understandable.

Belle motioned for Falk to follow her to the passenger side of the truck, where she opened the door and climbed up and plopped down into the middle seat. She then turned to Falk and motioned for him to join her.

He studied the door and the opening before taking hold of the interior hand hold and climbing in.

Belle thought about informing him about the seat belt, but then wondered if an angel would need it. She looked over at him, at his closed eyes, and wondered what he was thinking about.

He responded to her thoughts, "I am listening."

Jess started the truck and backed out into the driveway, where she turned the vehicle around and pulled out to the end of the asphalt driveway, and then onto the dusty dirt road.

Belle sat in silence as the truck lumbered down the road toward the highway. Her mind drifted to these outings and how they had evolved over the past several months. Their travel to town was limited to once per week, mostly due to finances. Things had grown tight and combining trips into one per week taught both of them to plan much better than before and allowed them to spend time together, "Off the clock," so to speak.

And now, she was sitting next to an angel. An actual angel was in the truck, right next to her. Of course she knew this, but the realization of the fact sometimes made her wonder if she was crazy. It sure sounded crazy, if only in her own mind.

She thought, *Of all the things I would like to ask him, the things anyone would like to ask, and here I am thinking about Walmart. This angel was the messenger that delivered the second scroll, had he delivered the first as well? Was he injured the first time and we just didn't know about it?*

Falk smiled even while his eyes remained closed.

Once on the highway, the silence in the truck, and her own thoughts were more than Belle could take, she decided to start a conversation. "So, what's on the agenda for today?"

Falk's eyes opened.

Jess glanced toward Belle, "What do you mean?"

"I know we're going to lunch, but I was hoping to run an errand while we're out?"

Jessica perked up a bit, "Oh sure, I need to get a few things, too, now that you mention it. Sorry, I'm in a bit of a daze, wanna hit Walmart before lunch?"

"Sure, that sounds great."

Jessica glanced over at Belle, "We're doing fine with food for the next week, unless there's something you can think of?"

Belle thought for a moment, "I'll grab some eggs and fruit, other than that we're fine for a while."

Jessica looked over at the quiet angel, "Falk might like to see more of the surrounding area as well."

Falk remained motionless, his eyes closed once again.

Silence.

When no response came, the two glanced at each other. Belle shrugged her shoulders.

Once inside the store the three walked over to the end of the first cash register, and Jessica picked up a tabloid and began leafing through it. Not normal behavior for her.

Belle glanced over to Jess, "I'll meet you up front here in, let's say..." she looked at her cell phone screen, "Twenty minutes? Falk, why don't you come with me?"

Falk bowed slightly.

Jessica pulled her phone from her purse and pressed the lone button on the front to activate the display, "Sounds good."

Belle walked toward the cosmetics section, angel in tow. As she turned to enter the hairspray aisle, she stopped to see where Jessica had gone, but Jess was right where she left her, thumbing through the magazine absentmindedly. Belle shook her head and continued on down the row. She decided to hurry since it looked like Jess did not need anything after all. She picked out hairspray, shampoo, conditioner, and some foundation. She could make it at least another week on the rest of her supplies.

She and Falk then walked to the produce section where they picked out some oranges, tomatoes, bananas, and kiwis. Falk held several of the produce bags for her. Then they made their way over to get a dozen eggs.

Belle turned to Falk as they walked down the dairy aisle, "This must be very different for you, what do you think of this store?"

"It is interesting that everything in this place is in short supply."

"What do you mean? This is a big store with lots of stuff, pretty much whatever you might need."

Falk looked around, "In Paradise there is a storehouse for snow, and it is much larger than this place, one hundred times larger, maybe more. There is another for hail, and you would not need to visit a storehouse for fruit or food, it is all around. Whatever is needed would be at your fingertips, and in such supply that there would never be a question of if it would be there."

Belle looked over at Falk and smiled, "That would be nice, no wonder it's called Paradise."

The two walked back toward the front of the store to see Jess still standing at a check out stand flipping through one of the tabloids. She wasn't sure if it was the same one as before.

Belle nudged Falk, "Now that's an unusual sight."

Jess turned toward the familiar voice, "What is?"

Belle raised one eyebrow, "You, looking though one of those rags."

Jess's brow furrowed as she focused on the paper in her hands. She flipped it closed and let out a sigh, "Wow, I don't know what's wrong with me today."

Belle placed her items on the checkout belt, "Uh huh," then reached over to her friend and pulled the non-newspaper free and placed it back on the rack. "Jess, you and the angel stick with me."

Jessica grimaced and put her arm around the messenger, "Alright Falk, you heard the lady."

———————

John put his new book in the passenger seat of his car and pulled out to find a place to hole up for lunch and maybe start reading his new book. He was looking forward to sinking down into some other world where he could forget some of what he saw in Afghanistan.

———————

Fiesta Mexicana was the lunch choice for the day. Jessica, Belle, and Falk walked toward the entrance. Falk stopped and for a moment neither of the ladies noticed, then all at once Belle pivoted to see Falk walking back toward the truck.

"Falk, what's wrong, did you forget something?" She had no idea what he could have forgotten, but those were the words that came out.

"I need to stay outside."

"Why?"

"I am not sure."

"Alright. Hold on and I'll unlock the door for you so you can sit in the truck."

His voice took on a soothing tone, "No, you do not need to," as he faded from view.

"Ok, that's weird. Jessica, what do we do now?"

Jessica shrugged, "I suppose we go inside."

"But there is an angel standing next to our truck."

Jess turned and continued walking toward the restaurant, "Pretend like you don't know."

Belle looked at Jessica dumbfounded. Then turned toward the truck and spoke louder than before, "OK FALK, WE'RE GOING INTO THE RESTAURANT NOW, COME ON IN WHEN YOU CAN, OR WE'LL SEE YOU WHEN WE COME BACK OUT."

She waited, half expecting a reply, then not knowing what to expect. Finally, she shrugged her shoulders, turned, and walked toward the building, "I *think* we'll see him when we come back."

Jessica smiled and held the door open for Belle.

The hostess seated the pair and placed two menus on the table. Their waiter walked up as they slid out of their jackets and settled into the booth. He took their drink orders as he placed a basket of chips and a bowl of fresh salsa on the table.

Belle dipped a chip into the red, chunky mixture, "Ok, so what's up?" She bit down on her salsa-covered chip, letting the cool yet mildly spicy sauce linger for an instant before chewing. Her attention remained on Jessica.

"What do you mean?"

The chip was in the way, but Belle managed to talk around it, her hand over her mouth, "You have something on your mind, I mean, you can barely function. So what gives?"

"I know, I'm sorry." Jessica reached into the chip basket.

The waiter returned with their drinks, "Are you ready to order, or," he noticed they hadn't touched their menu's yet, "do you need a few minutes?"

Belle looked at Jessica, "I'm ready if you are."

Jessica reached for one of the menus, "You're ready? You haven't looked at the menu yet."

"I know but I remember having some kind of enchiladas." She looked up at the waiter, "It was chicken enchiladas with a spinach sauce."

The waiters head bobbed up and down, but before he could speak Jessica said, "Oh that sounds good, I'll have that too," and she placed her menu on top of the other one.

The waiter finished scribbling on his note pad, "Alright, two Enchiladas Monterey, very good, I'll get your order in. Is there anything else I can get for you?"

Both ladies shook their heads and the waiter walked back toward the front of the restaurant, he stopped to ask another patron if he would like a refill of his drink.

Belle watched the waiter and she noticed that the other patron was thoroughly engrossed in a book. He nodded his head and barely glanced an acknowledgement at the waiter.

She then turned back to Jess who was staring down at a chip she held with both hands, "So? What's on your mind?"

Jess snapped the chip, "I had a dream and it's bothering me, that's all."

Belle replied, "I wanna hear it," as she slid the rest of her chip into her mouth.

Jessica sighed, "Let me think about how it started." She thought for a moment, "Let's see, everything started out white, I couldn't see anything. At least at first, you know how sometimes when you walk out into the bright sunshine and sometimes you can't see anything?"

Belle nodded her head as she scooped up more salsa on a fresh chip.

"Ok, then my eyes adjusted and I could begin to make out details, a long floor stretched out in front of me. Then I started to see the walls and ceiling, I was in a room. It was really long in front of me and not as wide."

"How wide?"

"I'm not sure. It might have been forty feet or so, maybe."

"Ok, so how long was it?"

"I would say, it was easily four or five times longer than it was wide."

Belle nodded her head.

Falk stood beside the truck, invisible to mortals, but very much there. He had become aware of a pause in the wind. This was not a wind that could be felt with physical skin. No, this was the real wind, the wind of reality. The wind that carries the very will of the Creator, issuing forth from His essence and flowing in and through everything in Paradise as well as our universe.

Mortals might want to pigeonhole this wind and see it as a network, a data stream if you will. That description would be partly true, but it is so much more than that. In a very real sense it is a living wind that can range from the lightest of breezes to the strongest hurricane.

Today, however, Falk felt something truly rare. In the truest part of everything, he felt a pause, and it was directed at him.

This was the reason he waited. To move from this spot when a pause was issued would be unthinkable, even unimaginable. He held his face into the wind, into the current of life. Waiting for a message, a calling, a purpose, even a next step.

———————

"I started walking toward the center of the room, along the right hand wall. Everything was white, but there was a texture to it. There was a very ornate molding along the wall, like a baseboard but it was around two feet tall. Everything looked really old, almost crumbly. I think all of it was made of stone, white stone. It was like the entire room was carved into one big white rock, but the room was so tall that I could not be sure."

"How tall?"

"I'd say it was probably twice as tall than it's width and there were chairs in the middle of the room. At first, I didn't know they were chairs, they were so big, from where I entered the room they looked like a pair of stone cubes."

"They looked like cubes?"

"Yeah, you know, like a very modern style of furniture. The sides and back are even at the top, and if the seat were not cut into the structure it would look like a cube. Know what I mean?"

———————

Falk heard Jessica sharing her dream with Belle, he heard the waiter asking customers questions and the answers that were given. He heard someone in the kitchen chopping vegetables and someone else swearing at the person doing the chopping, saying in Spanish that they were doing it wrong.

But there was one person, a man, he could hear among the others. He was saying something, like he was reading. It was something about the throne-chariot of the Creator. It was about the throne room of Elohim, or more specifically, it was a description of the throne-chariot, the Mercavah, on which the Creator sits.

The pause subsided and he raised his head. Falk had to learn more about this one, and what he was reading.

Belle dipped another chip into the salsa, "I think so. You walked over to the chairs? Did you sit in them?"

"No, that's just it, I couldn't reach, they were much too big. I mean the seat of the chair was probably around six feet high."

"Both of them?"

"Yep, and they were facing one another. Anyway, I was looking up at one of the chairs and something caught my attention. When I turned to look at the side wall, to my right, the one I had just walked next to, it was different. Before, it was just the ornate wall, but now there were columns along it. They were really big, probably five to seven feet in diameter, and there were maybe fifteen or twenty of them along the wall. They were completely smooth, more like Egyptian columns than the classic Roman or Greek styles. And they looked old like everything else. On top of each of the columns stood a huge statue of an eagle."

"One per column?"

From where Belle sat, the front entrance of the restaurant was in clear view so when the door opened and Falk walked in, it caught her attention. At first he looked lost, so she waved at him. His eye's and head locked onto her so fast it actually startled her. There was a sharpness to his movement.

As the angel approached, Belle scooted over and motioned for Falk to sit next to her. He looked uneasy but somehow found a way to fit in the booth, it wasn't made for people over six and a half feet tall.

Jessica waited for Falk to settle then smiled at him, "Glad you could join us."

Falk looked around at the different items on the table, "Thank you, I am glad for that as well."

Jessica thought about how his answers were always so awkward. "I was just telling Belle about a dream I had, would you like to hear it? I can start over."

"No need to start over, I have been listening, please continue."

She looked at Belle, eyebrows raised, she spoke to herself, "Ok then, let's see, where was I?"

Falk replied, "You were talking about the eagles that were on top of the columns."

"Oh, that's right!" Jessica's brows furrowed, as though surprised Falk actually knew what they were talking about. "Let's see, the eagles were on top of the columns, I was about to talk about their wings. It was weird because they held their wings to the front, covering their bodies, not back like a normal eagle. Oh, and their heads almost touched the ceiling. I stood there for a long time just taking in the detail of those statues until I heard something behind me."

———————

Jessica turned just in time to see the wall opposite the columns disappear and it was evident that the room in which she stood was in the mountains and outside the room was a downhill slope. The room must have been high in the mountains because the tree line was about seventy-five yards down the hill. As she walked to the edge of the opening she could see movement among the trees. The wind accounted for some of the movement, but here and there she could see where the tree tops moved back and forth as something, or some things, passed between them. Flames shot into the sky, first from the left, then the right, then in varying locations.

All at once several dragons burst from the trees and galloped toward her.

Her feet were frozen in place and her heart pounded against her ribs. She tried to move them with all her might, but they would not budge.

Then, all at once, five more exited the tree line, followed closely by several more. All of them ran with a hypnotic undulating motion that was both fluid and powerful, their muscles rippled with each stride underneath loose hanging skin.

In the sky behind them she saw a spinning vortex. The vortex opened from the center and light flooded out. She had to shield her eyes for it was too bright to look at, the dragons had a noticeable reaction to it as well. It seemed the light, which was behind them, drove them forward, toward her with even more speed.

She suddenly found she could move her feet again and when she turned to run back toward the columns something caught her eye. She looked up to see each of the stone eagles opening their wings in unison. Their movements were slow and deliberate. Underneath the wings, each of the figures looked silver, except that the silver rippled and moved. When the eagles wings were fully open, each formed a sort of dish, the inside of which was completely covered with the liquid silver.

The eagles caught the blinding light and the silver liquid acted to focus it back towards the dragons. Each of the eagle figures targeted an individual dragon who's multi-octave and clashing screams sent Jessica's hands to her ears in a vain attempt to stop the pain. Each dragon burned up into twisted heaps and then scattered like ash easily blown away in the wind.

Falk listened to Jessica's dream, but he also listened to the muttered reading of the man he'd heard from outside. Such things, such words, he wondered if the reader fully grasped what he was reading. He had found the man but could not see his book. In this form his abilities were severely limited. He decided to have a look at the reader.

Jessica continued with her dream, Falk rose to his feet and motioned for her to continue. In slow motion, Falk stalked the sound as if to allow each reverberation to continue as the cadence of the consonants pierced him through.

Jessica stood and stared. She tried to understand what she had just seen.

More movement in the trees. This time slower, but again from multiple places. The sounds became more even, like a rhythm. Then she saw them. Giant men exited the tree line wearing military uniforms. The figures moved toward her, there must have been a dozen of them. Every one had a powerful build and they were easily as tall as the columns. Without thinking she backed up against one of the chairs. She thought, *Those giant men could sit in the chairs.* Her heart sank, she realized that she was in their room and she did not belong there, they did!

The figures on the columns continued to target the big soldiers but nothing happened to them, they kept coming.

She called out, "Why isn't this working?" But there was no response.

––––––––––

Falk walked past the man in the booth and stopped. He paused, staring straight ahead.

The man in the booth stopped reading and looked up at the tall man.

Falk turned, "Please, keep reading."

"What do you mean?"

"Please, do not stop."

"You could hear me?"

"Yes, and it reminded me of..." Falk's voice trailed off.

"I'm sorry, I didn't mean to disturb you, I thought I was reading more quietly than that."

"You were, I am sorry to disturb your reading. May I inquire as to what it is you are reading?"

"It's a novel, I bought it this morning. Here, have a look," the man closed the book on his finger to hold his place, showing the cover to Falk.

Falk's eyes grew wide, "I have seen this book."

––––––––––

The group of soldiers separated into some sort of formation and one after another they all reached back and grabbed large machine guns that had been slung to their backs.

The light from the eagles continued to shine, and while the soldiers squinted, the light seemed to do nothing more than make them more angry than they already looked.

The first of the giants stepped into the room and advanced toward the eagles. Time slowed as his weapon came to life and the eagle, who's light was focused on the giant, exploded in a spray of gunfire. Others emerged into the room and the remaining eagles met similar fates.

She watched the last of the stone and silvery liquid fall to the ground, she then turned to the giant that had first entered the room, his face was toward her. Then, all at once, she realized all of the giants had turned toward her. She peered up to his eyes but could not see them because they were shrouded in darkness.

His gun raised to her head, then a muzzle flash.

Jessica continued, "I jumped up in my bed awake, I was so scared. It was probably a couple minutes before I knew where I was and that it was all just a dream, but I couldn't go back to sleep after that."

Belle reached across the table and took Jessica's hand. "That's a scary dream, what do you think it means?"

"I'm not sure."

Belle thought for a moment, "You could ask Falk."

"I thought about that, but he doesn't say much."

Belle grabbed another chip as her head bobbed up and down in agreement, "Did you know this is the first time he's been around people?"

"No, really?" She thought for a moment, "That sure explains some things."

Belle looked down at the chip and snapped it in half, "Still, he might know about dreams, it might be worth a try to at least ask." Belle glanced toward the front of the restaurant. "Jessica, you're not going to believe this."

"What?"

"Falk is talking to a man over there."

The man in the booth held out his hand, "I'm John."

Falk's brow furrowed, as he cautiously took hold of John's hand, being careful not to squeeze too hard, "I am known as Falk."

"Really? There's a Falk in this book and so far He's my favorite character. It's an unusual name. Would you care to sit down?"

"No, thank you, but I'm here with some friends. Actually, one of my friends wrote the book you are reading."

Belle sat up a little, "Falk is coming, and he's bringing that guy over here."

Jessica swallowed her chip to clear her mouth, "Maybe he's more social than we thought, though I wasn't expecting to meet anyone today." She rubbed her tongue over her teeth.

Falk and John approached the table. Falk stood to one side and looked at John, "John, I'd like to introduce you to Jessica and Belle, they are my friends."

John held out his hand to Belle, "Hello Jessica, Falk here tells me you wrote the book I'm reading."

Belle smiled and shook John's hand, "I'm Belle, but it's nice to meet you, I'm the editor."

John looked stunned. He pulled his hand back and smiled, "I'm sorry," he turned his attention to the other woman in the booth and apologetically held his hand out to her, "Jessica?"

"Yes, I'm Jessica Mozes."

"John Wilder, very nice to meet you, Ma'am. Good book, by the way, at least so far!"

Everyone except Falk laughed.

Jessica blushed a bit, "Thank you, I'm glad you're enjoying it."

The waiter approached the table carrying two plates of food. "Excuse me folks, hot plates here."

Falk and John stepped to the side and watched the waiter place the plates in front of Jessica and Belle. The waiter turned to John, "Your lunch will be out momentarily as well, sir." He then pivoted and walked back to the kitchen.

John looked back toward the ladies at the table, "I better get back to my table, it was nice to meet both of you, and sorry for the confusion."

Belle nodded her head.

Jessica smiled, "It was nice to meet you too, John."

Chapter 18

Inseparable

Jarod approached the cave he and his wife Baraka called home, with their nine children. The city Cain had started so many years before loomed behind him, spread out in all directions. This cave, while overlooking the city, was quite a distance away and completely hidden in the forest. Not that anyone from the city would be interested in finding this place, nor any of the inhabitants who were of the line of Seth. Jarod, the sixth generation of Man, lived among the few relatives not enticed to join the city below, or one of the other villages that had taken root farther away.

He walked out from the forest and into the clearing in front of the cave. Several of his children greeted him and his youngest daughter, Naka, age six, ran to him holding one finger in the air. He scooped her up into his arms and kissed her on the cheek.

She held her finger close, too close, to his right eye. "Look, Papa, I fell down and cut my finger."

"Oh no!" He took hold of her hand and gently moved it far enough away that he could take a look at the cut. "Let me see here, I wonder if this is one of the *baaaaad* cuts."

Her eyes grew wide as her mouth dropped open.

He studied the finger for quite some time before peering toward her, without moving his head.

"Is it Papa? Is it a *baaaad* cut?" She held her breath waiting for the response.

He waited until he was sure little Naka was about to burst at the seams, "No, this one will be fine." He raised his eyebrows at her.

She copied his facial expression and they both sighed together. She kissed him on the lips and started squirming, so he put her down and she ran toward the others, laughing.

Jarod stood with his hands on his hips.

Baraka spoke before he could ask his question, "Did you learn of the strangers in the city?"

Jarod's eyebrows raised, "Yes, and I made a small trade." He opened his satchel and pulled a small object out. It was wrapped in leather. "They made this." He held it out for his wife.

She took the object from him and pulled a small knife from it's sheath. "Two blades? Why on Earth would they make a knife with two blades?"

"I do not know, but the edge is very sharp, they say it is good for self defense."

"Self defense?"

"Yes. They call it a dagger."

"Why would we defend ourselves? The Lord of Spirits does that."

"Yes, I know. I only bought the knife to show you and I thought we could use it to cut bread and meat."

She looked back down at the knife, "I hope you did not trade too much for it, but it is finely made."

"Yes, that was the smallest one I saw. There were much longer blades with handles made for two hands."

She looked at him, "Did those have two blades as well?"

Jarod nodded his head, "Yes, just like that one, only larger."

Baraka grimaced, "Sounds dangerous."

"You should see them, they look dangerous, but like these the craftsmanship is very good. Some are exceptional."

"So what was the news? Other than the blades?"

"They also make a type of clothing, it looks like fish scales."

"Scales?"

"Yes, only made of metal. Finely crafted like this blade. Oh, and the women are now putting colors on their faces."

She scowled, "They're coloring their faces? What do you mean?"

"Red on their cheeks and lips, I think. I did not look too closely," his voice trailed off, "Where's Eini?"

Baraka smiled, "Where he always is, with Saba Adam, those two are inseparable."

Jarod, Enoch's father looked toward the watershed. It was in the distance, but he could see the rise of the tree line that outlined the ridge. "Eini can learn much from him."

Baraka took her husband's arm, "Do you think he spends to much time with Saba Adam?"

Jarod reached out to his wife, "No, it might be good for both of them."

Baraka pulled in closer to Jarod, "Next time you go to the city, I wish to go with you."

"Saba?"

"I am right here Eini."

The eight-year-old picked up one of the fallen leaves. "Would you tell me again about the time before?"

Adam looked at the leaf in little Enoch's hand, "You mean, before the first leaves fell?"

"Uh huh." Adam looked up at the surrounding trees as the little guy spoke, "Before that."

He closed his eyes, and could almost remember how bright and beautiful the world was back then. He let out a long even breath. "Very well, what would you like to know today?"

Enoch abandoned the leaf and had crouched down to pick up a stick. "What was it like to walk with Him?"

Adam looked at the little boy, "With Elohim?"

"Uh huh, what was that like?"

Adam watched his great, great, great, great grandson as he drew in the dirt, his chin on his knee. Enoch looked up at Adam without lifting his head, Adam's eyes were gazing at something far away, "Saba?"

Adam smiled. "You should have seen it." Adam sat in the dirt next to Enoch with a groan. "I remember the night sky would light up," Adam picked up a stick of his own and began to draw, "and a shaft of light would split the sky as high as you could see." Adam's drawing paused, "Oh, and the sound, it was so loud."

Enoch watched Adam's face, entranced. He could almost feel what his Saba said.

"It would come down to the ground so fast, making this kind of long line of fire and smoke straight down from high in the sky." Adam's eyes closed again, "It would come shooting down to the ground, and when it hit," Adam paused and looked over to Enoch, smiling.

Enoch's mouth had dropped open, then Adam stopped! "Saba! Don't stop!"

Adam placed his arm around Enoch, "It would crash to the ground, dirt would fly up into the air and the Creator's light would flood everywhere. You could feel it. I mean you could really feel the light. He called it Glory, it was light, but it was also thick, I could feel it and smell it."

"You could feel the light?"

"It was almost like water, but lighter than water. It was warm, but not like warm water, it was warm inside me."

"Inside?"

"Yes, you know how when you eat warm soup, you can feel the warmth inside you?"

"Uh huh."

"I cannot think of anything closer to the feeling than that, except it was everywhere inside, all at once. Then," Adam paused, a single tear plunged down his cheek, Adam's voice trailed off to a whisper, "Then the Creator would speak, His voice was big, I mean really big, like thunder. But not really, more like a thousand thunders at once, all different kinds at the same time. You know the kind of thunder that you can feel in your stomach?"

Enoch nodded his head, all of his perception was squarely aimed at Adam as the memories flooded into his Saba's mind. The little boy could almost feel what Adam felt.

Adam placed one of his hands on Enoch's stomach and one on his own. He shook his hands, vibrating them up and down, "All of my insides would shiver when he spoke, like that only a lot more, and faster." Adam turned away, and rubbed the tears away from his eyes with the heel of his hand.

Enoch held his breath as he watched Adam. He could almost feel the emotions flowing through his Saba's heart. "I wanna feel that."

Adam reached over, pulled Enoch to him, and kissed him on the top of his head. "I miss walking with Him," Adam wiped his nose, "He made everything good, I miss Him, so much."

"What are you two talking about?"

Enoch turned at the sound of Eve's voice, "Savta!" He flung himself toward her and she bent down, arms open to the little boy.

"Hi Eini, how are you today?" The six-hundred-and-twenty-four-year-old Savta wrapped her arms around Enoch. The youngsters embrace was tight around her neck and she cherished these moments with this persistent little guy who always seemed to want to be with Adam.

Enoch loosened his grip and puckered his lips. Eve took hold of his face and kissed him. She stood and looked over at her husband. His head was down, held up by one hand. It was obvious to her what they were discussing. She took a deep breath and turned toward Enoch, "Eini, how about we make dinner, together. Are you able to stay? Do your parents mind?"

"Oh no, they don't mind."

"Would you like to help?"

"Sure! What are we making?"

Eve moved next to Adam, her hand drifted to his shoulders, "I was thinking about making a nice fruit salad and cook the fish you and Saba caught today." Her nails lightly stroked back and forth across her husband's shoulders.

"Ok! Can I cook the fish? I can start the fire by myself now!"

She held out her hand, "You can do it but I want to watch."

Enoch took her hand and the two began walking to the cave, "You do not have to watch, I can do it by myself."

"Just pretend I am not watching. How about that?"

"Oh, alright. I will pretend."

Enoch released Eve's hand, his pace slowed to a stop as he turned to look back toward his Saba.

Eve turned to see why Enoch let go of her hand. She could see a sadness wash over him. He stood there for a long moment before he finally turned and reached for her hand once again, his head down.

The two walked together, quietly.

———————

Jessica put her pencil down, "Enoch? Enoch knew Adam and Eve?" She had learned that Michael would be with her when she had a question.

"Of course."

Jessica scowled, "Not 'of course,' What do you mean 'of course?'"

"Jessica, Adam lived nine hundred and thirty years. He was only in his six hundreds when Enoch was born."

"I just never thought of Enoch knowing Adam. I mean, Adam was still so emotional about the fall. I never would have thought that."

"You have endured great loss, but he lost most of who he was. You have never lost as much as he did. You have never known who you really are, so you have not known loss as he knew it."

"I suppose not."

"There is no supposition about it. Adam's knowledge of loss was far more than any man, until the last Adam that is."

Jessica thought for a moment, letting this new concept sink in. "So, what does a six-hundred-year-old woman look like?"

"She was beautiful. You have seen women that have similar appearance. In your eyes she would have looked closer to fifty years old."

"Can you describe her to me?"

"Dark, curly hair, brown eyes, dark brown skin, and the brightest smile. She was truly beautiful, almost beyond measure."

"And Adam, what did he look like?"

"He was more rough, you might say 'ruddy.'" He thought for a moment, "His skin color carried the color of the Earth he was made from."

"He was red?"

"Reddish, like a clay color. That color never left him."

"How tall was he?"

"He was approximately nine feet, maybe a little more, he would have a hard time walking in buildings now."

"That tall?"

"Yes, Eve was not quite as tall."

"How tall?"

"She would not have to duck down in your hallway, but she would in the basement. She was around seven and a half feet tall."

"They were giants!"

"No, not giants. That was the size the Creator made them."

"How come we're not that tall now?"

"The weakening of man's genetic code is but one of the losses Adam experiences."

"Experiences? Adam is still experiencing loss? Isn't he in Paradise?"

"Yes, Adam still experiences loss, as he sees what his failure has led to."

"But the fall is over, we just have normal life now."

"Nothing here is as it should be, nothing is as it was created. All is marred. All of creation experiences frustration because of the sin of your kind. Frustration takes on many forms, it can be the atrophy of muscles, the degradation of the senses over your life span, even the weakening of your genetics over the course of the millennia. There are many frustrations brought on by sin, throughout this creation."

Jarod swallowed his last bite, "It seems like Enoch takes in everything Adam feels. I've never seen a child so focused on anything, especially at his age."

Baraka began gathering up the dishes from the table, "You mean focused on Adam?"

"More than that, like he is focused on what those memories have done to Him. He wants to know what it was like before, but he also wants to somehow experience the consequences."

"You mean, it's like he wants to take in the whole thing?"

Jarod nodded his head, "Yes, all of it."

Baraka thought for a moment, "Elohim is doing something, Enoch is a special little boy."

"Yes, he is."

Chapter 19

Light and Shadow

Michael arrived earlier in the day and spent some time over a late lunch talking to Jessica, Belle, and Falk. He had explained a few things to Belle, now that she knew more of the reality around her. Jessica watched his demeanor as he handled what would otherwise be a delicate conversation. He listened with such patience and displayed a gentleness that almost seemed out of place coming from this huge warrior.

Michael slowed his speech for emphasis, "Belle, do you understand all that I have told you?"

She sat silent for a long moment, then looked up at Michael, "So, you're an angel too?"

"Yes."

"We're surrounded by angels, and I didn't even know it?" Her tone was stern and she was disappointed to be left out.

Michael answered with a flat tone, "Yes. Such is normal for your kind. We are at war, and that war is all around you."

"Angels are protecting us?"

"Yes, we have a perimeter set up round about this home."

Belle glanced toward Falk, "And what about Falk?"

Michael leaned back in his chair, "Falk is one of Gabriel's messengers, he was injured delivering the scroll you and Jessica are now working with and now that he has been healed to a certain level, he has been reassigned as a protector. His role is different than it has ever been before."

She looked into Michael's eyes. "You asked if I understand. Yes, I understand. It's a lot to process. But, I'm glad you told me all that you did. Thank you."

"You are welcome." Michael smiled, looked out the window, pushed his chair back, grabbed his backpack, and rose to his feet. "Thank you Belle, the acceptance in your heart honors us."

He looked at Jessica, "Would you mind coming with me?"

Michael and Jessica hiked to the place where Jessica had seen the other archangels once before. She was just as tired this time as the first time they had ventured here. The area was an open, grass-covered hill top and the two of them wandered here and there taking in the clean mountain air. After twenty minutes passed she thought that maybe she was wrong, that the archangels might not be coming. The temperature dropped as sunset approached.

Jessica began to wonder why they had come to this place, She crossed her arms in an effort to stay warm. "Do you want to start a fire? Maybe warm us up a little?"

"No, no fire tonight, it will be dark enough soon." Michael pulled a white sweater out of his back pack and handed it to her. She pulled first one arm through a sleeve, followed by the other.

They continued to wait.

After another half-hour or so Michael broke the silence. "I want to show you something, it will not take long."

"Alright."

In the distance she could see a bright light, in the shape of a man.

"Jessica," she heard his voice now coming from the distant light, "take note of all you can see."

She muttered to herself, "It's pretty dark out here."

"Yes, that is right."

She had forgotten he could hear so well.

She held her hand up and could only see its outline because of Michael's light. She looked around and saw how the light filtered through the trees. Bands of light that cut straight through the darkness.

The light went out.

"Alright Jessica."

"AH!" She jumped at the nearness of the voice. He was beside her again, "You scared me."

"I am sorry. I want to show you one more thing, and then we can go."

She crossed her arms in front of her chest, once again, "OK."

Michael again began to glow. This time the light was soft, at first, and built up slowly, allowing her eyes to adjust until he was again a brilliant light.

He turned to her, "This is going to be strange for you." He offered her his hand.

When she placed her hand in his, he pulled her in front of himself, her back to him, and placed his other hand on her shoulder. She felt a warm sensation flow over her body, thick like honey. Her eyes drifted down and she could see that her body was beginning to glow. She turned to look up at Michael.

His eyes met hers, "Please, look straight ahead."

She turned back and their combined light was reaching out for a good distance. She marveled at how the trees, thin grass and even the boulders around them had a luminescent quality to them. She had never seen the ordinary things look so radiant and as she looked more closely she could see the light and color pulsing on them, even the rocks seemed to have life, their own modulation.

Michael broke her silence, "Look carefully for differences in how you see things now and how you saw them when I was far from you."

She closed her eyes for a moment, long enough to remember the previous scene, then opened her eyes again. She had not seen the light as "living" the first time, but she had seen shadows. There were no shadows this time, since she was at the source of the light, if there were shadows she could not see them.

Michael removed his hand from Jessica's shoulder and all went dark. There was a burst of light, an instant flash, and she found herself in the front office of her parents house, standing at the desk. Down the hall she could hear the printer spitting out multiple sheets of paper, Belle must have finished editing a chapter.

She closed her eyes once more to remember the sights from the woods.

Michael's voice drifted into her mind, "Do you understand?"

"I'm not sure. You wanted me to see the two vantage points of light?"

"You saw at least part of the answer that you seek about Man's fall."

Jessica turned to see the archangel standing at the window that looked across the driveway, "I did?"

Michael turned to face her, "Yes, when I stood with you, did you not see everything around you perfectly lit?"

"Yes, it was beautiful, and I saw no shadows."

"From that vantage point, though all around you would otherwise be in darkness, you saw only light."

"And the other view?"

"You saw a light in the distance, though you stood in the darkness. You were separate from the light so you could see the light, but you could also see shadows and ultimately darkness. Both views were from the same location, only you were different."

"So, in darkness, I could see light, but I could also see darkness. But as the light, I only see light."

"Close. You only see things as they can be seen in the light. You would never see darkness or shadow."

Jessica thought out loud, "So Adam and Eve moved from being the light to being distant from the light."

"Right, but of course it is much deeper than that. Remember, Elohim gave all of this creation to Adam. So his fall affected everything. From the core of his being, to the most distant of stars. All of it was affected, in fact, degraded. Man chose to move away from being the light and in so doing stepped into the darkness. To have the knowledge of good and evil is to occupy a position to judge between light and darkness. Elohim did not move away from Man."

Jessica interrupted, "But that was only because the serpent tempted them, he lied to them."

Michael continued, "Being tempted is not sin, they moved out from under the protection of Elohim when they lifted themselves up to judge the Creator's decree. Now all of creation suffers from Man's arrogance, and Man continually tries to fix his mistakes using methods that ultimately will not work. We have seen all of this before, but this is the last time."

"I'm not sure what you mean, what have you seen before?"

"There are many methods being employed," he paused. "many attempts to invalidate the effects of the fall, your scientific community is ripe with them. You can see it all around you."

Jessica had a puzzled look on her face, "I don't see it."

Michael looked out the window, "Sure you do, you just haven't thought about it. You see it in the scientific efforts to extend life. Some of your scientists right now are saying life spans will rise sharply in the coming decades, into the hundreds of years. They are even talking about life without death, they are trying to erase the curse of death from the world.

"Just as Eve attempted to clothe herself and her husband, science is also trying to cover over the cost of sin. They want sin with no cost."

"You said you've seen all of this before. What did you mean?"

"The manipulation of nature to meet the needs of your oppressors. The fallen one convinced your kind to follow him and his kind. Making you enemies of your Creator."

"Enemies?"

"Well, more like creatures afraid of their own shadows. That singular act of rebellion changed everything. We could see it, down to the smallest level of your existence, down to the components within what you call DNA. Not just yours, but all life under your charge, all was changed on that day.

'Before that moment, Adam and Woman would have born children in the image of Elohim, because they were His image. Instead they bore children in their own, fallen state. They produced images of themselves, fallen images of the Creator."

Jessica turned to look out the window toward the darkened driveway. "So it wasn't the tree itself, it was the act that condemned them."

Michael's voice became stern, "One day you will understand the first sin more fully. Then you will understand the truth of what was lost."

"You mean there was more to it?"

"Yes, however, that is not for me to reveal even though the revealing of that truth has already come to be part of mankind. It will take some time before Man will allow himself to see it, and feel the weight of it."

Jessica sensed a sadness, that Michael felt a heaviness for mankind, and the revelation that would eventually take hold. As though the entirety of Man was still given over to the thing that tripped up Adam and Eve.

"It sounds like you carry a weight just thinking about it, did you know then that the Creator had a plan for redemption?"

"It affected us all, all of my kind." Michael shook his head, "No, we did not know of a plan. As far as we knew all was lost, the goal of Elohim had been thwarted.

'Raguel was affected more than the rest of us, he was in Paradise when it happened. He saw how the heart of the Creator mourned."

"Was it the same when Lucifer fell?"

Michael shook his head again, his eyes distant, "No, it was nothing like that. It was unlike anything he had seen before. Raguel said in later years that the grief Elohim expressed was more like the grief of a parent who had lost a child, His only child."

She turned back toward the big archangel. "You said you had seen all this before?"

"Yes and each time it failed and your kind looked for outside help. Our enemy has been all too eager to lend a hand. Which is what happened here."

"So there was technology back then?"

"You can say that, but the truth is that our kind knows how to do things. Technology is this generation's method, a way to make certain things palatable to the masses. Technology is a wrapper. Many things are called 'Tech' when what it really means is a new way to do something that has been done before.

Today mankind thinks it is at some sort of pinnacle of development merely because you have figured out how to harness the microscopic world. Your scientists map out your DNA and they think that enables them to know how to make a man. It does not. Man does not understand life because life is not DNA, life is not made up of certain chemicals or molecules that are arranged just right.

"Time and time again, scientists have placed all the right chemicals into a flask in an effort to make life. It has never worked. Man cannot make life. Life flows from the one that is *life*. DNA is a result of life, in a matter of speaking."

Chapter 20
Longing Heart

Enoch woke before the rest of his family, that is, *if* he had slept at all. He had a big day ahead and, as a result, had tossed and turned all night long. That feeling of anticipation that completely ruins a good night's sleep had gotten the best of him.

He was glad the night was over, it was morning and his big day could begin. If all went well he would see someone he had never seen before. But right now he had to get his chores done. Like every other morning, he arose before sunrise to milk the cows. That always took quite a long time.

Then he had to get the morning water, so he snatched the two wooden pales from the kitchen and hurried to the well. Once he'd returned with the water, he grabbed a couple of handfuls of fried einkorn cakes his mother, Baraka, had made the night before and put them in one of the large pockets of his outer garment.

The cakes were nice and crisp on the outside, moist on the inside, and each was a single bite of goodness. He loved his mother's cooking, and the fact that she had made them in anticipation of his big day made them even better.

Right on time, he started his journey, the destination was several miles away and he would get there around mid-morning. The sun was just beginning to rise when he left the family cave and followed a well-worn path that would take him to Saba Adam's home, then the two of them would continue on to the watershed divide.

The nineteen-year-old had grown into a tall, husky young man, with just a wisp of a beard. His stride was long and there was a slight rise to his step that had become a trademark. People that knew him would recognize that step from a long way off. He was a serious young man and not prone to foolishness—he did not like games.

There was a purpose to him, like something was continually pushing him, driving him. His parents could see it, indeed, it was like a hunger that motivated his every deed, every thought hinged upon this unseen quest.

About halfway into his morning journey, the trail came to a fork. The path to the left wound many miles down the mountain and into the valley, toward the city that shared his name. He could see it in the distance. As he continued on to the right, he considered how many changes had occurred over the past few years, and how the arrival of the sky people, the Watchers, had marked the beginning of that change and sadness for his small tribe.

Within the few years since their arrival the people's knowledge of materials and building methods had gone in a direction no one could have foreseen. Stories were told of how the strangers taught the people all types of things. From the large-scale production of various textiles and metals, to the use of plants for medicinal and even magical purposes. His brothers and male cousins had gone to the city to see the women there. There were rumors that the Watchers had taught the women there to apply various cremes, lotions, and color to their skin and lips, making them quite alluring. His female kin had gone as well, as they wanted to learn all about the ways of the city. The ways of these strangers.

Not a single one returned.

Enoch, so far, had not been to the city. He had no need to go, and for that he was glad.

"Why go to a place like that anyway? All it would do is tempt me to follow in their ways." He hoped he would never have a reason to go there.

The sun began to shine through the trees, he could see the clearing and beyond it the cave entrance that was elevated several feet. There was a large fire pit in front of the cave's entrance and a few stone benches.

Then he saw her. A smile spread across his face. She sat on one of the stone benches, weaving. It would not be a stretch to say that Enoch loved this woman like his own mother, she was in fact his Grandmother, his Savta. She was a number of generations removed, but such things were not as much of a concern back in those days.

He thought to himself, "The Creator called her the 'Mother of all living,' and yet here she is weaving a simple basket." It was a poetic thought, however, on the other hand he could imagine her trying, in vain, to sew together fig leaves in an attempt to cover herself and her husband.

This was the place she and Adam had come when they had lost their garments of light. When they desperately sought a rock over their head, a strong covering. For their covering was lost. Their Creator had been their rock but now this cave stood as a poor representation of the one they had abandoned that day.

There were scorch marks around the mouth of the cave from when Satan himself had tried to keep them out of there. He claimed it was his cave, and he hated that they had found comfort there, displacing him.

Enoch entered the clearing and continued toward this beautiful woman, "Good morning, Savta!"

Eve glanced up from her work, "Good morning, Enoch." She placed the basket on the bench and rose to greet him.

Enoch gave Eve his customary tight hug, "Where's Saba? Is he ready to go?"

She pulled away to look into his eyes, "He went to the divide early this morning."

Enoch's eyes grew wide with a look of concern, "I thought we were going together today?"

Eve sat back down to continue her weaving, "An angel came this morning and said he should go early."

Without warning Enoch turned and ran.

Startled, Eve looked back up to see the young man disappear into the brush. "No! Enoch! There's more...to tell you." It was no use, he was gone and would find out soon enough. She smiled, "They are expecting you."

Enoch ran as fast as he could. Through brambles and thistles, thorns and dense underbrush. Every short-cut he had ever learned would pay off now.

There was a huge cloud up ahead, dark and menacing. It looked like it covered the very place he was headed, and the closer he got, the cooler the temperature. He took note of the cloud, but pushed forward as fast as he could.

Questions flooded his mind. *Had Elohim returned? Would the pillar of the Creator be there? Would Enoch be able to find them if they left the divide for a walk? Sure I will, Saba said the pillar stretched up high into the air, I will be able to see it! Why can I not see it now?*

Perhaps the questions should have stopped him but so strong was his longing for one glimpse of the Creator that stopping was not an option. *Could this actually be happening?* He blocked it out of his mind and pressed on.

The young man came, at last, to the watery moat that surrounded the shallow, rounded summit. He pushed into the water up to his thighs. The brisk water made his hot muscles spasm and took his breath away, but he pressed on. He was swallowed up to the top of his waist, his arms above the current, and he moved forward in exaggerated lunges, right then left. Back and forth until the water level began to subside.

When he emerged, the cold caused his body to shiver. Without a thought he lunged forward the final half-mile, out of breath and now cold. Just shy of the summit he stopped to catch his breath and noticed that the trees ahead were lit up in an unnatural way, and bent toward this strange light. He wiped his brow with the inside of his wrist and made a forceful effort to slow his breath.

The cloud was directly overhead and spanned as far as he could see, in all directions. It was so dark underneath.

He heard talking up ahead, and took a few quiet steps forward, his breathing stopped in an effort to listen. He heard his name about the same time he saw the source of the light ahead. It looked like the top of someone's head, except it was white. Not just white, it had a brightness to it, like the air around it coursed with currents of light, white yet colorful at the same time. It was beautiful beyond anything he could imagine. With the dark cloud as a backdrop, this figure's brightness took on a brilliance like nothing he had ever seen before.

The figure's head turned toward him, at least he thought it turned toward him, Enoch panicked and ducked behind a large thorn tree. Footsteps approached, no longer cold, his body continued to shiver only now out of fear. He closed his eyes and buried his face into the tree's bark, his fingers gripped it tightly.

"Enoch?" The voice was familiar. His Saba's voice. "There is someone here I would like you to meet."

Enoch's heart pounded, he could hear the pounding in his ears. He wondered if Saba could hear it as well.

Adam pulled at the young man, "Enoch, come with me."

Enoch looked at Adam with terror in his eyes, "Who is that?"

Adam could see the frightened eight-year-old in Enoch's eyes, "Come meet him."

"But He does not look like the one you described."

"Come meet Him. You need not fear."

"Nothing is as I thought it would be, I thought I would see the pillar..."

"Enoch, stop. Things are rarely as we think they will be. Come, come, He wants to meet you."

"He wants to meet me? Why? Does He know who I am? How does He know me?"

"He told me about you, long before you were born. He has known you were coming for a long time. He came here today to meet you."

"What? How can this be?"

"Enoch, why did you come here? Was it not to see, to experience your Creator?"

"Yes, but Saba," he peeked around the tree to see the one in the distance looking at him. He jerked back, suddenly out of breath once more. Tears streamed down his face. "I am so afraid, my legs will not carry me there. I am ashamed, I am like a small child. Now that I am here I fear for my very life."

Adam's voice soothed the young man, "There is nothing to be afraid of, this one is good, very good. Come, I will help you."

Adam put his arm around Enoch and walked him out from behind the tree.

The one on the hill was draped in white linen, His light brown hair was long and wavy and blended with His beard. The air around Him crackled and popped with ripples of living light. His face, apart from the long beard, looked like the face of a young man.

As the pair approached, Enoch's legs gave way, Adam could not hold him and the young man fell to the ground, kneeling, head down. Adam slowly knelt next to him and wrapped one arm around the young man.

The stranger spoke, "Do not be afraid, I come for Enoch, the seventh generation of Adam. Now, let me see your face."

Enoch looked at Adam.

Adam's expression reassured him and Enoch rose to an upright position, face toward the stranger. His tears formed rivers down his dirty face.

The stranger walked toward him, His movements so smooth and effortless, it appeared as though he drifted above the ground. When He reached Enoch, He bent down and placed one hand on the young man's shoulder. "Yes, you are the one I seek."

The words coursed through Enoch's mind, tears continued down his face. "You know me?"

"Yes," the stranger's eyes looked young and full of joy, "and I have great plans for you."

"Who are You?"

The being's shoulders lifted, as he flung his head back in laughter. He held out his hand to help Enoch up.

When Enoch took His hand his skin tingled in a wave that coursed through his body. He rose to his feet as the one before him began to speak.

"That, is an excellent question! You may think of me as the Angel of Elohim, and I am leaving for my home just now, would you care to join me?"

Enoch's eyes grew bright and he glanced over at Adam. Adam gave Enoch a big smile, clenched his jaw, and nodded his head slowly. Enoch looked back toward the angel, the inside corners of his brows up, he pushed his lips together. His breathing grew more rapid as his eyes scanned every feature of the stranger's face.

"Yes, I would like that very much." The words were slurred and muddled, but the Angel of Elohim understood.

The angel smiled and again held out his hand and when Enoch grasped it a wind began to swirl around them.

Adam backed away as the wind strengthened.

The air swirled round and round, and took on the semblance of a whirlwind. The two in the middle of this twisting air began to rise from the ground until they slipped from the Earth realm and out of site.

The air slowed to a stand still and Adam sat down next to a tree.

Chapter 21

Marvels

The two accelerated through the sky and all the while there appeared to be something like a dome over them. Enoch could see the air passing around them, yet felt only a light wind on his face. The two flew through large fat clouds, and above them until the circle of the Earth was clearly visible. Darkness above and the Earth beneath, Enoch marveled at this perspective of the world on which he lived.

The Angel of Elohim spoke, his voice calm, "Enoch, no other man has yet seen a view like this, but they will. I have brought you here to show you a very special concept. Something that will help you to know and understand the times and seasons."

As they continued to fly higher and higher, Enoch turned from his view of the Earth and saw something in the blackness of space.

Another whirlwind, swirling in the emptiness ahead of them. There were no references around it that would allow him to know how large it was, and it continued to grow in size and colorful complexity, until they finally entered through it's open mouth.

Enoch's senses were all but overwhelmed, his skin tingled as they entered a boundary layer to another atmosphere. Then new smells filled his nostrils and had an awakening effect. He suddenly felt more alive, more alert. The air seemed more tangible, full of thought, and energy. His tongue tingled.

The colors inside the vortex behaved in ways he had never seen before, or maybe his vision was also affected by the different air here. Certainly, there were many more colors than he had ever seen on Earth. He thought for a moment on how he would ever explain what he was seeing to anyone else. *Surely that would be impossible!*

They emerged out the far side of the vortex and into what appeared to be another world. With grass and trees, buildings, and angels round about. They settled in a large grassy field, and one of the angels approached, very fast, and came to rest in the field in front of them. He was covered in raging purple blue wild fire, and his eyes shone with light blue swirling flames.

The Angel of Elohim turned to Enoch, "This is Uriel and he will show you around. I want you to get to know him." Then the Angel of Elohim faded from view.

Uriel motioned with his hand, "Go ahead, look around. You will notice things are quite different from the world you are used too."

Enoch looked around, but it took some time before he realized how big everything was.

These same trees on Earth were not half the size of the specimens in this place. And the buildings were of a construction type he could never have imagined. A mixture of living trees and metal that combined in an intricate and beautiful way. The results were buildings so large and tall that again, he could not have imagined them on Earth.

They continued higher still, soaring above the highest of the tallest trees and buildings. Uriel leaned over to Enoch, "I am going to show you something and it will help you."

Enoch's head bobbed up and down, as he continued to look all around.

The angel reached out his fiery hand and Enoch paused and looked up at his face.

The archangel responded, "It is alright, I will not harm you."

Enoch smiled and grabbed ahold of the angels hand. Up and up they went until the edges of the city could be seen. The city was circular in shape and Enoch at once saw demarcations in the ground that formed radius lines running from the center of the city to its edges.

The angel pointed to one section and said, "that part there represents winter, then up above is spring, then on around is summer and the last section is autumn, or the time of the Fall."

Enoch had the look of someone concentrating.

The angel smiled and continued, "There is a space between each section, it represents a single day, do you see it?"

Enoch squinted his eyes, "No, I do not see it."

The angel pointed in another direction, "Look over here between autumn and winter, it should be more evident there, do you see the sliver between the sections?"

"Yes! I see it! That represents a single day? One day in the year?"

"That's right."

"Why are those days set apart from the other days?"

"The day between autumn and winter is the shortest day of the year, and the day between spring and summer is the longest day of the year."

Chapter 22
Quick Outing

Jessica pushed her cart through the aisles of Venture Foods, the local grocery store in Divide, Colorado. Belle walked to the opposite end of the store, she had a hankering for a nice apple pie and maybe some vanilla ice cream to top it off.

In the freezer section the ice cream lids were always threatening to come off and an extra layer of plastic struggled to hold the tops down. The fact that the atmospheric pressure at 9200 feet is somewhat lower than it is at sea level causes the air that is whipped into ice cream to expand, which pushed the tops open and the ice cream out over the sides if the extra plastic were not present, and often when it was. This was just one of the odd things that comes with living at this altitude.

Jessica made her way through the produce section and stopped to look at the tomatoes. She pulled a plastic bag from the roll below the counter and pushed a medium-size fruit into the bag to open it.

"Succulent produce, wouldn't you say." A man's voice startled her. A middle aged man pushed his cart next to hers, "This store always has great tomatoes. The pair you have are very nice, I must say..." He winked at her and began to laugh.

"Uhhh, yeah, they do." More than a little creeped out, Jessica decided that would be enough and moved on. She put the open bag into the child seat of the cart and moved toward the back of the store. The man followed at a distance and she felt a familiar presence. Her eyes began to shift, she could feel the dizziness that accompanied her vision change, but was more used to the sensation now.

She looked around for Belle but did not see her. She stopped at the spices section to find sumac. The man walked past her. She noticed he was very tall, maybe not as tall as Michael, but taller than anyone she had met in this small community. His hair was completely white. Then she noticed the other side of him, or his form in the other realm. Long dingy hair, dark armor and chainmaille, and that purplish vapor that covered his wings. Her heart began to pound. She thought he might be able to hear it. This was the same angel she had seen in the bookstore.

She turned back to the spices and found the sumac, thyme, cumin, paprika, and salt.

"Did you find what you needed?" Belle's cheerful voice was a welcome surprise.

"Yes, I'll have to experiment a little, I'm not seeing cumin seed, so this powder will have to do. You're gonna love this."

"What did you call it again? Zubar?"

Jessica corrected her, "Zatar, it's just a mixture of spices and can be used for lots and lots of things. We have olive oil, don't we? I forgot to check before we left."

"I don't know, maybe we should get some just in case."

"Ok, I'll get it and meet you at the check out."

"Alrighty." Belle turned and walked toward the front of the store.

"So you're making zatar? You're right, it would be better with cumin seed."

"You know of it, Remiel?" She turned to see him again. He obviously had not been aware that she had recognized him. He was a handsome man, different in appearance than in the bookstore, but now his other side was again spinning.

He spoke with a steely tone, "Of course, I know of it."

She began to back away. Then noticed another man behind the former archangel, he had on a denim jacket and had been looking at a can of something or other. It was the man from the restaurant. Now he was looking at Remiel.

Remiel's face stopped, he now had a protruding jaw, high cheek bones, his face was pale and somehow dark at the same time, as though in shadow. He grabbed her wrist. "Do not back away when I'm talking to you, I don't want to make a scene."

The soldier from the end of the aisle put down the can, still looking at the angel, "Hey, leave the lady alone!"

Remiel's head jerked around to see the man at the other end of the aisle walking toward them.

Remiel turned back toward Jessica and spoke in a hushed tone, "I'm not here to make a scene, if you stop writing we will leave you alone."

Jessica trembled and looked up from Remiel's painful grip, "I won't stop, and I don't believe you anyway."

Remiel spoke quickly, "I feel bad for you, you're a good woman, I can see that, you could still have a good life. None of what is about to take place needs to happen. I would ask you to rethink your stance, but I can see my request would do no good." He looked back over his shoulder, the man had covered about half the distance. "Just remember the name, Hook, Jesse Hook. Look him up." Remiel let go and hurried toward the front of the store.

The soldier walked past her a couple of steps, looked around the corner, then back, "Ma'am, are you alright? You're Jessica Mozes, I remember you from the restaurant, you're the novelist, right?"

She rubbed her wrist, "Yes, I remember you too, thank you, I'll be fine."

"Do you know that guy?"

"No, I don't know him, but I know who he is."

"What would make him act like that? Someone needs to keep an eye on that guy."

"I really appreciate you coming to my rescue. I don't know what he might have done if you hadn't been there."

"You're welcome, I'm just glad you're alright." He turned to leave.

Jessica reached out and took hold of his arm, "I'm sorry, but I don't remember your name."

The soldier turned back and stuck out his right hand, "Wilder, ma'am, John Wilder."

She grasped his hand, "John Wilder, OK, I won't forget it again. Thanks again, I do really appreciate your intervention."

"I'm glad to be of help, ma'am."

From the front of the store Jessica heard a familiar voice, "Jess, we're next!"

Jessica turned back to John, "I've lost all track of time, thank you so much for your help." She noticed John looking at her hand, still grasping his. She let go with an embarrassed laugh, then turned to find Belle.

Chapter 23
Return

Adam sat against a tree very near the spot where he had introduced Enoch to the angel. He sat with his arms draped over his upright knees and his head slung to one side, his mouth open. His eyes were closed and his breathing deep and steady.

Enoch bent over and placed his hand on his Saba's shoulder.

Adam's body jerked, "What is it? What happened?" Adam sat up, his neck still bent to one side. His hand involuntarily moved to the side of his head, and pushed it up to its normal, upright position. His eyes flicked open as he licked his lips, adding back a bit of moisture.

Enoch crouched down in front of Adam, "Are you awake?"

Adam's brows furrowed, "I was not asleep."

Enoch smiled, "I can see that."

Adam's eyes opened and his eyes flicked up to see who had disturbed him. The man's face was unfamiliar, with his long beard and hair. Then after what became an awkward several seconds, the man smiled again and Adam could see that this was the one he had been waiting for, "Enoch! You are back!"

"Yes, I am. I wish you could have come with me. It was a most amazing journey." Enoch stood up once again, "How did you know when I would return?"

"I did not know, I waited here for you."

"You could not have waited! I was gone too long, perhaps four or five years!"

"No, it has only been a day. I think I must have fallen asleep earlier this afternoon, but I waited for you here, just where I watched you leave, yesterday morning."

Enoch, combed his fingers through the full beard, it hung down to his chest.

Adam eyed the young man's face and rose to his feet. "You had no beard when you left."

"Nor could I grow one, at least not a thick one like this, when I left several *years* ago."

Adam walked over to where Enoch departed, "This place has become a doorway to Paradise. You must tell me everything."

"I wish to, but I am hungry just now, is there anything to eat?"

"No, I do not have anything here, come with me back to the cave," Adam began walking along the way he and Enoch had come, "surely Eve will have something set aside for us."

Enoch walked next to Adam, "It is a doorway Saba, but Paradise is but one of the places it leads to. There were other places as well."

Enoch paused, then looked at Adam once again. "Why did you wait so long?"

"Like I said, it was not so long, here. You left yesterday morning and the sun is only now rising."

"Right, as you said, only one day."

"Yes, not long. But, I am hungry as well."

Adam turned to leave and Enoch placed his right hand on Adam's shoulder, slowing him to a stop. His left hand held his own face.

Adam peered back at Enoch, "What is wrong?"

"I must rest for a moment, I am dizzy."

Adam helped Enoch to the ground next to a large tree, then sat down against another tree. "We will rest here as long as needed."

Something startled Adam once again, this time he knew he had fallen asleep because night had fallen around them. Once he regained his composure a sound broke through into his mind.

He looked up at the moon, then around at the trees. He looked over at Enoch, who sat with his feet pulled in tight, his arms wrapped around his knees, head buried.

Adam rose to his feet and walked over to the young man, he heard quiet sobbing as he approached. He touched Enoch on the shoulder and felt the younger man relax a little.

Enoch wiped his face on the arms of his robe and looked up at his Saba.

Adam helped Enoch to his feet and held him by the shoulders. Enoch reached out and fell into Adam's arms.

For much of the night the young man sobbed. His tears so thick, Adam was sure he could feel Enoch's soul pouring out. It reminded him of when he thought the world was dying, when he had experienced sin. Adam held Enoch tighter.

Then the wailing began. Enoch spoke though Adam had no idea what those words were, so garbled by his pain they were. He had never heard anything like this before. The pain of the younger man caused Adam's emotions to break open as well.

All at once, the out of breath Enoch fell silent, his body shaking. He pulled back from Adam's shoulder and whispered, "Saba, I need to sit down."

Adam helped Enoch to the ground once again, then sat next to him.

Enoch looked off into the night.

Adam waited.

They sat for a couple of hours.

Finally, Enoch spoke without breaking his stare, "Saba, I wanted to come back, but now that I am back, I do not want to be here. Everything about the place is different. I did not know it would feel like it does. I was used to it before I left, now I feel it, and I do not like it."

"What do you not like? What do you feel?"

"The colors are muted and dead. The air here feels dark, it looks dark. Everything is twisted and pressed down, like some unseen force presses everything down until it is hard to breathe." He looked over at Adam, "Surely, you feel it?"

Adam pulled a blade of grass out of his mouth, "It is night, of course it is dark here."

The moon lit up Enoch's eyes and Adam noticed something, a knowing that he did not expect. Adam turned away and thought for a moment, "I think I know what you mean, for myself and your Savta

Eve, many things changed all at once, but the atmosphere changed over time. You must have felt it all suddenly."

"Yes." Enoch replied.

Adam pulled the blade of grass apart, the action reminded him of the first time Eve made garments for them, "How are you feeling now?"

"Shaky, but perhaps it is time to get up and get to it. It is almost morning."

"Very well," Adam tossed the grass to the side and rose to his feet. He turned to help Enoch up, once again.

As the two began the trip back to Adam's cave. Adam kept one hand on Enoch's shoulder. Enoch could sense different emotions rippling though Adam and when Adam's hand slipped from his shoulder he stopped and turned to see his Saba had slowed, something was wrong.

Enoch asked, "What is it?"

"I was just thinking..." His voice trailed off.

"What is it? What is wrong?"

"What you must think of me."

"I do not understand."

"This world is like it is, because of me. Because of my sin. I see now what my sin did to you when you returned. I have always felt a great deal of regret about what I did, or what I did not do, but to see now how it has affected you, how it affects us all..." His eyes became like glass, "I wish I could go back and change it, I have always wished that. I get this pain in the bottom of my stomach, and I would go back and do the right thing, if I could."

"Saba, I saw you from the great Paradise, the one with me told me something about you and I believe it was said so I could tell it to you, now."

Adam straightened up and looked at Enoch, "What was said? By whom?"

"Uriel, one of the archangels, told me that you sinned once. Once, only. Yes, that sin separated you from your Creator, but there is a path to righteousness. There is a way back, for mankind. Others blame you for the state of the world, but they willingly sin all the days of their lives.

"You need not be concerned with what I think, Saba, I do not judge you. Your life changed my life, from my youngest days you gave me a glimpse of the time before.

"I have seen your sorrow, for I know now what was lost, I have seen the garden with my own eyes."

"You saw it?"

"Yes, it is intact."

Adam looked away, "All of it?"

"Almost, there is a void in the midst of it. The Holy One told me that the void will be healed one day."

"Did he say when?"

"No, he would not say, or, perhaps he did not know. But the garden is growing, and not just the height of the trees, though they are truly wondrous, its borders expand outward as well. The Holy One said the garden was made for us and we will one day be back there. Do not lose hope Saba, we will return. It was made for you and you will have it again, but now our kind must travel a long road to reach it. There is much to repair, and there are forces at work in this world that you do not understand. You have seen them, but they did not reveal their true selves to you, and now their kind is tampering with our kind."

Enoch leaned forward, almost too far, "I have been called as a teacher, to let the city which bears my name know what is happening. I must warn them!" Enoch took a step to keep from falling.

Adam reached out to steady Enoch, "Easy there young man, let us get some food into you first, and I think you need some rest as well."

Enoch smiled, "I suppose you are right, but then I must go to the city to tell them what is happening."

Adam put his arm around Enoch and the two began walking once more, "Come now, we will go back to your home, I am sure your parents are wondering where you have been."

"I am glad it is a long walk, it will give me time to think what I might tell them. Maybe I should cut this hair off, or they'll never recognize me!"

The two laughed at that thought as they walked slowly through the tall grass.

Chapter 24
Drawing

Jarod rose from his bed and kissed Baraka on the forehead. As he stood upright he was overcome by the urge to stretch. He moved toward the front of their home, a nice deep cave, which of course caused his eyes to squint against the brightness of the morning light. In the distance he could see his son scratching in the dirt with some kind of contraption.

Enoch had returned a couple of days prior and Jarod and his wife had not recognized him at first. He claimed to have aged a few years on his last trip and Jarod was not sure if he should believe him or not. He could see that his son looked older but how was it possible to age so fast?

He watched as Enoch scratched here and there, then back to the first spot again, then he would stop and stare at the ground, pull at his beard with both hands, only to then set off again. His movements were frenetic and his motionless concentration, staggering.

Jarod paused at the opening of the cave and thought for a moment, he wanted to see what his son was doing, but he did not want it to be obvious. He knew Enoch had been affected by his trip with Adam, but wanted to leave room for his son to be able to return to normal. After all, anyone can be affected by certain life events, especially when they are young. Eventually though, things tend to return to normal.

Just then he spotted the well, and it gave him a plan of action. Jarod walked over and picked up a bucket from the lip of the cave and carried it outside. His path would take him past Enoch, and whatever he was doing, which would work out just fine. As he walked past his son, he could see a large circle on the ground, it must have been twenty yards across. There were two smaller concentric circles inside this larger one. Enoch had used a length of rope staked at the center of the circles and fastened to the bottom of the walking stick he was using to draw with. Then there were straight lines running outward radially from the edge of the center circle to the edge of the outer circle.

Jarod called out to Enoch on his way to the well, "Good morning, son."

Enoch looked over at his father, "Good morning."

"What are you drawing?"

"It is a way of keeping track of time."

"Ok, son. That is good, right?"

"Yes, it will help with planting and harvesting, lots of things."

"Very well, son. I am just going to get some water."

As he reached the well, he tried not to look toward his son, but his eyes kept wandering. Enoch had told him that he had gone on a journey and now, apparently, his head was filled with wild imaginings. He certainly did not want to make Enoch feel strange, though he sure acted strange.

Something inside him wanted to see what Enoch had seen, to embark on an adventure. But a part of him was afraid. It seemed all too abnormal. He liked normal, he liked routine.

But still, here was his son. Not being normal, not acting as expected.

Jarod noticed his sons face. That beard! How did that happen so fast! But then, past the beard, his sons eyes. They were so full of life, so full of wonder!

He filled the bucket and turned toward the house. As he approached his son and the drawing, Enoch called out to him.

"Father?"

Jarod stopped and smiled, "Yes?"

"Would you like to see this calendar I've drawn?"

That look, the emotion of his son, it was contagious. "Yes, of course, son. Show me." He set the bucket on the ground and looked up. Enoch walked into the drawing and stood in the center.

Enoch cleared his throat and smiled at his father, "See, there are two rings, the larger outer ring, and the smaller inner ring, then there is the central circle."

"Yes, I see."

"The inner ring is split into four sections, quadrants. These represent the four seasons, spring, summer, the time of the Fall, and winter.

"Yes, keep going, this outer ring is also split into four, but then there are three more divisions inside of the four."

"Yes, those divisions coincide with the cycles of the moon, they are called months. Each one is thirty days long."

"So, you are saying there are ninety days in a season?"

"Not exactly, see this sliver at the end of each quarter?"

"Yes."

"This sliver represents one extra day, a special day. Every three months there is a special day, at the end of spring is the longest day of the year. Opposite that day, between the time of the Fall and winter is the shortest day of the year. The slivers after winter and summer are when the days and nights are of equal length."

Jarod crossed his arms and held his chin in his right hand, "So, each year is 360 days long, no, plus the four special days. So, a year is 364 days long?"

"Yes, 364 days in a year. Now, this is a very simple version of the calendar, the one I saw in Paradise was much more detailed. I am missing a few things, I think."

"You were in Paradise?"

"Yes, and a whole city was laid out in this shape and there were markers that coincided with parts of the calendar that were made of polished stone."

Jarod glanced up at his son, "Polished stone?"

Enoch, replied, eyes wide, "Yes, you should have seen it."

"So, you really did leave."

"You did not believe me?"

"I did not know how to believe it, never has anyone been taken from this world before."

"Saba Adam introduced me to the angel who took me there."

"Who took you?"

"The one who took me said I could call him the angel of Elohim, but he introduced me to a fiery angel in Paradise who's name was Uriel."

"You have always been a good boy." Jarod thought for a moment, then asked, "Is that why he took you? Because you are without sin?"

"That is what he told me, yes. He said my time with Saba changed how I see the world, how I see sin."

Jarod closed his eyes.

"Father? Are you alright?"

"Yes, son."

A tear wandered down Jarod's face.

"Father?"

Jarod turned toward the house. "I am proud of you, son."

"What is wrong, Father?"

Jarod walked, without speaking, toward the cave.

———————

Falk stood at the sliding glass door and stared out into the woods. He looked up, past the trees and watched as a pair of guardians descended from the east, and into the faint glow of the surrounding troops. He took comfort in knowing more of his kind surrounded this place, and were there to protect them against the evil intent of the fallen ones.

He had lived a fairly solitary life, the job of messenger had always been mostly solitary.

He had rather enjoyed his many errands, even with the fighting. Rare was the parcel that did not make its destination once handed to him. And though this was not the first time he had sustained injury—

had the scars to show it—he had never been through anything quite like this.

As he stood, he could hear Belle in the kitchen. Every night she made a point to take a glass of water to her bedroom before retiring for the night. He could also hear Jessica in her room above him also preparing for sleep.

He pondered the idea of sleep, it was so routine for these children of Adam. Did they know that the first man and woman had not slept or even laid down before their fall? Adam had been such a majestic being, his spirit with all of its glory had been his covering. But then everything turned inside out. Now his flesh was on the outside, with its frailty and vulnerability exposed to all. Where formerly their flesh was protected by their spirit, now man's might was covered in weakness, for flesh can never be as strong as spirit.

Falk turned and walked toward the center of the room. He mused over a story Ariel had told him on the night he arrived in this house. She told him of a fight that had taken place in this very room, when a deceiver had set up residence in the ceiling above his head in an attempt to poison Jessica's dreams. Katriel had dispatched the little dragon, and the small seraphim was no doubt in the Crypsis nursing his broken jaw, health comes more slowly in that realm. Even slower than in this world. It would be decades before his mouth would be usable again.

His mind moved from the dark Crypsis to the light of Paradise. Life was so abundant there, much more than the place he now stood, this world had become so dingy and pale. In Paradise, there was a perpetual freshness of life and vitality among the people and animals, it even showed forth in the life of the trees, mountains, and stones. Indeed, even the ground itself had purpose and strength. Here, the ground's voice was muted and it sat with almost no life at all. It was merely a surface which existed outside of thought and reason. It was overlooked and taken for granted, when it was meant to have life and purpose.

Then there was the thicker atmosphere in Paradise, and thicker matter, as well as the substance underlying the matter which was much more robust than here.

When compared to Paradise this realm struck him as thin, stretched out, as though something were pulling at its edges with no regard for what might happen if it were to stretch too far. There was a strain on everything, and that strain was taking a toll on a creation that was not renewed, or filled in, moment by moment. The substance of creation had its flow cut off when the first man and woman fell. And now, through the millennia the toll had become apparent.

"All of creation surely groans, for the offspring of Man to arise. The true sons, the ones made complete by the Creator of all."

Just then he heard a familiar voice from beyond the glass, "*Come outside.*"

Belle closed her bedroom door behind her and removed her robe. Just then she heard something, but was unsure of what it was. She grabbed her robe and slid one arm into a sleeve and opened her door to listen through Jessica's door. She slid her other arm into the other sleeve and could hear the sink running in Jessica's bathroom.

She suddenly had a thought, *Falk must have gone outside.* She walked down the hallway and pulled the robe closed over her night shirt and sweat pants. Rounding the corner to the office area she pulled her chair out and leaned over the desk to look and separated the wooden blinds enough to look out the large plate glass window. It overlooked the rear deck and woods behind the house. She could just see Falk's head, as he walked down the pathway toward the fire pit. She reached down and tied the robe shut, "Where is he going?"

———————

As Falk approached the fire pit he caught the sweet, sharp scent of the throne room. From the woods he heard, "Falk, over here."

———————

Belle had made her way down the steps and to the basement glass door. She watched as the angel walked off the path and into the woods.

She eased the door open and slipped outside and with great care, closed the door behind her. She stood for a second, face toward the glass, not sure this was something she should be doing. But her curiosity overwhelmed her. She turned and walked slowly down the trail as quietly as her slippers would allow.

Just before the fire pit she turned into the woods, and moved from tree to tree, searching. It wasn't until she had reached her fifth tree that she noticed something. It was low to the ground and she eased closer, behind a larger fir tree, she gripped its bark and peered around it. Falk knelt, face to the ground, arms outstretched.

Then from behind a tree stepped another form. He was much shorter than Falk, like a normal man, and he had long hair like Falk did, but unlike Falk he had facial hair, long, wavy, and flowing. This man stooped down and helped the messenger to his feet. She could hear them talking but could not make out what they were saying. She closed her eyes and pushed her forehead against the tree. Her fear of getting caught was her only impairment to moving still closer.

She bit her lower lip, opened her eyes and eased around the tree, there was another fir about ten feet away and she carefully eased up to it. Her heart pounded within her chest but she slowed her breathing and listened.

The man smiled, "You fulfilled your mission, in a most unusual way, I must say."

"I am sorry for that, it seemed to be my only option at the time, I hope I did not disappoint you."

Belle peered around the tree to see the man reach beneath Falk's jaw and gently lift the angel's downcast face.

The man's head tilted to one side, "You do not disappoint me." His voice had an unusual tone to it, like joyful music.

Falk rose to a more upright position, his hands on his knees. "I live to please you."

"I know you do."

The angel continued, "And I am full of thanks for the healing that was sent through Raphael's choir. Although," Falk paused, his head and posture sunk once again, "I do not understand why I have been left here."

"You are here to endure with Man. Your existence had been on the outskirts, seeing but not experiencing. Your time here has allowed you to gain understanding. You will not truly understand by hearing from others alone. True understanding comes first from revelation and then by experience of that revelation. This is but the smallest taste for you. Your time here is almost completed, but for the remainder of your stay, you will have your wings."

Belle's eyes grew wide as she saw two protrusions on the angels back grow and tear through his shirt. She watched the entire process of regrowth, down to the plumage forming. She had expected his wings to be pure white, she had grown up thinking all angels wings were white, but Falk's were striped, much like the red-tailed hawk's. And his wings were enormous, not as large as the wings of the angel he had talked to at the edge of the woods, but much larger than she had imagined.

Falk rose to his feet, he looked to his right, stretched his wings out, and moved them all around. They were beautiful, agile limbs. His body rose from the ground with a single thrust, then he settled back to the ground and embraced the man.

———————

Without a word Jarod entered the cave and sat down, Baraka sat next to the fire pit, just inside and in the center of the cave's opening, a small distance from her husband. She arranged the small pieces of firewood on the still red embers from the night before, "You fetched the water? That is unusual."

There was no answer.

She picked up a few more sticks from the ground next to her, "Jarod?"

Silence.

She turned to see her husband with his head in his hands. "What is wrong? Are you feeling alright?"

Jarod's muffled voice escaped past his hands, "No, I am not alright."

Baraka tossed the sticks into the fire and brushed off her hands, "What happened?"

He lowered his hands from his face, "Have you seen what your son is doing outside?"

"No." She peered out the cave's opening as he spoke.

"He was taken to Paradise. An angel took him."

"Yes, that is what Saba Adam told us. It is a miracle!" She paused, then looked back toward her husband, "why does that upset you?"

Jarod walked to the cave entrance, "At first I was not sure I believed it, but now I know it is true." He paused for a moment, then looked at his wife as she stirred the fire, "Do you know why he was chosen to go?"

"No." She turned from the fire, "Why?"

"Because he allowed Adam to change him. Because he allowed the memories of Adam to change how he sees the world."

She thought for a moment. "Jarod, we discussed this many times, we knew they were good for each other. He loved being with Saba Adam from such a young age."

"I know."

"I do not understand why this upsets you."

"Truly, you do not understand. All of the years of my life, Adam has been there."

Her brow furrowed.

Jarod exclaimed, "He was there all of my life."

She turned again from the fire, "He has been there all of my life as well."

"He was there, and I was not. I did not go to him and allow him to change me. He has a treasure inside of himself, and I did not want him to affect me. I wanted to be normal, Saba Adam was always different. I did not want to be like that.

"So, I was not changed by him. The same opportunity that Enoch seized with all of his might, I shrugged off."

Just then Enoch walked into the house. "Good morning, Mother." Enoch noticed the red of his father's eyes.

Baraka looked up at her son and smiled, "Good morning, Son."

A look of concern washed over Enoch's face, "How is Father?"

"He will be fine. You were drawing something outside?"

"Yes, a calendar, would you like to see it?"

She rose to her feet, "I would love to see it, Son!"

"Alright, and after that, I will help around here today because tomorrow I need to go to the city."

His mother reeled back, "The city? To Enoch?"

"Yes."

"Whatever for?"

Jarod looked up at his son.

Enoch answered, "I have a message for the people there."

Jarod had lost all of his other children to that city, so he stood and asked with a stern voice, "What sort of message?"

Enoch looked down at the floor, "I cannot say, the message is for them." Enoch paused and looked at Jarod. "Father, would you go with me?"

For a split second Jarod thought, then the words blurted out of his mouth, "Yes, I will go with you."

Enoch smiled, "I feel better already."

Jarod's eyes squinted, "Your message is not a friendly one?"

Enoch looked into Jarod's eyes, "No, not friendly."

Chapter 25

Enoch to Enoch

Jarod led the way through chest-high grass, while Enoch kept pace. Both men remained quiet for most of the morning. Jarod served as a guide, since Enoch had not been to the city before. They began the trip in the dark of night, and enjoyed the first beams of sunrise to their right.

Sometime around mid-morning the tall grass gave way to thick woods. The pair stopped in the growing heat, removed their outer robes and stowed them in their packs, then continued on.

"Enoch?" Jarod broke the silence.

"Yes, Father?"

"I understand there are things you cannot say, but what can you tell me? Why are we going to the city?"

Enoch thought for a moment, "I suppose I can say that I am going there to tell the Watchers that I know what they are doing and that they need to stop now."

"Are you talking about the men that came to the city not long ago?"

"Yes, they are wicked creatures, Father. Not what they pretend to be."

Jarod spoke over his shoulder to his son, "They said they are from another world, they have brought advanced knowledge, knowledge that has helped the city and will continue to help make life better for all."

"Father, while it may be true that they have brought knowledge, they are using that knowledge to barter for what they need. They need agreement from our kind to perform their works on this world and now they have bought agreement with knowledge. Does this knowledge help Man? Yes, but it is knowledge that would have been discovered anyway.

"If they were to reveal who they really are, I doubt they would have received the agreement they needed."

Jarod asked, "What is it they pretend to be?"

"They pretend to be like men."

Jarod froze, stopped cold. Enoch pulled up in time to avoid running into his father. Jarod turned to face his son, "What do you mean, what are they?"

"Great winged serpents, for the most part. All of them are angels that have turned against the Creator." He paused, then said, "They are not here to benefit us, they are here for their own selfish reasons. They hate mankind, Father."

"They look like men, Son, I have seen them, they are not serpents!"

"They have an ability to change their shape and they have used this ability to take on the form of men. Because they look like us and because of the knowledge they have shared, they deceived the people into accepting them."

"Son, the Watchers also came to us, to teach us new things."

"Yes they have. The Watchers pushed us forward with ideas that allowed us to be more productive and have made our lives better. But what those angels in the city teach is not for now, they are bartering knowledge that was supposed to be for the future in exchange for access to the one thing they lack."

"What do you mean? What do they lack? They seem to have come here to take wives and..." Jarod's voice trailed off.

Enoch put his hand on his father's shoulder.

Jarod continued, "They want a way to make their descendants flesh," he turned to face his son, "is that it?"

"They seek descendants, and they want their offspring to be 'of this world,' because if they are part Man, they do not need agreement *from Man*. They barter their knowledge for the right to distribute their seed."

Enoch let that statement set for a moment, then continued, "Going back to what you were saying before, about the timing. There is a time and place for everything, every hidden truth is hidden for a reason. We are to either discover those truths, or we must be taught them. But only in the right timing. The Watchers in the city are teaching things that further their own goals, that is all."

Jarod asked, "Why would they teach men things, when they know we will learn them later, on our own?"

"When they show men things early, they can shape how we view them. For example, they teach the refinement of iron into a much harder metal, and they make weapons from that material. Everything they reveal, they reveal in such a way that Man leans more on the visitors or on himself and less on his Creator. What they are really teaching is how to be independent and how to force one man's will onto another."

Jarod thought for a moment, "Son, most of the newcomers have taken wives."

Enoch turned away from his father and gazed up into the trees, "Yes, I know, and those women will soon bear children, terrible children." He glanced back toward his father.

Jarod returned his son's glance, "Terrible? What do you mean?"

Enoch looked back up into the trees, "They will be like nothing you have ever seen before. Many of them will be giant in stature, two or even three times the height of a normal man, but all of them will be fierce fighting men. They will lead our world into great destruction."

"How can you be sure?"

Enoch sighed and looked at his father, "I have been there. I have seen it with my own eyes. That was one of the purposes of the angel taking me on my journey. I have to be the voice of the Creator to these children of Adam, because they have turned their back on His voice."

Jarod looked toward the city, though he could not see it through the trees, "If they have turned their back on Him, why does He not leave them to their fate?"

"He loves them, and he wants them to return to the knowledge of their Creator and His purposes. The fallen Watchers are lying to them in order to perpetuate their kind on the face of the Earth. But their kind is destructive. Their children will be evil and cold from birth, and there is nothing that can be done about that.

"These children, by their fifth birthday, will have the stature of a normal man. They will be able to take wives and husbands in their sixth year, and reproduce.

"At first, if these children marry their own kind, their offspring will either die or will be born misshapen, for their bloodlines are too similar. I say marry, but these will not truly marry as we think of it, it's rather more just breeding."

"You mean like the animals?"

"Yes, that's right. But in successive generations they will be able to breed among themselves, and when they do, they will establish themselves as great tyrants of the Earth. No one will be able to resist them and nothing on Earth will be able to stand in their way. Only the Creator himself will be able to stop them.

"Whatever they lust for they will take and then throw it away. They and their fallen Watcher fathers will corrupt all the bloodlines on Earth. Not just the bloodlines of men.

Jarod's head tilted down, his eyelids blinked at an accelerated rate, brow furrowed. "How?" In his confusion he had asked the wrong question, he shook his head very slightly, "Why, why would they do this?"

Enoch again turned away from his father. "There will come a time when some of the Watchers will reveal their true selves to the people. Their true forms, for nothing stays secret forever. They will reveal their secrets, because their intentions for the people are cruel and hard.

"This will be their undoing, at least in the short term. The revelation that the Watchers are not men, and that they have taken women and creatures, both domesticated and wild, in order to turn the world's life into their kind; will unhinge the minds of some, while others will refuse to see, much less believe the truth.

"The Watchers wish for this world to be reworked to bear their image."

Enoch paused for a moment, to allow his father to work out, or somehow absorb what he was saying, "If you do not want me to continue, I will stop." He turned to face his father.

Jarod stood silent, still facing downward. His world was literally spinning. He wondered how this could possibly happen. "People, mankind, You and I, our kind, we want to live our lives in peace. I do not want to make trouble for anyone else. Who would want to go out of their way to ruin the world for everyone? I do not understand how this could possibly be?" He looked into his son's face.

Enoch breathed out a long sigh, "Jarod, my father, you are a good man, which is why you would not have such thoughts. But the Watchers, the fallen Watchers, are not men. They hate men. They use our kind for their purposes and when they are finished with us, they will seek to rid this world of our kind. But first, they will force men to serve them, and their wishes."

Jarod turned away and crossed his arms, "What do you mean, they will force men to serve them?"

Enoch took a deep breath, "The Watchers and their children will spread out across this world, each with a group from among mankind. These will serve as their livestock of brood mares and stallions, cows and bulls, chickens and roosters, and ewes and rams. Mankind will be allowed and encouraged to multiply into cultures that can be loosely controlled.

"Men will find happiness in their work and relative prosperity, while their cultures thrive. The cities will branch off and form new cities which will eventually become nations. Each nation will have at its core one of the Nephilim families."

Enoch looked over at his father to see his brow furrowed at the strange word.

Enoch continued, "That is what they will call themselves, the Nephilim. They will consider themselves to be to us, as we are to livestock, since they will have angelic blood lineage, which they will call "Royal Blood."

"These Nephilim will establish themselves as monarchs, kings really, and will rule with the lightest of touches, at first. Over time, the light touch will gradually become more intrusive, the demands on the populations of the world will grow.

"National allegiances will grow, as people from each country will strive against those of the other kingdoms. Instead of the natural order of cooperation, mankind will be raised to believe their nation, whichever nation they are in, is better than all others, this will ensure that the culling can take place seamlessly."

"Culling?" Jarod interrupted.

"Yes, there will come a time when the national populations will grow to levels that will be almost unmanageable. At that point, the Nephilim will meet to find ways to shrink their populations. They will discover many ways, but the most favored will be war. This tool, will be the easiest to implement and will be found to be incredibly profitable to the Nephilim and the nations that support the wars.

"The Kings will eventually go so far as to engage in lies and falsehoods that cause their citizens to call for war, leading their fellow men and their children to their deaths on the basis of lies and elaborate hoaxes."

Jarod placed his hand on Enoch's shoulder, "You said earlier that the Creator will stop it, when will He stop it?"

Enoch thought for a moment, "When a delay would mean that no men would survive, that is when He will stop it."

"How?"

"He will destroy the world."

"What? How?"

"He will save a remnant of man, but he will destroy the world out from under the hybrids for He hates mixture."

Jarod's breath was taken from him, he sat on the ground. "Son, I am not sure I wanted to know this."

"All flesh on the face of this Earth will be killed, except for the chosen few."

"Chosen few? Which chosen few? Will we be among them?"

"No, we will not. But Father, we must continue on." Enoch held his arm out toward his father, who took hold of his son's hand and pulled himself up to his feet.

Jarod motioned for Enoch to follow him, and after another hour of walking he again turned to his son to speak, "Son, I have only ever heard truth come forth from your lips. But this is beyond anything I have heard before, beyond anything I would have, or perhaps could have imagined. Please do not take offense at my hesitant nature, it has been with me since birth."

"Father, I take no offense with you, what I have seen defies description. I have only told you what I could describe, and then only to the best of my ability. So, we will see the reality of it together, at least so long as we are upon the Earth. We will obey the word of Elohim, who alone can protect us."

"So, what is this message you have to deliver?"

"I will tell the Watchers to repent of this evil they are engaged in."

"If the Watchers are what you say they are, do you not think that message will arouse them to anger?"

"They will be angry. But we will be safe, we have an escort and the Watchers will be fully aware of them."

Jarod looked around and, seeing no escort, grimaced as he continued walking.

John drove down the mountain, his month-long vacation came to an end, and for his next assignment he would be part of a security detail of a base just outside Colorado Springs, Colorado. It would be a nice assignment, in that he would be close to home, only a forty minute commute. On the down side, it would most likely be dull. He'd had his share of dull assignments before, but he would be here as a duty assignment, so it would be a regular job. Most likely his last before the end of his enlistment, just a year away.

The blue mustang eased into the parking lot of the Cheyenne Mountain complex. John parked his car and walked across the parking lot, briefcase to his side. He noticed three men walking toward him from the gaping mouth of the facility. The first two wore uniforms he did not recognize, but the third looked like an Air Force Para-Jumper, or PJ uniform, none of them wore rank insignia, and as the first two passed, the third held out his hand.

"Sergeant Wilder?"

John reached out and shook the man's hand, "Yes, sir."

The other man continued, "George Matthews, It's nice to meet you, Sergeant. If you'll come with me, I'll get you situated."

George turned and walked at a brisk pace toward the entrance of the base, a wide concrete mouth that plunged into the side of the mountain.

John kept pace, "What's with the rank insignias?"

"What do you mean?"

"I notice no one is wearing them."

"Oh right, we're not military. I'm a contractor and I work for GenCon, a genetics research firm, we occupy a portion of the the Cheyenne Mountain complex. You'll be briefed on how everything works around here."

"I see."

The two continued into the mountain, and past a set of twenty-five-ton blast doors. George motioned with his head toward the doors, "The Air Force is in that part of the complex."

John replied, "That's where I thought I'd be."

George smiled, "The military likes to keep their orders vague when it comes to these types of facilities. As far as anyone else should know, you work in the Air Force section. That's what you're to tell people."

John nodded his head, "Roger that."

Enoch and Jarod walked several more miles, homes dotted the edges of the main road into the small city.

Jarod's pace slowed to a stop, "Here we are son, this is the road into the city."

Enoch eyed the road, shocked, "I remember this path being much larger, with many horse-drawn carts. Three or maybe four could fit in the breadth of it."

"When was this, you have not been here before today, Son?"

"On my journey, Father. This city will grow many times larger before the first end."

Jarod repeated his son's words under his breath, "The first end."

Enoch looked at his father, "I will not finish this task if I do not begin."

Jarod laughed and slapped Enoch's back in a gesture meant to lighten the mood a bit. "Right you are! Off we go then, Son. Perhaps we will be able to leave this city before nightfall."

Enoch began again, in front this time, and heavier. "I would like that."

———————

George led John to a large metal cube, around forty feet long.

John noticed that the entire building was supported every couple of feet by large coil springs. The pair stopped about ten feet from a set of stairs that led to a normal looking metal door.

George turned to John, "This is one of our office buildings. There are four floors and it's climate controlled and plumbed. You probably noticed that it sits on springs, those are in case of Earthquake or nuclear attack, the structure is designed to absorb those sorts of impacts, so all of the electrical and plumbing lines have to be flexible as well."

John nodded his head, "It all has to be able to move together."

George smiled, "You got it." He motioned for them to walk around the side of the building where they could see several more buildings with different configurations.

George continued, "We have twenty-six buildings in this part of the complex. That's double the number of buildings the Air Force has in the bunker."

John asked, "So GenCon has more in other parts of the complex?"

"That's right, most of our offices and labs are here, but we do have a few more buildings elsewhere. I'll show you those later on."

John turned to George, "So, what's next? I'm sure I have some paperwork to sign."

"Not your first rodeo, I can see that. Yep, I'll take you to the administrative office and they'll have you sign your life away. But first, do you have any questions for me? I know this is different than you expected."

John crossed his arms, "I've never been 'loaned out' before. What's that all about?"

"It actually works out well for us and the government, and for that matter it works out pretty good for you too. For example, pay. You'll receive your normal pay from the Army, same as always. You'll also receive a salary from us, it'll be a little more than you receive from the Army. So, your pay as of now has effectively doubled."

John's eyebrows raised, "That's good for me."

George replied, "Bingo, but it's also good for the Army, because for the price of your normal pay, they have a presence in an important research facility. For us, well we only have to pay half of your salary. It's a win all around. We have quite a few employees 'on loan' as you call it."

Kokabiel saw them first and the bile of disgust rose in his throat. The righteous angels of light walked into the city strong and well-nourished. The light they gave off soaked into the exposed bits of skin of each of the Watchers. One by one, and from everywhere in the city, each Watcher turned, at first not knowing why, then the overwhelming scent of Paradise filled their nostrils and their spirit bodies breathed a collective sigh with the onset of nourishment so long deprived. Several of them smiled as they turned to see what was different in the air. Semyaza and Azazel, though far apart, each knew immediately what surrounded them, and while Azazel turned with a snarl, Semyaza simply gazed up into the sky.

From all over the city the Watchers moved toward a central location, where the two main streets intersected. Semyaza was there all along and stood frozen. Onlookers, men and women alike, in turn stared at Semyaza. They could not see what he saw, but his strange behavior caused them to have a foreboding sense about whatever was causing their leader to stand frozen, gazing at the sky.

When Azazel arrived he approached Semyaza, "What do you make of this?"

Semyaza responded with a flat tone, "I do not think they are here to render our judgement."

"And still, they are here. There must be a purpose."

―――――――

Karmiel, Katriel, Leibel, and Feivel, all from Michael's choir, flanked the two men that walked into the center of town.

One of the two men was known to come from the people of the caves, from the line of men that still adhered to Adam and his God, the so-called "Elohim." Semyaza, had not paid him much attention, he was harmless enough, and had never required an escort like this in the past. But the other one, the younger one, something was different about him. A faint glow swirled all around him. Semyaza was sure the men of the city could not see it, but it was there. This one was the reason for the escort.

Just then, from above, something caught the Watchers attention, the sky began to light up in a wave that moved from east to west across the city. It grew in intensity, until the angels could finally be seen above. Not just a few, but more and more, they kept coming, until the sky was full.

Armaros leaned toward Azazel, "There are seventeen hundred and twenty eight of them, sir."

Azazel thought for a brief moment, "Twelve cubed, how appropriate. The government of Elohim has arrived. The young one needs protection, apparently."

Semyaza agreed, "That's a lot of protection for one man." He glanced back over his shoulder, "Armaros, bring Remiel to me."

"Very well." Armaros acknowledged the request, and was off.

Mankind would not see this sight, not on this day, their eyes had been too dull since the time of the Fall. Now their eyes could not even see as much as the animals around them, in either the physical or spiritual realms. Pitiful creatures, these fallen men.

Enoch and Jarod walked straight through the gathering crowd, toward the taller, pallid Watchers. Jarod had always noticed their hair, all of them had long whitish hair, the fact that there were so many of them stunned him. Sure he'd seen them before, but he had not realized how many there were. When the pair were within thirty yards of Enoch's target, the younger man reached out to stop his father's progress. "Wait here Father, I must do this alone."

Jarod protested, "Son, let me come with you."

Enoch turned to face his father. Jarod saw something he'd not seen before, light swirled around his son, it moved around and through him. And his son's eyes, held him transfixed. Then he heard a voice, it was his son's but somehow foreign, "You must stay here. Everything is as it should be, trust Elohim to protect us both, He will." Enoch smiled.

Jarod gave his son a hesitant nod, and Enoch continued on.

From the crowd someone shouted, "Jarod, is that your son?"

Enoch looked at the many Watchers that stood before him, unaware of what most of them gazed at. He scanned the group as his pace slowed. He noticed his hands were shaking. Then he saw the one he was looking for. One of the two was already staring at him, as though they expected him. He walked through the group, each of the strangers at least a head taller than himself, until he reached the leader. He stepped in front of Semyaza and realized his lips were dry, and his throat felt as though it were swollen shut. He tried to compose himself.

It seemed as though the entire city fell silent.

Semyaza broke the tension. "Did you have something to say, or did your path end here in front of me?"

"I umm, came to say something to you."

Semyaza's face lit up with a grin, he motioned for the crowd to come closer, then he spoke with a grandiose tone, "It seems this young child wants to 'Um me.' I'm not sure if that is good or bad, do any of you know? Is this a local custom I have not yet heard of?"

The city's residents broke out with an uneasy laughter.

Enoch smiled and a hoarse whisper escaped his lips, "If I may...."

"Of course you may, you look harmless enough, whatever you like young man."

Enoch cleared his throat.

Semyaza's eyes squinted and he ducked his head to see into the eyes of the stranger more clearly.

Enoch forced out a word, "Semyaza..."

Semyaza was surprised, "You know my name? How do you know my name?"

Azazel stood toe-to-toe with Katriel and snarled up into his eyes, daring him to reach for his sword.

Katriel, a head taller than the nine-foot tall Azazel, stood with quiet resolve, unmoved by the challenge.

A fifth angel, who had approached from the crowd, stopped next to Semyaza, opposite Azazel. Semyaza's eyes remained fixed on Enoch with only a half blink to give away his anxiety. They were protecting this one man, this mindless animal.

Enoch continued, "Semyaza, you have broken the laws of the Creator."

Semyaza's head jerked back.

"You have forsaken the lofty station, the highest Paradise, which was your eternal dwelling place, and have defiled yourself with women." Enoch paused.

Semyaza glanced up at the angel to his left, his smile returned, and his eyes darted back to Enoch, "You are one of those that live in the woods, near the mountains?"

"Yes."

"You have some strange, backward notions." Semyaza turned his gaze toward the crowd, "See, this is what happens when you allow yourself to be filled with superstition and backward thinking. This young man still believes in an all powerful being that made everything from nothing."

The crowd laughed.

Semyaza continued, "I suppose this 'Elohim' of yours sent you to me?"

"No, not directly, His messenger did."

"And which messenger would that be? Does this messenger have a name?"

"I do not know his name, but he sits in a great throne room."

"He sits? How can he sit and not be Elohim, isn't there only one throne?"

Enoch felt a warmth in his body and he spoke with confidence, "He sits, past the crystal sea, past the burning stones, past the seven torches, he sits next to the blue crystal throne upon which dwells the fires of the living Elohim, of whom there is no end or beginning. Yes he sits, and he writes."

A faint texture swept over Semyaza that revealed scales and the course skin of the hidden dragon. The change was nearly instantaneous, and Enoch was unsure what he had seen. His eyes squinted as he again spoke, "Semyaza, I saw where you were created, I saw the slaughter of your son and the sons and daughters of these Watchers, and I saw how you and your allies will all grieve for them. The cry will issue forth from your kind. A perpetual petition for your beloved will rise from your inward beings, and you will know no mercy or peace."

Semyaza leaned toward Enoch and spoke in a hushed tone. "If these warriors were not here, I would rip you limb from limb, but as it is I will let you live. Do not cross my path again, or your fate is sealed."

Enoch spoke again, "Azazel."

Azazel's eyes jerked toward the young man, his head followed.

"You, oh Azazel, will know no peace. You have been weighed and judgement has come full force against you for the evil you have brought to the Earth. Your godless deeds and the unrighteous revelation you have revealed to the kind of man will not go unpunished."

Azazel's body turned, his anger now visible.

Enoch continued, "A mighty and powerful sentence has gone forth from the throne, and you shall be bound. You will cry out for relief but your petitions will not be heard. For you have shown men the metals of the Earth and how they should be worked to produce weapons of war, and antimony for the mixing of metals, energy storage, and resistance to fire. You have taught them to work gold and silver in order to fashion it for bracelets and ornaments for the women. And you have taught the women to draw men to themselves through the use of eye paint, precious stones, and dyes."

Azazel, his anger's strength gone, looked at Semyaza, then toward Katriel, then his eyes shifted toward the young man.

Enoch continued, "Semyaza, you have judgement placed upon you as well, for you taught the use of plants to alter the conscious states of men and women. You have taught them to leave their bodies and move between this realm and that of darkness.

"Kokabel, you have taught the signs of the stars, Arteqoph has taught the signs of the Earth, and Hermani has taught men to be skillful in the loosing of spells and magic.

"For all these things and more, each of you angels who swore an oath to each other on the mount called Hermon is to be bound until the eon of judgement, when you will be released for a short while, after which your judgement will be set."

Semyaza and this cohorts had been silenced by the man who had seen things no other man had seen, including Adam himself.

Enoch and his escorts turned and walked away, silent.

Semyaza and Azazel watched as the young man walked through the crowd, joined up with his father and the two continued on the road that led out from the city.

Chapter 26
Second Thoughts

Jarod and Enoch had walked past the edge of the city and all the homes along the main road when Jarod stopped to look back the way they came. He scratched the back of his head and started to laugh.

Enoch turned toward his father, "What happened, why are you laughing?"

Jarod turned back to his son, "What? Oh nothing. It is nothing. I am relieved. It looked like that Semyaza fellow wanted to eat you alive!"

"I am sure he did. Wait until you meet the children, they will not be as kind as their fathers."

Jarod followed his son, "That was kind?"

Enoch looked into the sky, then with furrowed brow, turned to continue the trek home, *why does our protection remain?*

———————

As the two continued on, Jarod thought about his son and how he had changed. Physically he was different, he seemed like he had aged but having only spent two days with Saba Adam, he'd come back much more mature and focused. Sure, Enoch had always been more serious, or perhaps more focused than the other children. But he had also been happy, the happiest person Jarod knew.

He wondered if that happiness was gone, or momentarily replaced with the purpose of this trip. This was a side of Enoch that Jarod had not seen to this point. He was a man that walked with such purpose, a man who knew why he was on the Earth.

Funny, that was the one question most people struggled with, their purpose. Most give up on finding an answer, but Enoch wanted the answer from a young age and never gave up his pursuit of it. Perhaps Adam kept him pursuing.

Enoch began talking, but Jarod did not know whom he was talking too. He tried to listen, maybe he was talking to himself.

Jarod strained forward to hear.

No, he was in a conversation of some sort.

Enoch glanced back toward Jarod, then turned away to gesture some sort of agreement. Jarod felt uneasy and now Enoch came toward him.

"Father?"

"Yes?"

"Something is about to happen to you that will open your eyes. You will see."

"What will I see?"

"It will be helpful if you take hold of my hands, I will steady you."

Jarod's concern was evident on his face.

Enoch held his hands out to Jarod, "Father, please take my hands."

Jarod's hands moved to grip his son's. Immediately, a warmth flowed through his body, radiating out from his right shoulder. He began to feel dizzy and was glad to be holding onto his son.

He saw columns of light all around, encircling them. Then another wave of dizziness and with a blink of his eyes the columns began to look like massive men, but different.

Then with another blink or two, these men took on more definition and each looked very tall, and even more massive than before. He had seen an angel before, during his time of invention, but that angel was in the form of an ordinary man, these were something else entirely. He had had no idea how large they really were, in their natural state.

That's when he noticed the hand on his right shoulder. He turned to see another of the angels behind him. He turned around and took a couple of steps back. This one wore clothing similar to his own only he also had a belt with a large sword hanging down his left side and a shield slung over his other shoulder.

He had enormous wings held behind him, he thought there were four. Then he noticed the angel's arm, his right arm was uncovered, and his muscles looked powerful with deep striations. They seemed to have a different arrangement from those of a man.

His hair was long and other than his brows he had no facial hair, and his eyes—what amazing eyes this being had—swirling blue fire that surrounded a deep black pupil. He felt as though he could be swallowed up by them.

Jarod heard his own voice before he decided to speak, "What is your name?"

The brawny angel smiled, "I am Katriel, the leader of your security detail today."

Jarod's eyes drifted to the left, pausing at each of the other angels that stood guard around he and his son. His head turned as far as it could, then he looked to the right, again pausing at each of the angels.

"Son?" Jarod's voice was unsteady.

Enoch took another step toward his father and held his shoulders with both hands, "I have you."

Enoch could feel the tension in his father's body relax a little.

Jarod turned to face his son, but peered around him to look at the angels.

Enoch smiled, "Father, we have been asked to a meeting and you need your vision for any of this to make sense."

Jarod blinked his eyes several times, "A meeting with these angels?"

"No, not these angels." Enoch glanced up, and into the face of Katriel, "Some of the Watchers."

Jarod's attention was firmly on his son now, "The fallen ones?"

"Yes. Katriel will stay with you, to help you."

Jarod nodded that he understood as he peered up at the massive angel.

Enoch nodded back, "Are you ready? They are up ahead, there is a clearing up over that next rise. We should be there before too long."

"Yes, I am ready."

Enoch smiled and turned to walk up the path.

Jarod followed his son, about ten yards behind with Katriel beside him. He could not help but notice that the angels, there must have been thirty, walked along with them as well. Something caught his eye and he looked up to see what looked like hundreds of these same beings flying above.

George led John into the building, it was rather cool inside and John noticed there was no receptionist, just a series of offices, a stairwell, and a small elevator. It was a no-nonsense affair that made perfect sense given the secrecy of this place, and it made sense as to why George met him outside. Apparently, George was the receptionist today.

John followed George down the main hall and to an office with an open door. The two walked inside to a tall countertop, bar height.

John was surprised to see a woman in casual clothes. She had long gray hair, parted in the middle and straight. It had an unkept look to it. She wore a navy blue sweatshirt and jeans.

As they entered the office the woman looked up at them through ornate glasses.

She pushed her glasses up higher on her nose, "Good morning George, who do we have here? Is this Mr. Wilder?"

"Yep, right as always," George turned to John, "John, this is Sandy Magee, she'll be helping to get you through in-processing."

John reached over the counter and Sandy took his hand.

John said, "It's nice to meet you Sandy."

Sandy released John's hand and replied, "It's nice to meet you as well, I have your paperwork right here, how about we get this over with?"

John smiled, "Sounds good, what's first?"

George interrupted, "I'm going to get a cup of coffee, can I bring some back for you two?"

Sandy smiled, "Sure! I'll take a cup, with cream and sugar."

George turned to John, "How about you?"

John answered without thinking, "Sure, I take mine black."

"Well that's easy," George turned to leave, "I'll be back in a few."

———

At the top of the rise, Enoch and Jarod stopped to survey what was ahead. Seeing a group waiting below, Enoch pushed forward without a word. Jarod followed with Katriel at his side.

Jarod watched his son move with confidence. As they neared the group, one moved toward Enoch, until the two stopped some ten feet apart.

Jarod could just hear the two as he approached from behind his son.

Enoch spoke first, "Greetings."

The tall pale man returned the greeting, in silence.

Enoch continued, "If you wish to speak with us, speak with no deception, show your true form."

The pale man's brow furrowed as he pursed his lips, "I'm not sure what you mean."

Enoch turned to his father, "They are not serious. Come, let us return home." With that, the two turned to leave the way they came.

Then from behind them came a voice, "Wait! Wait! We will show ourselves."

Enoch and Jarod stopped and turned to see the fallen angels in their native forms.

To Jarod's eyes several of the once pale men now looked similar to their escorts, though darker in substance, but most were massive serpent-like creatures the likes of which he had not seen before. Their huge bodies were covered in scales, with tremendous membranous wings. These were huge reptilian creatures and he had no understanding of how they could take on the shape of men, nor how they could produce offspring with women.

Enoch took up his former position, opposite of one of the man-like angels. "What is your name, and what is it that you want?"

Jarod thought the angel looked annoyed, "My name is Remiel. You described things no man has seen, and you have pronounced judgements you could not possibly have put together yourself, having not seen." Remiel looked down and sighed, then his eyes looked up toward Enoch, "And yet, you *have* seen and you *have* heard." Remiel's head rose until he faced the sky, "So, you must have *been* there."

"Yes, I was." Enoch said with a flat tone.

Remiel's head still skyward, his eye's glanced in Enoch's direction. "You have pronounced judgement from the Creator upon us, your words have shaken us, have shaken me, to the core."

"They were not my words."

"Yes, we know this. We could smell the scent of Paradise on the words you spoke." Remiel fell silent. His head made a slow decent until it faced down just slightly. He turned to view his cohorts, his eyes drifting over each of them. He could smell the fear emanating from them.

Enoch broke the silence, "What is it you want from me?"

Remiel's head snapped back to face Enoch, which caught the young man by surprise. "We wish to petition the Creator, of course."

Enoch's head twisted sideways, "So, petition Him."

"That's just it," Remiel's eyes remained fixed on Enoch, "We forsook our place in the highest Paradises, and we cannot return to offer petition, the way is heavily guarded."

———————

George and John walked out of Sandy's office, coffee cups in hand.

George turned to John, "Glad that's over?"

"Yeah, I hate paperwork. Sandy's nice though." John sipped his coffee.

George swirled his cup and downed the last bit of the dark fluid. "She's really good at her job, but sometimes she's a little odd."

John sipped his coffee, "Yeah, I picked up some kind of weird vibe from her. Like she knew about me already."

George's head bobbed up and down, "She knows stuff alright. She's been here at this facility longer than anyone, she does her job well, but she can be, as you said, weird. I stay clear of her when I can."

John's eyes widened, "Sounds like a good plan."

———————

The two continued on for another hour before they reached the edge of the forest. As they entered amongst the trees Enoch thought he heard something in the distance, behind them.

Jarod looked back the way they had come as well, "What is that sound?"

Enoch glanced at his father, "I am not sure."

The sound grew louder, and louder. Building upon itself, time and again. Until suddenly a group of figures shot past them, overhead.

Enoch's head followed them until he could no longer see them through the trees. He then turned back to his father, "Did you see that?" Jarod was no longer standing, but was on the ground, "Father! What happened?"

Jarod rose to his feet, and brushed himself off, "I am not sure, son. I thought I felt something rush past, something gray in the air. Or many things, I do not know what it was."

Enoch walked back toward his father, "Are you alright?" He began to brush off his father's shoulders and back.

Jarod's face blushed, "My legs gave way beneath me. What was it?"

As Enoch's company of men and their angelic escorts pushed forward, the brightness of the day began to fade.

Jarod looked up into the sky, the sun was toward the west, but not yet setting. He would not have expected the forest to be this dim yet.

Jarod's attention snapped to Katriel as the big angel began to speak, interrupting his thoughts, "You are seeing beyond the light that you are accustomed to. You are seeing with more than your eyes now."

Jarod looked down toward the path, to keep from stumbling, "What do you mean?"

Katriel continued, "We see with more than our eyes, your kind has forgotten this, or more accurately, has decided to be solely physical. Like the fallen ones, your kind has forsaken your first estate, you were created with much more than you are now, only with much struggle will your kind rediscover what was cast off."

Jarod glanced back up toward his protector, "How long will we struggle?"

"Until the end of the age." Katriel's blunt tone caught Jarod by surprise. "The gears have been dislodged and will one day be set right."

Jarod did not know what gears were, but he could surmise that setting them right was a good thing. He looked toward Katriel and smiled.

———

Belle walked to the back of the grocery store, to the bakery section, this time for bagels and donuts. As she walked past the bakery counter she looked over to see if Nick was working. Not seeing him, she proceeded to the display case and took her time selecting items for herself and Jessica. Falk had tried a donut and did not care for it at all. She wondered if he would like the taste of bagels better.

"May I help you with anything?" Belle turned to see one of the bakery employees walking in her direction.

Belle smiled, "No, I'm almost finished here, but thank you."

"Well if there's anything I can help with, just let me know." The woman turned to leave.

"You know, there is something you could help me with." Belle placed the last donut into the box and closed the lid.

The woman turned back toward Belle and smiled.

Belle thought for a moment, "I was wondering about that young man that works here, I believe his name was Nick? I haven't seen him in a while, does he still work here?"

"I'm really not sure," the woman's face tilted to the side, "I remember you, Nick watches for you so he can talk to you. I think he's kinda shy."

Belle was surprised. "Really? He watches for me to come in?"

The woman replied, "Yes, he does, or at least he did, I haven't seen him for at least a week." She removed her thin plastic gloves and held out her right hand. "I'm Cara."

"I'm Belle, it's nice to meet you, Cara."

"As I was saying, I'm not sure if he still works here or not, I know he was hired quickly because they needed someone for the night shift, it's hard to find people to work so late."

Belle replied, "Yeah, he told me his hours a couple of times, sounds miserable!"

"Oh believe me, we go through a lot of people in that position. It pays more, but the hours are terrible."

Chapter 27
The Oracle

Enoch and Jarod walked for a couple of hours before the adrenaline in their bodies began to subside. Their time in the city and then their time with the fallen angels had made for quite a day. Once the chemicals in their blood ebbed, they quickly realized how tired they were.

The two walked side by side, until Enoch began to slow.

Jarod turned to his son, "Tired?"

Enoch let out a quick laugh and nodded his head.

Jarod continued, "I am too, perhaps we should spend the night in that next clearing up ahead."

Enoch nodded again, his eyes half closed.

The two laid next to a small fire. Bugs made their various sounds all around them, and the stars shown bright and clear. Jarod slept and Enoch wrote the request of the Watchers in a small book that was full of empty pages. Once he had finished, he read the request aloud before putting the book and quill away. Then he laid down and closed his eyes.

Enoch awoke with a start. He quickly rose from his bedding and woke his father, "Father, we must go back!"

Jarod sat up and rubbed his eyes, "Go back? To the city?"

"No, back to where we talked to the fallen ones."

"Why? Surely, they're not still there."

Enoch thought for a moment, "Perhaps the angels can regather them?"

"Perhaps. I don't know how to summon angels. They seem to appear on a different schedule than mine." Jarod laughed.

Enoch rolled his bedding into a tight bundle, "There must be a way. I have an answer for them, regarding their request."

Jarod sat up and turned to see his son's frenzied activity. "Are we leaving now?"

Enoch shoved his bedding into his pack, "Yes, we must go," Enoch turned away from his father, "or I can go back and you can continue on." Enoch picked up his cloak and put it on.

Jarod raised his hands, "Enoch stop, give me a moment, I want to come with you. Settle down."

Enoch took a deep breath,"Alright, I can wait." Enoch turned back to face Jarod, "I am glad you are coming."

———————

Enoch heard a quiet voice beside him, "We are here."

Jarod looked surprised.

Enoch crept toward his father and whispered, "Did you hear that?"

Jarod's head bobbed up and down.

Just then, Jarod saw Katriel appear behind his son.

Enoch saw his father startle, then relax. Jarod motioned for his son to turn around.

Enoch turned to see what was behind him.

Katriel said, "Our assignment is to protect you, until you reach your home. We have not left you."

Jarod inquired, "Did you watch us sleep?"

"We stood watch over you."

Jarod's brow furrowed.

Katriel continued, "What else is there to do? We do not sleep." Then he turned to Enoch, "You have received a new assignment, I have sent for the fallen ones to meet us. We will depart at your leisure. I have also sent for provisions."

Two smaller angels appeared next to Katriel, one on either side. The one on the right held out his hand.

Enoch walked over to him, and saw two wafers of bread in his outstretched hand. The angel spoke with a deep voice, "There is one for each of you."

As Enoch took the wafers he wondered at how small they were, they were the size of his palm, "What are these called?"

The angel responded, "Bread."

Enoch took a bite as he handed the second wafer to his father. "Interesting."

The second angel held a ladle.

Enoch helped his father up, "I do not think there is another ladle, we should go to him." Enoch smiled.

Jarod finished the wafer as he approached the angel with the ladle, "Is this the food you eat?"

Katriel spoke, "Sometimes. Normally we have no need for this type of sustenance."

Jarod looked up at the angel's face, "You don't eat?"

"We can, and we do on occasion, but we have no need to eat."

The angel offered the ladle to Jarod. He grasped it and took a slow draw of the fluid inside.

The water was cool and smooth, slightly sweet. It had an aromatic quality to it.

Jarod smiled at the angel, who was already smiling at him, then handed the ladle to his son.

———————

Katriel remained visible during the trip back to the clearing where they had first heard the petition of the fallen ones. Jarod had rested well during the night, and Enoch would find his rest later. He had slept, but not as well as his body needed.

As they surmounted the last hill they saw that the fallen ones had gathered and were milling about. They seemed anxious and Enoch could understand why.

Katriel pulled up next to Enoch, "Are you ready?"

Enoch spoke in a low tone, "No."

Katriel looked toward the fallen Watchers, "You have nothing to fear, you know we are with you."

"They are not going to like what I have to say."

The big angel turned toward the prophet, "You are responsible to say what you were given to say, that is all. You have delivered a difficult word before, what makes this one different?"

Enoch thought for a moment, "I have received a warning before, but this is an answer to a direct question." He looked at Katriel, "They asked for forgiveness, for themselves and their children, and the Lord of Spirits said no. Why would He say 'no' to these Watchers when He is forever ready to forgive Man?"

"We are different from you, we have a different role in the ultimate outcome of creation. Your kind is highly favored."

"So if you sin, there is no forgiveness?"

"If we purposefully act against the will of our Creator? It is as you have said, there is no forgiveness. Redemption is for Man."

Enoch and his father approached the band of fallen Watchers. Remiel studied the prophet's face, in hopes of finding the answer to the Watchers petition. He found nothing.

As the prophet and his father approached the fallen ones, one from Katriel's guard pulled up next to Jarod and steered him to the side and stopped. Katriel and Enoch continued forward.

As the two approached Remiel, the other Watchers approached as well until there was a large gathering huddled in a semi-circle around the prophet, his guardian, and Remiel.

Enoch again stood before various angels, several of which looked very much like men. These were larger than he and likely larger than

Adam, the largest man. The remaining angels were of the winged serpent type with massive wings. He had seen more of these in Paradise, though the ones there seemed more healthy than these. There were fifty or so individuals, and they were all here to listen to what he had to say. Or, more accurately, they were here to listen to the message he was about to relay.

Remiel approached Katriel and Enoch with a wide grin, "Greetings Enoch, we hope you have good news for us today. I must admit, I was quite surprised to hear you had received an answer so soon."

"Yes, I wrote your petition out last night so that I would not forget and spent the night in a vision of sorts. I will tell you of my journey leading up to the message if that is alright with you."

"Yes, yes, of course. We are anxious to hear what you have for us. Tell us everything!"

Enoch cleared his throat before he began, "I wrote your petition and last night I had a vision.

"In my vision, clouds called to me, shooting stars and lightning beckoned me up. Upon a wind I was lifted up to Paradise, and I entered in, through a small gate, a narrow path, and I walked near to a wall. A wall made of hailstones and tongues of fire encircled it round about, and I was frightened.

"And I went into the the tongues of fire and found that this wall was part of a great house. I entered the house and the walls of the house became like great stone slabs, yet made of snow. The floor was of snow as well.

"The ceiling was like shooting stars and lightning, flashing this way and that. Among the lightning were great and fiery cherubim, and their Paradise was water. A flaming fire encircled all their walls and the doors blazed with fire.

"Inside the house, which was as hot as blazing fire and as cold as snow, I found no delight for I was in fear. There were doors round about me, blazing with fire.

"Yet one door stood open. Through that door was another house, greater than the former one, built of tongues of fire. It so excelled in majesty, glory, and splendor that I am unable to describe its brightness.

"The floor of this house was fire and above were lightning flashes and shooting stars. This house was not on fire, it was fire. Everything —the walls, floor, doors, the ceiling—all of it was fire.

"Then I looked and saw a massive and tall throne, it stood there like ice and it's wheels were bright and fiery like the sun, each one was a sun.

"The sound of the Cherubim issued forth, and from beneath the throne issued forth a river of liquid fire.

"Then I was unable to see.

"And a Great Glory sat upon the throne, who was adorned in the whitest clothing, whiter than snow and brighter than the sun.

"Most angels could not enter into this house and none could look on his face for great was the fierceness of the glory and majesty that sat upon the throne, and no man could look on Him.

"Brilliant fire encircled Him and a great fire stood beside Him.

"Ten thousand times ten thousand angels stood before Him, but He needed no counselor, He needed no one to offer Him wisdom.

"His every word was deed.

"And the four holy ones of the Hayyoth, did not leave Him by either the dark of night nor did they depart from Him by day."

Enoch noticed that the Watchers attention hung on every word he spoke.

He continued, "I fell prostrate, trembling before the throne and remained there for a time, until the Lord of Spirits called me by the word of His mouth and said, 'Enoch, come here, and hear what I have to say to you.' And behold, one of the fiery holy ones came down to me and raised me up, all at once, and brought me to the door, though my face remained bowed.

"Then the Lord of Spirits answered and said, 'Fear not, come here, righteous scribe, and hear my voice. Go and say to the Watchers of Paradise, those who sent you to entreat for them, and on their behalf...' and this is what I am to tell you, 'You were made to petition and entreat on behalf of Man, and not Man on behalf of you. Why is it that you have forsaken your former home, the true Paradise, the everlasting sanctuary. Why have you lain with the daughters of men, and defiled yourselves and taken wives unto yourselves, and done as the sons of Man, and begotten for yourselves sons, giants?

"'You were my holy ones, I made you to be spirits, and to live forever. But now, with the blood of women you have desecrated yourselves, and having become flesh, you have begotten, and having learned from Man, you have lusted and done as they do—you have done as those of flesh and blood do, those who die and rot.

"'Because of this I gave to men, women. That they might beget children by them, that their kind might remain upon the Earth.

"'But you were of the spirit realm, wholly different from them, living forever throughout all the ages of eternity. That is why I made no women among you. You were made for, and belong in, Paradise.

"'But you have lowered yourselves and these begotten giants, who were conceived of spirit and flesh, they will be known as evil spirits on the Earth, they will dwell where they were conceived.

"'When they die, and they will die, their spirits will remain on the Earth and they will be called evil spirits for that is what they shall be.

"'Spirits begotten in Paradise should dwell in Paradise, but spirits begotten on Earth will dwell on Earth.

"'The spirits of the giants are restless, tormented in themselves, being of two places but dwelling in the lower of the two. They do violence, attack, and wrestle upon the Earth. They cause illness and vomit violently upon the Earth. As spirits they will eat nothing, but abstain from food and will have a terrible thirst. They shall rise up against the sons of men and against the women, they will hate them, for it is because of them that these evil ones must remain captive upon the Earth.

"'From the day of the slaughter, and destruction, and death of the giants, those who's spirits will be released at that time, they will make desolate without judgement falling upon them. They will therefore ruin the Earth until the culmination and judgement, when the great age will be ended. It will be ended all at once.

"'You were in Paradise and although no mystery was revealed to you, you learned a mystery that was stolen. And this mystery you have taught to the women. In your hardness of heart you have taught the women, and through this mystery women and men multiply evils across the surface of the Earth.

"Then the Lord of Spirits instructed me to say to you that there will be no peace for you."

Enoch looked down and waited for what he could only imagine would be an angry response.

Most of the fallen ones had already left, though some were in the process of leaving. One of the dragons approached. Remiel, the smaller cherubim stepped aside to make way for the larger serpent.

Katriel placed his hand on the hilt of his sword. He looked directly at the seraphim serpent, "Semyaza, I did not expect to see you here."

"Of course you didn't, and I expected the Creator to have a better message for us."

Semyaza stood firm and stared at the prophet. A long moment passed before his eyes flicked over to Katriel, then back to Enoch. Then he blurted out, "Is that it?"

Enoch thought for a split second and then words stumbled out, "Yes, that is all." He looked at Katriel, who stared at the fallen Watcher.

The prophet looked back at Remiel then toward Semyaza, "What do you mean?"

"I just want to be sure you got it all out. It is clear from your description that your vision was true. The Creator is petty and lacks compassion. He was right to surround you with so many guardians, makes killing you an unwise venture."

Semyaza turned to leave and whipped his tail toward Katriel.

The big cherubim's sword launched from its sheath, cutting a fiery blue arch in the air, and stopped the dragon's tail spikes mid-air.

Semyaza turned back toward the guardian and laughed, then shot into the sky with Remiel close behind.

Anarkum pushed his host to continue on, ever since Nick's SUV had been destroyed, he had been outside in survival mode. He figured it was a good thing he had the demon inside him, since he didn't know how he would have survived without his help. Anarkum knew how to survive and helped every step of the way.

As he approached the crest of Pike's Peak his lack of proper clothing suddenly began to matter. He knew that the tourists on the mountain would wonder how he could be here with no jacket, though he didn't feel the cold, he had lost his ability to feel it, and he was glad for that.

Nick decided to have a look around. He surveyed the surrounding landscape, with the railway and tourists at the far end of the parking area, and a small building covered with quite a few antennas, not far from him.

He felt drawn to the small building, *That's an odd little building.*

Chapter 28
Doom Sayer

Enoch thought about the eighty-eight years that had passed since that first fateful trip to what was then a small city. And in those years the city had grown, and the population had become more and more corrupt. Every foreseen event had come to pass in an orderly succession and now Enoch again traveled to the city to pronounce the judgement that would arrive soon if the city did not turn back to Elohim.

There would be no getting lost on the way to the city now, the two had walked many years by the same route and Enoch's oldest son, Methuselah, had begun making these journeys with his father and grandfather some years back, when he was a youth of merely three decades. The ground had given up any notion of growing anything where they walked, instead it helped them by marking an unmistakable path. This trip to the city was different than any of the others. Over the decades Enoch had pronounced the love of Elohim toward the people, and how He desired that they learn of His love for them. This trip would, however, be much different, at least in how it would end. It was their choice, but either way, it would end much different than before.

They walked through the night and there was an urgency to this message that propelled the prophet foreword. He looked up into the sky and saw the great mass of the host of Paradise that circled above. Over the years his perception into this other realm grew more and more clear. He had never seen such a large gathering, it was comforting, and on the other hand, it was not. He looked up into the swirling mass of light, a vertical tunnel of life. If there were thousands on his previous trips there had to be hundreds of thousands this time around. A vast number of angelic messengers sent to protect the people in the city, if they chose to accept the protection.

Jarod interrupted Enoch's thoughts, "Son?"

Enoch looked over his shoulder, "Yes?"

"Do you know how this will turn out?"

"I feel something is coming, but we will live. Was that what you wanted to know?"

"Yes, and no. What is coming?"

Enoch looked up into the sky again, "Something terrible, but with the boy here with us, we will live."

Jarod playfully swatted Enoch's son on the back, "Because of him? What's so special about this young man?"

Enoch winked at his father, "I have certain assurances about he and I. You, on the other hand, there are no assurances, so stay close to us."

Jarod grimaced, "Thanks! That is really good news."

Nick walked over to the building, he was a good distance from the parking lot and was sure no one had seen him. He walked carefully around the building looking for a normal-sized door but the only one he saw was a garage-style door on the end facing the parking lot.

The demon inside him interrupted his thoughts, "You're not looking hard enough!"

Nick's shoulders slumped, "I don't see you helping, you said there was a doorway into the mountain, not a building."

"It's *near* the building, not *in* the building."

Nick threw his hands in the air, "Fine I'll look around. Feel free to help."

Nick began looking but he had to be careful because Pike's Peak toll road wound around the slope beneath the building, and motorists, though probably forty yards away, would be able to see him from there. It was a good thing there were lots of large rocks he could hide behind.

Just then Nick saw a metal handle sticking up past one of the rocks, and as he approached, he could just make out a cover, about the size of a manhole cover one might see in a road.

Adam and Seth roved through one of the fruit tree groves. Unlike the groves around the cities, consisting of singular kinds of trees. Here in the wild, the trees grew wherever they saw fit. So these wild groves had many types of fruit trees growing together.

Both men carried a large sack on his back, almost like a back pack, except they were completely open on top. The fruit Adam gathered he placed in Seth's sack and vice versa. It was an efficient way to harvest fruit to take home.

In the distance Seth saw a pair of strangers approaching.

"Father, do you know them?" Seth said to Adam.

"No, I do not." Adam squinted his eyes, "They look tall."

"Taller than you."

"Yes, I should say so."

Seth shook his head, "Crossbreeds."

One of the strangers held up his hand as he drew near. "Greetings, Saba Adam!"

"Greetings," Adam replied.

The stranger sensed Adam's unease.

Seth turned to Adam and whispered, "Did you see his hand has six fingers?"

Adam nodded his head, very slightly.

At nine feet tall, Adam was the tallest man, every generation after him had lessoned in height so seeing someone taller than himself meant these two were not of his line, or not fully.

The pair of strangers stopped around thirty feet from Adam and Seth. "Saba Adam, we have come to meet you, and to bring you news."

"Very well, what are your names?"

The stranger held his hand to his chest, "I am Tubal Cain, and this..." he motioned toward his companion. "is my sister, Naamah."

Adam replied, "And what are you known for?"

"Excuse me?"

"What do you do, I know of your kind. You have been taught of the angels. What did they teach you?"

"Our kind?" Tubal Cain laughed under his breath, "What do you mean?"

"Come now, did you come to play games with me? You obviously know more about me than I know about you."

Tubal Cain was silent.

"Your kind, you are part man and part angel, you bear all the signs. Obviously, you are much taller than I am, your heads are very tall, though you try to hide that under all that hair. You have very large eyes, and you have six fingered hands. Obviously, you are crossbreeds."

Tubal Cain laughed, "Yes, what you say is true enough. And you ask what we are known for, what our skill is. I tell you, my skill is metal working with copper and iron. Naamah, is skilled at weaving."

Adam's eyes brightened as he focused on Naamah, "Weaving? You work with plant stalks?"

"Yes." Naamah smiled.

Adam took a step toward her, "What sorts of things do you make? Baskets?"

"Yes, sure, baskets and much more. I also make large containers and furniture to sit on."

"To sit on? And they bear up under the weight of a man?"

"Oh yes, they are really quite strong. I also make a form of light armor."

"Armor?"

"Yes, you know, for protection in battle. Of course, Tubal Cain makes maille out of iron strands which is better, but heavier."

Adam frowned, "I would not know of such things. We here on the mountain are peaceable folk."

Naamah raised one eyebrow, "Of course. But then you have protection."

Adam's frown grew deeper, "What do you mean?"

Naamah motioned toward the sky, "The angels, do you not see them?"

Adam looked up into the sky. Other than a few clouds, he saw nothing out of the ordinary. He replied, "No, not anymore."

Tubal Cain looked up, "They are all around you. I would not lift a finger against you with the protection you have."

Adam looked around. Then back at Tubal Cain, "Did you come up here to meet me, or was there another purpose? You said you had news for me?"

Tubal Cain's hands clasped behind his back, head down, his eyes glanced toward Adam, then at Seth, "Cain is dead."

Adam stopped what he was doing, but his eyes stayed fixed on the fruit he was about to pick, "What happened?"

"His house collapsed, while he was sleeping. It collapsed and crushed him, he and his wife."

He looked at Tubal Cain, "Awan?"

"Yes."

Adam's eyes closed then he glanced back at the fruit. He reached for it and plucked it from the tree.

Tubal Cain laughed, "Saba Adam, I have a question for you, so I will get right to it.

"It is well known that two great catastrophes are coming upon the Earth. One will be fire and the other water."

Adam, still looking at the fruit, raised his eyebrows, "Who told you this?"

Seth approached his father and helped to remove his sack.

Tubal Cain plucked an apple from the tree next to him, "Azazel told us."

Adam watched the bigger man study the apple, "And why would he reveal such things?"

There was a pause, and Adam continued, "Certain information is not to be spread around. Like your metal working. Azazel would do well to keep some things to himself." Adam looked straight at Tubal Cain. "What is the price for this knowledge? I am sure it has a high price. He is trading what does not belong to him."

Tubal Cain spoke with a steady, almost eery tone, "He takes any woman he wants for his wife, whenever he wants. He has many children now." Tubal Cain tossed the apple into his mouth and chewed loudly.

Adam probed a bit more, "Is he your father? Did he take your mother as his supposed wife for a day and now her real husband is raising you for him? That must not sit well with him."

Tubal Cain swallowed, "Saba Adam, I'm sure that is none of your business."

"Do not worry, the truth is self evident." Adam looked away, then turned back, "What of these so called catastrophes?"

Tubal Cain felt uneasy, "Azazel does not know when they will happen, nor does he know which will come first."

Adam plucked several apples and placed them into Seth's pack, "So, you want me to tell you, Yes?"

"Yes, of course."

Adam reached up for two more apples, "There are things I can say, and there are things I cannot say. I can say nothing about the topic at hand." He placed the apples into the pack with the others.

Tubal Cain glared at Adam, "You cannot, or you will not?"

Adam turned back toward Tubal Cain, "Either way, you are not getting an answer today. Unlike your real father, I know when to hold my tongue." He could see the giant's anger rising.

Tubal Cain looked at each of the angels, then back at Adam. "Be glad you have protection, Old Man." Then he turned, took his sister's hand, and stormed off.

Adam looked around, unsure of where his angelic protectors were, "I am very glad to have protection."

Adam looked toward his son, "Seth, this old man needs to sit down."

"Yes, of course." Seth kept his eyes on the strangers as he helped his father to sit down against one of the fruit trees.

The morning sun rose and the city of Enoch slowly came to life as people moved about the streets. If they happened to pass through the main intersection of town they saw three men in robes, with their heads covered and facing the ground.

From one of the streets a woman yelled out, "The Doomsayer is back!"

Then a man across the road from her bellowed out, "Who cares!"

To which another man said, "Come on, let's go see what he has to say this time. If nothing else, he's entertaining."

And so it went, the news that Enoch, the Doomsayer, was in town spread throughout the city over the course of time. Enoch and his companions did not move, nor stir, until Enoch's guide, Uriel, whispered into his ear, "It is time."

Enoch mouthed a silent prayer, pushed the hood of his robe back from his head, and looked up to see the majority of the city gathered round. He turned in a slow circle, and made eye contact with as many as would let him, which turned out to be very few. He had just about completed his rotation when his eyes found a small girl, held in her mother's arms. His eyes locked onto hers, she smiled. He wanted to smile, he wanted to comfort her and all these people, but he could not. His task crushed him.

Enoch addressed the crowd, "People of Enoch." The words wheezed from his mouth, it had been a long time since his throat felt so dry when trying to talk to the people of the city. He coughed a couple of times into his fist to clear his throat and tried again. "People of Enoch, I have come today with a special message for you."

"Spit it out, Doomsayer!" came a voice in the crowd. From the sound of it, many in the crowd agreed.

"I am here to tell you that your Creator loves you and He would save you if only you would allow it."

The man who's voice was heard earlier moved through the crowd to confront the prophet. "Save us from what? The star people are gone, we drove them out."

"Yes, Jabal, this city drove them out, and where do you think they went?"

Jabal shook his head, "I think we don't know, and we don't care where they went. Why would we?"

"You would have done well to keep track of them. For they spread out to the other cities."

Jabal puffed up his chest and held his chin up, trying to make himself seem larger, "Again, why do we care about that, they're someone else's problem now."

"Actually, they control the other cities. They have taken control of them and now the most powerful of them is returning. And when they do, you will not like what you see."

Jabal crossed his arms. "If they come back here, we will drive them out again. We do not need your Creator here. Go back home and dream up more stories to tell your children."

Enoch's eyes pleaded with the man in front of him, "You must listen to me! All these years I have taught you about the Creator and how much he loves you. I have begged you to come under His protection, please ask Him to save you, He wants to save you!"

Jabal was indignant, "Your backward notions cannot save anyone. Maybe you are one of them, maybe you desire to deceive us into following you."

"Do I look like a Watcher? No, I would have you follow someone far greater than I."

Jabal was indignant, "What were the two laws again? You said it was so simple, but we cannot remember the two laws."

The crowd was growing restless as evidenced by the noise level growing to a point that he knew they could not hear him. Not only that, but the prophet could see the direction this conversation was going, he lowered his voice, "They are not laws, not really."

Jabal continued, "If He is the Creator, why would He beg us to follow Him? You've been coming here for so long, each time telling us that He loves us, yet, if He is real, why does He not show His face? And why would he put such a burdensome set of laws upon us?"

Enoch's voice remained low, "He wants to save you from what is coming."

Jabal's head tilted to one side, "And what is that? What is coming?"

Enoch's voice became hoarse once more, "Something terrible."

Jabal paused. Then, fearing he had lost his momentum, he seized Enoch by the arm.

Uriel pulled his sword from it's sheath and Enoch motioned for him to remain calm.

Jabal pulled Enoch's sleeve, "You must leave and never return!" Then, as though some signal was given, the crowd rushed Enoch, Jarod, and Methuselah. All the while Enoch motioned for Uriel to stay his hand. The crowd hustled them to the edge of the city, where they were pushed to the ground.

Jarod watched the crowd leave, then turned to his son, "Did I miss something?"

Enoch brushed dirt from the front of his clothing, "What do you mean?"

Jarod wiped tiny rocks that had imbedded in his palms when he fell, "What two laws?"

Methuselah's head bobbed up and down, "I wondered that, too."

Enoch grimaced as he shook his head, "They are not really laws, more like the way things should be."

Methuselah asked again, "What are they?"

"You know them, and you live by them, you do not recognize the term because there is no law when we live according to the love of Elohim." Enoch's eyes found his Son, the question was still in his eyes, so Enoch continued, "As created beings, we belong to the one that created us, we owe our Creator all of our being, of course. This goes without saying, really."

Methuselah's head bobbed up and down, "Of course, without Him, we would not exist."

Enoch half-smiled, "The other is to treat all fellow creatures, great or small, that can acknowledge the Creator, with respect, and with honor.

"Those are the laws."

Jarod rolled his eyes, "Is that all? The people find those two things to be a burden?"

Enoch smiled, "That is what he said."

Methuselah stood to his feet and walked over to his grandfather.

Jarod grabbed his grandson's outstretched hand, "To think they would even have to be spelled out like that."

Enoch stood up with a groan and the three men continued to brush themselves off.

All at once Enoch stopped and stood transfixed on the city, his countenance changed before their eyes, his very life seemed to drain away in front of them. Jarod watched his son, then turned toward Methuselah, brow furrowed. Methuselah shrugged his shoulders.

Jarod interrupted his son's thoughts, "What do we do now son?"

Enoch turned from the city, "Now, we go home."

Jarod and Methuselah led the way and the prophet of Elohim followed at a distance. Uriel walked next to, and spoke to Enoch, while the angelic host circled above.

Chapter 29

Conquest

"Look someone approaches from the east!"

Great clouds of dust rose into the air, then the sound of thunder, rolling but never ending. It was the sound of mighty animals galloping toward the city on the dusty flesh of the Earth.

A pair of runners were sent, and through the streets they went in search of Jabal, the current magistrate of the city.

Jabal had only just returned from the far side of the city where he had hurried the public nuisance, known as the Doomsayer, out of the city. There would be no more need of him here, and Jabal had seen to it that he left for good.

"Jabal! Come quick!"

The sound came from the city center and Jabal with his friend, Ermiel, walked at a brisk pace to see what was happening. They traveled along the road that led to the west side of the city. As they arrived at the outskirts they saw the two boys that had originally sounded the alarm, and a dust plume in the distance. Only now it was obvious that there were at least a handful of entities, each kicking up its own trail.

Jabal walked out past the others and leaned over a mud-brick wall, "Who do you suppose it is, the Watchers?"

One of the boys cupped his hands and held them over the top of his eyes to block the sun. "I can't tell, looks like two of them. They don't really look like horses."

Ermiel smiled, "I'm sure there are riders on those horses."

"If those are horses, they're the fattest horses I've ever seen. And there's something on their heads."

Jabal cupped his hands over his eyes, "What is that on their heads? Is it a shield?"

The runner looked more intently, "A shield? Are you sure?"

Jabal shook his head, "Too much dust to be sure of anything."

One of the boys muttered, "They've stopped."

"The one on the right has his arm in the air. Wait, now they've both stopped."

The others cupped their hands over their eyes. One asked, "How far is that?"

Jabal answered, "Three miles? Maybe more."

Ermiel broke in, "Now he's making a motion in the air."

Jabal nodded in agreement, "Uh huh, I see. Wait, is that...?"

Ermiel interrupted again, "Those, my friend, are more riders."

The boy muttered under his breath again, "...and more, and more, and more."

The group of men watched as the men on strange beasts walked in either direction around the small city. The line of riders almost looked as though it emerged from the first two, the line behind them must have been staggering in length.

Jabal looked at his friend, "How many swords do we have?"

Ermiel glanced toward Jabal, then down, and finally back toward the riders, "Not enough, not if they want to fight us."

Jabal thought for a moment, then said, "Get the strongest men, give them the maille, swords, and shields. Get them here now."

Ermiel nodded his head, "I'll be back in one hour."

The procession outside the city continued, in a slow, hypnotic cadence. The desert heat drifted up, distorting the view of the riders. The promised hour had come and gone with no sign of Ermiel or the men from the city, but the boys that stood with Jabal had remained at his side. Little help they would be in a fight, since he would send them into the safety of the city anyway.

His mind drifted back to the Doomsayer. Jabal did not know his real name. He thought about this man who claimed to know things that would happen in the future, and how none from the city actually believed him. The things he talked about always seemed so far off. Yet now, outside the city of Enoch, something straight out of one of the man's sayings could be playing out before his eyes. And he'd just escorted the Doomsayer out of town. Surely this must not be what the man had talked about. Surely, the timing was by chance.

Jabal heard a group walking toward him from behind and soon Ermiel once again stood next to him, this time dressed for battle. Jabal looked up into the sky, "You're late."

Ermiel placed a clump of chain maille, a sword, and a shield at Jabal's feet, "It took longer than I thought, I had runners keep an eye on the stranger's progress so I knew we had more time." Ermiel held out a bulging calfskin. "I brought water, it's warm by now."

Jabal took the skin, and pulled the top off, "You didn't miss much," and took a long draw. He looked to his right to see the boys parched lips, and tossed the skin to the closest one, "Here, you boys' have the rest."

One of the boys caught the skin and took a long draw, the other waited his turn.

Two more hours passed, and still the riders continued, on and on at the same slow pace. Jabal, now dressed for battle, had long since sent the boys home, and most of the men were sitting next to the various homes, out of the sun. They ate a hurried dinner, as the day cooled off and the sun was in retreat behind the strangers. Just then the last of the riders emerged from behind the original two. These took no more than twenty steps before they all came to a halt as one, then turned in unison to face the city.

Ermiel looked to the right and then the left, he was sure they must have completely encircled the city. He looked back at Jabal, "Have you ever seen anything like this?"

"No."

Ermiel leaned on the wall next to his friend and let out a long breath, *Jabal always gets quiet when he's tense.*

―――――――

Nick's progress was slow, he had figured out that the handle he had seen was attached to the cover, and once open, there was another handle on the underside of the cover.

Inside, he found a ladder that went straight down. He pulled the cover closed and except for small holes in the cover that let a tiny amount of light in, he was in darkness. He looked down into the gloom beneath him but could not see anything, he had no idea if the ladder was ten feet, or one hundred feet. Heck, for all he knew, it could be a mile.

The voice inside him urged him on, not with words, but he could feel it straining against his will, urging him down the ladder. He began a slow, careful decent into the blackness.

Jabal and Ermiel watched the motionless strangers. Not one of them flinched, not one of them stirred. The sun disappeared over the horizon and the silhouettes remained, until even the silhouettes could no longer be seen.

The moon made a brief appearance, late into the night. There was but an edge of shine to it, not enough to see clearly, then it disappeared over the horizon. Jabal wondered if this too was part of the plan.

What they did not see, indeed what they *could not* see, was the movement of the beasts. Slow and silent, they crept closer to the city. Hour after hour, they moved in unison, but not together. That is to say, they progressed in intervals, meticulously planned and orchestrated. This strategy had worked on so many of the other cities, and now it would work on the crown jewel, the city that had labeled each of these riders as outcasts.

Sometime around three o'clock in the morning Jabal heard a sound he had never heard before. It came from behind and moved overhead, toward the riders. A large *woosh* and rustling, like heavy cloth blown in a strong wind.

Ermiel found his way in the dark to Jabal's side, "What was that?"

"I don't know."

"Sounded big."

"Very."

The sound continued in the distance, followed by a series of soft thuds, and finally a gritty silence.

Nick continued his decent, he had lost count after the first couple hundred rungs. His hands hurt along with his feet, and he stopped to look back up, and could no longer see the light from the cover.

He looked down and could just make out a dim glow, maybe it was the bottom. He couldn't be sure of course but the thing inside him compelled him to continue. So he took in a deep breath and continued on.

Jabal yawned and searched the darkness for any sign of the riders, anything that would tell him they remained where he last saw them.

There were two truths that would have served Jabal well at this hour. First, darkness, true and utter darkness, never betrays those hidden in it. Second, and probably more important, the beasts and their mounts shared a type of vision he would never know. From their fathers, the Watchers, they had inherited the genuinely reptilian ability to see the type of light given off by heat. This infrared vision was at this moment allowing the riders and their mounts to progress with silent confidence, on a night when Jabal could not see his own hand held mere inches from his face.

About the time the distant horizon began to glow a beautiful blue, foretelling the rising of the long awaited sun, Jabal and Ermiel both realized something was in front of them. They both looked up to see the silhouette of an incredibly tall figure and they had trouble grasping the reality of the situation, as though their minds had slipped into a kind of shock, they both believed this was a dream.

The Watchers had been around the same height as Cain's father, Adam, who was a little over nine feet tall, and the tallest man. This figure would have been almost double the height of the Watchers, and much more robust in build.

Ermiel wondered how long this "man" had been there.

Jabal saw something in the distance, past the silhouetted figure. He caught a glimpse of greenish black, membranous wings that almost glowed in the light of the horizon.

The two men found themselves in some kind of stupor. Whether it was from the lack of sleep or some other reason did not matter. The bottom line was that their reactions were much slower and dulled down from what would normally be the case.

The sun finally peeked into view and Ermiel realized that the figure before them was one of the riders, and before he could come up with a coherent thought, his hand reached for his sword.

Jabal's eyes drifted over the man's armor, it was as much adornment as it was protection, when suddenly the giant figure burst into action, slicing through the men's maille, bones, and organs with a single swipe. Both men's faces were caught in a spray of red.

Neither man realized what had just happened and Ermiel, now completely disoriented, thought he saw a green monster glistening in the distance. *Couldn't be, animals don't breath fire.*

Ermiel's sword tumbled from his hand as the two men crumpled to the ground and fell to their backs, gasping for air to the sight of huge creatures, with boney head shields and long pronounced horns on their heads, crashing through the wall, carrying riders headlong into the men behind them.

Jabal closed his eyes, *the Doomsayer was right,* then slipped from this life.

Chapter 30

Confession

As Enoch and Edna approached Adam's cave, Enoch could see that every generation was represented. From Seth to Jarod, everyone had gathered. This was a gathering unlike any they had experienced in the past, it was not full of good times and good food, this was a time of uncertainty and sadness.

Seth approached the couple and spoke quietly, "Edna, you are as radiant as ever! I trust you and Enoch are well?" He reached out and hugged Enoch's beautiful wife.

Edna whispered, "Saba Seth, Yes, we are well, and how are you, and Savta Azura?"

"We are well," Seth answered. He motioned toward the cave entrance, "You two should both go in, He is asking for you."

Enoch and Edna greeted the other family members as they passed through the gathering and into the cave. Up ahead, Eve sat on a short stool next to a blanket-covered straw bed where Adam laid, covered by a sheet of linen and a thick woolen blanket.

Enoch dropped his outer garment on the floor next to Eve and knelt down on it. Edna stood just behind him and to one side, a hand on his shoulder.

Enoch looked at Eve. Her hands were folded together on her knees and she rocked back and forth ever so slightly. Her eyes were closed and her mouth moved as though speaking. *She is praying.* He thought.

He reached a hand over and grasped hers. She placed one hand on top of his and gave it a squeeze. She opened her heavy eyes and looked into Enoch's. He leaned over and kissed her on the forehead.

Eve closed her eyes and bowed her head once more.

Enoch pulled his hand from Eve's and looked over at Adam, whose eyes were also closed. He spoke softly, "Saba Adam? I am here."

Adam's eyes remained shut, but his hand lifted a little, trembling.

Enoch slid his right hand under Adam's hand.

Adam grasped, his grip was weak.

Adam's eyes opened and he whispered, "Tell everyone to leave, but you stay."

Enoch turned to Eve, as she turned and motioned for those who had gathered to exit the cave. She followed them out.

Enoch turned back to Adam, "We are alone now."

Adam's eyes began to well up, "I could have paid for it."

Enoch leaned in, "What do you mean?"

Adam was emphatic, "The garden, I could have paid for it!"

Enoch's head lurched back, in a slight motion. "Saba, What are you talking about? Paid for what?"

Adam's grip tightened on Enoch's hand, strong now, and getting stronger.

Enoch felt his Saba's grip crushing his hand. He resisted as best he could, but the pain continued to grow. He wondered where this strength had come from.

Adam closed his eyes, "Our sin! Her sin..." Adam's voice cut short, he paused to catch his breath, "What you don't understand, no one understands. Do you see, how can you not see it?"

Enoch placed his left hand on top of Adam's hand, pain pulsed through his knuckles causing him to wince, his left hand grasped Adam's hand in an attempt to pry it loose.

Adam's eyes opened once again as he released Enoch's hand, his head raised up. "Oh! I am sorry."

Enoch pulled his right hand away and grasped it with his left. Rubbing it to help the blood return to his fingers. Enoch cleared his throat, "What do we not understand, Saba?"

Adam's head fell back to the bedding, "I could have stopped it."

"Saba, you are not making any sense. What could you have stopped?"

"When she ate of the fruit, I had to choose. I could have stopped it right then. But I did not."

"Help me understand, Saba. What are you saying?"

Adam spoke in a soft tone, and Enoch leaned closer, "Do you remember? The cost of sin is death. Can you not see? Can you not see what I did not do? What I did not do, until now, but now is too late, for I have sinned. Once I sinned, I could no longer do it, can you not see?"

Enoch squinted, trying to understand, "Are you speaking of death?"

"Yes!" Adam practically shouted.

Enoch looked back toward the cave's opening to see his Savta peeking in. Enoch motioned for her to come closer. "Are you saying you could have died then?"

Adam looked at his counterpart, "Yes, I could have been her friend that day. I could have shown my love for her by laying down my clean life for her sin." Adam began to weep, "I could have been her champion that day," his voice sputtered through the tears, "but I was afraid." His eyes welled up once more and he shouted, "I was selfish!" Adam could no longer see clearly, his tears flowed in a continuous stream now. "I was unworthy of her. I failed to redeem her."

Enoch closed his eyes as he placed his hand on Adam's forehead. His mouth began to move, though no sound could be heard.

Adam fell silent, except for his labored breath.

Enoch opened his eyes, though they focused on nothing, "Adam, father of mankind, you have seen the failing that was yours alone. But I say to you, there will come another Adam who will not fail to lay down his life for his bride. He will lay down his life and save her, and she will learn over the course of time what it means to be His bride. She will learn to be spotless and pure, then Adam, the last Adam will wed his pure and spotless bride. Then He will no longer wait, because it will be finished."

Enoch, with a puzzled expression, looked at Adam's face. "Do you know what that means?"

Adam nodded as Eve took his hand. She knelt next to his bed, leaned in, and kissed him. Her tears mingled with her husband's.

Enoch asked Eve, "Savta? What does it mean?"

"It means that the Lord, the Creator, will redeem His people, and we are to be His bride. We did not want Him to wait, but He was waiting for us. He has been waiting for us all along."

Enoch shook his head, "I am not sure I understand."

Eve continued, "Not long after Adam was created, he realized he was alone, just as Elohim is alone. We believed that Elohim would one day have a counterpart, and we did not want Him to wait. He is telling us, that He has a plan and our failures will not last forever.

"He said there is hope, because all will be set right."

Chapter 31

Expansion

And so it was that the unborn, the first, the beginning of man, died. It was his 930th year of life, and as 1000 years is like a day in Paradise, so Adam lived his life, complete, within the day he had first partaken of the forbidden fruit.

Representatives of all the generations that followed him gathered as a sign of respect. His body, wrapped in cloth, was taken to the cave of treasures, and laid next to the bone box of his son Abel, where it was to remain for one year. Once the year was completed his bones were to be collected and placed in a stone box, with a lid, which was to be made of either limestone or chalk and placed next to the box which contained the bones of his second born son.

When the Creator, Elohim, formed this man from the dust of the Earth, the soil he used, that red dirt, was loaned by the Earth. As with any loan, conditions may be put in place contingent upon the repayment of the loan. On this day, the Earth accepted the body of Adam, the loan repaid, and the conditions removed.

The conquest of the city of Enoch was quick and messy. It was not the first city these children of the Watchers, the Nephilim, had conquered. It was, in fact, the last. After this victory, all cities on Earth were controlled by the giants.

There were many cities in those days, the children of Cain had spread out across the world, building their cities in ways very similar to how the city of Enoch was built up. Through time and many generations, mankind had moved across the landscape.

The routes that connected these cities served as paths for the Watchers. Their mission had evolved over time, and now, instead of taking wives, they spread their seed across the whole planet—be it men, women, children, livestock, or wild animals—all were but creatures to to be used by these fallen angels. They were determined to corrupt the ancestral lines of everything on Earth. To reform the blood lines to their own image and to their own putrid mindset.

In their conquest of the cities, many people were killed. This presented the problem of what to do with the bodies. Cain learned that bodies could not be buried. He had tried to bury Abel several times, and the Earth spit him out each time.

He learned later that the Earth would not accept bodies until the Creator's debt had been repaid, that is the debt of the body of Adam, that had been taken from the ground. In other words, once Adam was buried, others could be buried. Until then, burial was not an option.

The burning of bodies was the logical outcome of all this. Therefore the giant heathen kings of old, the Nephilim, adopted the practice of burning the bodies of the dead.

—————

A group of children wandered off from one of the cities. It would have been fine, except that this particular city sat on the edge of the Duidain region.

They began playing tag amongst the fallen and broken trees. Jumping and playing and having a good time. After just a few minutes one of the children looked up. He could feel the ground shake and in the distance he saw fire and smoke rise. Then the shaking took on a rhythm, like a horse, only much larger.

All at once, the children looked at each other and started to run for home.

—————

It had been one week since the death and burial of Adam, and now the same group had gathered once again. In the moments before Adam passed, Enoch and Eve were called upon to come to his side, as they could most easily identify with the first man, they knew him best. Adam used his final moments to express to them his final regrets. Regrets from a time long past, and a world his actions forever changed.

It was now one week later and Eve's life was coming to an end. She also had a secret to reveal, but, unlike Adam, she asked for all of her children to gather around her.

Those who remained on the mountain did indeed gather to hear what she had to say. There were many tears, for this time they understood more of what this "death" was. They knew that Eve would no longer be with them, but what would come after her departure from her body, they did not know. Once Adam died, many of the children began to fear this thing called death.

The sobering thought was that it was a path they would all take, but that fact did not make it any less fearful. They knew their Creator, the Lord of Spirits, as Enoch called Him, loved them. He loved all that he had created. But they did not know if this "death" was an end, or a new beginning. Enoch told them it was a doorway into something else, a waiting area. A path to a place where they would wait for the Lord to finish His plan of redemption, after which time He would personally set them free. There was comfort in that notion, and they hoped it was true.

With everyone gathered and quiet, Eve looked up at them. All of these were descended from her, she was indeed the mother of all living.

She cleared her throat and smiled at her children, "Hello, my children. You are all special to me and I am so sorry that my life has come to the end. I introduced sin into this world, but our Lord, the Creator, is gracious. His redemption will come into the world through a woman."

She paused as a tear rolled down the side of her face, to the edge of her ear. Her head lifted slightly as she began to speak, "You must all hear this, but it must be kept as a secret upon the mountain. Do you all understand?" She took the hand of one of the children standing close to her. She looked into the little boy's eyes, "Do you understand?"

His eyes brightened as he spoke, "Yes ma'am, I understand."

Everyone in attendance agreed and a hush fell over them once again as she again cleared her throat, "Very well, this is what I have to say.

"This world will be destroyed, but not everyone in it. The water will rise and the rains will come such as the world has never seen before, and will not see again.

"The Lord is faithful to those that belong to Him, and He will lift up His chosen ones above the destruction, and He will save a portion of his creation to set the world right again after the destruction has been completed. And the Earth will be utterly changed.

"But the world will flourish again, and the animals will populate every part of the world, and man will once again walk as pure mankind upon the surface of the Earth for a time. But the root of bitterness will also be carried through the destruction and it will burrow deep into the fresh soil and it will spread like a weed.

"And the pure race of man and the mixture of man and angel will once again strive against one another for dominion of the Earth. And the striving will continue for many ages until the seed of the serpents will once again seek to purge the pure men from the world and take the world as their own.

"And in those days, at just the right time, when the children who are free of mixture, would no longer be found upon the Earth, the second great calamity will come upon the Earth, but this time the world will be cleansed with fire. And all those with mixture will be consumed, and the Earth will be pure as it was in the beginning. And the Lord will establish His reign upon the Earth, and he will rule with power and authority, justice and mercy."

With that, Eve laid her head back and closed her eyes. The color left her face and she passed from this life into the next.

She was made from a portion of Adam, one week after he was made, and now her life would end one week after his death.

Chapter 32

Dream Vision

Jarod, Seth and Enoch stood just out from the inner circle of children. The evening was cool, but not cold, and a small fire burned in the center of of the gathering. Several children threw sticks into the fire, and they watched them light up, burn bright, and turn to embers. The process would never get old no matter how many times it was repeated.

Jarod leaned toward his son, "They said you would have one year?"

Enoch's head tilted toward his father, "Yes, and that time has almost come."

"What remains for you to do?"

Enoch pursed his lips, then said, "I have written the visions I was given, and have written much more. I will give it to Methuselah as instructed. As for my work," he paused and silently counted off an imaginary list with his fingers, then he pursed his mouth and nodded his head, "It is finished. Yes, my work is finished."

Seth smiled, "Earlier you mentioned someone that would usher in a new age of man, that the one would rise above a great calamity."

Enoch moved closer to Seth, "This one you speak of will replace you on the Earth, as you replaced Abel.

"There is a silver chord, it is the righteous generations of Adam. This chord, though fragile, will not break.

"This one you speak of, and I do not know his name, will indeed rise above the destruction of this world. He and his children with him. And he will begin again. The corruption you see from up here on the mountain is worse than you know and it will become worse still. Self-governance is all but forsaken, and as the people allow others to define what is good and evil for them, when they allow the rulers of their cities to lower their standards, they will experience horrors and atrocities that no one was meant to see.

"When the great calamity comes, there will be no doubt that it is needed, and warranted. The Earth itself will bear witness that a great cleansing must come."

Just then one of the children ran over to Enoch and grasped his hand.

Enoch looked down at Methusalah's daughter, Kasi, as she pulled him toward the group of children.

Kasi looked up at him and asked, "Saba Enoch, would you tell us a story? Would you tell us one of your dream visions?"

Enoch's eyebrows raised as his face erupted in a wide grin. "Of course, I'll tell you a story. Let me think." He scratched his chin through his long beard. Then suddenly his eyes lit up and he turned to the children.

"If I tell you, do you promise you will not be scared?"

The children responded more or less in unison, "Yes, we promise!"

Enoch smiled, his eyes scanned them all, "Alright, close your eyes and imagine with me.

"Once there was a great mountain. From this mountain emerged a white bull, he was a grand bull, but alas, he was alone. For he was the first of the cattle on his world. Then there emerged a young white heifer, she was beautiful and the two were happy together. From these two came a black bull and a red bull. The black bull chased the red bull and once it caught the red bull, the black bull killed that red bull."

The children gasped and some of them covered their mouths.

Enoch continued, "The black bull departed with a heifer and went to a large field next to the mountain. From them came many bulls and heifers.

"Now that first heifer departed from the side of that first white bull for she had not seen the red bull for many days. She lamented and searched everywhere until she finally found his body and saw that he was dead. She mourned greatly and sobbed aloud.

"Now I saw that the first bull, the white one, came to her and quieted her. He comforted her and together they mourned for the red bull and she no longer cried out. Then, one day, she bore another white bull. After this, that first heifer also bore many other black cattle, and they each joined the other black cattle in the valley below. And that white bull, which had been born and replaced the red bull, he looked very much like that first white bull. And that younger white bull grew large and strong, and a very large number of white cattle came from it, and they each followed after the other.

"And I looked up and saw the Paradises open and I saw what looked like a star falling to the Earth, as fast as lightning. And all those large black cattle became uneasy and bellowed out with their voices, but that star arose and began eating with the cattle. Then I saw the Paradises open once again and many stars fell to the Earth, and those stars took on the appearance of those large black bulls and began pasturing among those black cattle. And I gazed at those bulls and look, those bulls began to mount the cows of the bulls and they all conceived and birthed elephants and camels and asses.

"Then the bulls feared them and were sorely frightened, and the elephants and camels and asses began to bite with their teeth and devour and gore with their horns. They began to devour those bulls, and look, all the sons of the Earth began to tremble and quake before them, and to flee.

"Then I looked again and saw that they turned on one another, they gored and began to devour one another. The Earth's voice was heard and it cried out.

"I looked up and saw the Paradise open up and beings came from Paradise shining and bright with the appearance of men. Four came forth and three came with them, then those three that came after took me and lifted me to the heights and sat me on a high tower, and there I stood. Then one of those three spoke to me and said, 'Remain here and watch and see what happens to the elephants, camels, and asses and to the stars and cattle and all the rest.'

"And I looked and one of the four that came from Paradise seized that first star, that had fallen from Paradise, and bound it by its hands and feet and threw it into an abyss. The abyss was narrow and dark and desolate and deep.

"And a sword was given to the elephants and camels and asses, and they began to fight one another and the whole Earth shook terribly. And I saw one of the four rise back to Paradise and he began to throw stones back toward the Earth, then he rounded up all those remaining stars that had fallen to the Earth and bound them up by their hands and feet and threw them into an abyss that was within the Earth."

Seth turned his head to Jarod, "Isn't this his dream vision?"

Jarod's head slowly bobbed up and down.

Seth turned back toward Enoch and the children, "When will his year end?"

Jarod glanced over to Seth, "Tomorrow."

Mahalalel leaned in from the other side of Jarod, "I did not realize it was *that* soon."

Jarod stared at his son, soaking up memories for when Enoch would no longer be with them. "Yes. Tomorrow is the day he will leave us." Before they could ask, he answered what he was sure would be their next questions, "I am glad for him, but I am also sad that he will be gone from us."

Seth and Jarod both glanced toward Enoch, then back toward the group, and Mahalalel, Jarod's father, put his arm around his son.

Enoch's story continued through the night, and the children's attention hung on his every word.

"Commander!" The General bowed low before the red dragon.

Long in thought, Satan turned to see Arteqoph bowing to him. The Commander slowly turned his body to face the General, and sighed out a response, "Yes, General Arteqoph, what is it?"

341

The General faced Satan and delivered his report, "Sir, it has come to my attention that the monster, known as Behemoth, has destroyed one of the cities."

Satan erupted, "What? How did that happen?"

The General continued, "The city was not far from Duidain, and some of the children from the city were playing and strayed into the wasteland that the Behemoth patrols."

"Patrols, heh, you're kind to that brainless brute. He no more patrols, than he knows how to speak!"

"Yes, sir. You are right, of course."

"Did you say he destroyed the entire city? Every structure?"

"Yes sir, it has become part of the monster's wasteland."

"The land he's not patrolling?"

"Yes, sir."

"And what about the people of the city?"

"Some of the children of Adam escaped, though not many."

"I don't care about them! Good riddance! What of the Watcher's children? They were in charge of the city were they not?"

"Yes, sir, they were. They were able to escape the carnage with only minor injuries."

"That is a relief!" He thought for a moment, before turning back to the General. "Something must be done about that pathetic creature. I've tried to reason with him and that did not go so well. He is as brutish as he is stupid!"

"Yes sir."

"I believe he has his uses. If he could trample the spirit of man, as efficiently as he can turn a forest into a wasteland, we would have something useful!"

Chapter 33

Departure

The time had come.

The group that made up the "silver chord" walked to the watershed divide and stood at the edge of the river. The line from Seth to Lamech, all of the descendants of Adam, at least those that remained on the mountain, walked with Enoch. Though the path was narrow and the river deep, none would miss this event.

The dark cloud had already begun its approach when the group entered the river. One after the other, the men helped the women and children across. Either by walking with them or placing children on their shoulders.

They walked in near silence, taking their cue from Edna on who's face could be seen the pain of a long foreseen loss. She walked close to Enoch, closer than normal. She embraced his arm and held his hand. Tears streamed down Enoch's face as he thought of his beautiful wife.

Overhead, the massive, dark cloud, began to swirl.

Enoch stopped the group around thirty yards short of his destination, then continued on with Edna. They walked the remainder of the trip in a slow cadence.

The swirling overhead picked up speed and a funnel of cloud lowered from the center of the cloud. A light shown down through the funnel.

Enoch kissed his wife and the two embraced for what would be the last time in this life.

Edna, still holding Enoch's hand, backed away from her husband until just their fingertips touched.

The funnel swirled down and covered the prophet. As his body rose into the funnel, their fingers separated. Enoch smiled at his wife for as long as he could see her, then he looked up, into the light.

The funnel closed with a deep boom and a pressure wave spread out in all directions. Its intensity surprised the people, a few stepped backward with the force of the shockwave.

Enoch knew that Edna, and the remaining members of the family, those that would remain on the mountain, would have to endure this fallen world until their deaths, and for most of them their deaths would be centuries away. He found comfort in what he had seen of the future, he knew his kin would be safe, their angelic guardians would see to that.

The Earth had become a playground for the fallen angels and their children who sought only to corrupt and pervert the bloodlines of the world. In so doing, they sought to remake the world and force it to conform to their fallen image and steal it from its Creator. They sought to rule man, to subjugate him to their will, to the will of their Commander.

———————

Jessica laid her pencil on the yellow pad of paper. She sat for a moment.

Then she looked up at the wall opposite her desk and asked, "Michael? Are you here?"

"Yes." Came the answer from the corner of the room to the right of where she was looking.

The archangel began to come into to view and she reached for the scroll and started to slowly roll it up, "Do you want to know what I remember?"

He spoke softly, "You are remembering Steven?"

She continued to roll the scroll, without thinking, "I remember his last night. We had a hospital bed in our home, it was in the den." She stopped talking, and sat motionless.

Michael walked to the desk and pulled up a chair that sat next to it. He sat down and looked at her, "Why did you have a hospital bed in your home?"

She glanced up into his eyes, "He didn't want to die in the hospital. He wanted to die in his own bed. He was in the hospice center in the Hospital and he didn't want to die there, in those surroundings. I arranged for him to be taken home but he had to use the hospital bed, because nurses would be coming and going. They needed to have more access than what a normal bed would allow."

He spoke again with the kindest voice she had ever heard, "What else do you remember?"

"I remember those last few days, he was no longer conscious but his body was fighting to live." A tear ran down her cheek.

Michael asked, "What else do you remember of that last night?"

She thought for a moment, "His sister had come to stay with me, he had not been awake for a couple of days and his breathing was just terrible. I think it's called a death rattle." She paused.

Michael urged her on, "Go on, I'm listening."

Jessica glanced at her companion, "She slept on the couch and I was right next to him in the recliner. It was just after two o'clock in the morning when I got up, I'm not sure why I woke up, but the house was silent for a number of seconds, then he gasped for air.

"I slipped from the chair and stood next to the bed. I told him it was alright to let go." She sat with her eyes closed for a long moment.

Then the angel spoke softly, "Then what happened?"

She looked up, but her eyes did not make it up to his before they fell back to where they had started, "I prayed over him and kissed him on the forehead. Then I crawled back into the recliner and fell asleep.

"The next thing I remember was Hannah, that's Steven's sister, waking me up, telling me he was gone.

"So I got up and stood by his bed again and waited for his next breath, the time between breaths were sometimes longer than others so I assumed she just had not waited long enough.

"So I waited, and waited, but it didn't come.

"I remember thinking before all this that I was ready, but in that moment, I wasn't. I was so foolish to believe I could ever be ready.

"I couldn't believe he was gone.

"That's when I looked at the clock and realized it was 2:15, I had only been asleep for a few minutes before Hannah woke me."

Michael looked away, "We all have those that we have lost, and we wonder what we could have done differently."

"You have lost someone? I didn't think that was possible."

"We have been at war with our own kind ever since Lucifer began his rebellion." He thought for a moment, "Your kind calls it a civil war, when brothers fight brothers. It's a strange term, really." He looked back at Jessica, "We have all lost. It is the payment for rebellion, and the payment is made by us all, not just the rebels."

Jessica slid the scroll into it's pouch and secured the top. She asked without looking at her angelic friend, "Do you know why I am having such a hard time financially? I'm doing this work, the work the Creator asked me to do, and now I can't seem to get paid. Do you know what's going on?" She held out the scroll to him.

Michael took the scroll from Jessica and said, "Come with me, you need to see something."

Jessica followed Michael out the back door and the two walked out to the railing on the back deck.

Michael pointed to a spot in the distance, toward a gap in the trees. "Look right through there, I will open your eyes." He placed his hand on her shoulder.

She looked and saw various mountain ridges, one behind another, staggered. Her brow furrowed, until she felt the familiar wave of dizziness that forced her to blink several times and take hold of the railing.

She shook her head slightly and looked again, then her eyes widened. Movement amongst the mountains, one of the mountain ridges moved toward the east.

"What is that?" She asked, still looking at what appeared to be a moving mountain.

Michael spoke with a flat tone, "That is one of several beasts assigned to you by Leviathan. She is working to cut off your supply."

Jessica leaned against the railing, squinting, "What do you mean, They're keeping checks from me? Food? What?"

"Provision begins in another realm, one you do not see. Provision is made by one of two systems, either the rulership of this world, or by the Creator. The ruler of this world gives bountiful resources to those who follow him, those who allow him to corrupt them. To the rest, you are treated as livestock, you are allowed to 'earn a living' because he has discovered over the millennia that slaves work harder and longer when they are motivated by self interest.

"Your desire to become more is what he uses against you."

Jessica looked up at Michael, "I don't understand how that answers my question."

Michael's tone remained flat, "Those he *allows* to participate in the system, he can *disallow*. He is shutting you off from the system, with the hope that you will be dissuaded from your calling. He is attempting to frustrate you. For most people, that's all it takes to get them to turn aside and quit.

"You must decide if you will quit, or if you will finish."